Navy SEALs + Hot Shapeshifters =
the Ultimate Alpha Males

Praise for *SEAL Wolf Hunting*

"Once again, Terry Spear has created a top-notch paranormal romance that will captivate and thrill readers from beginning to end."
—*The Romance Reviews* Reviewer Top Pick, 5 Stars

"A sultry nail-biter…the suspense will keep readers flipping the pages feverishly."
—*RT Book Reviews*

"I'm very eager for the next book! Highly recommended series."
—*USA Today Happily Ever After*

"A steamy page-turner! Author Terry Spear has another winner with this one."
—*Fresh Fiction*

"An exciting and fast-paced story with interesting characters, strong women, and plenty of romance, and I can easily recommend it to both shifter and romance fans."
—*Bitten by Books*

Praise for *USA Today* bestseller *A SEAL in Wolf's Clothing*

"A delightful and tantalizing read. The characters are spirited and realistic... You'll be captivated."

—*Thoughts in Progress*

"I have a thing for Wolves and Navy SEALs...put them together and I'm in HEAVEN."

—*Book Lovin' Mamas*

"Another riveting, fun, and sexy read by Terry Spear. If you love werewolf books, you don't want to miss this one."

—*Star-Crossed Romance*

"Excitement, hot and sexy love scenes, and situational humor that has me laughing out loud."

—*Fresh Fiction*

"Navy SEALs are the bomb to start with, and the one in this book is a shapeshifter to boot. Very sexy!"

—*Debbie's Book Bag*

"Spear, you did it to me again. I am in love with the wolf world you created and wouldn't mind an alpha SEAL wolf of my own."

—*United by Books*

"Tantalizing and suspenseful... Terry Spear is an alpha in her own right."

—*Anna's Book Blog*

Praise for *A SEAL Wolf Christmas*

"Spear's wonderful gifts as a writer [are] on clear display...the story is thrilling, containing edge-of-your-seat action."

—*RT Book Reviews*

"A complete, adventure-filled romance overflowing with the best of what keeps me addicted to books by Ms. Spear."

—*Long and Short Reviews*

"Terry Spear once again delivers... Well written, entertaining, and all around an incredible read."

—*BTS Reviews*

"A masterful storyteller, Ms. Spear brings her sexy wolves to life."

—*Romance Junkies*

"Escape to a world of amazing characters and intriguing adventure...Spear's extensive research and eye for detail brings this tantalizing tale to life."

—*Thoughts in Progress*

"Delicious, intense, and charming."

—*Anna's Book Blog*

"This book is a roller-coaster ride of mystery, intrigue, and wolfy love... Terry Spear is a masterful storyteller."

—*HEAs Are Us*

SEAL WOLF IN TOO DEEP

TERRY SPEAR

Published by Sourcebooks Casablanca, an imprint of Sourcebooks, Inc.
P.O. Box 4410, Naperville, Illinois 60567-4410
(630) 961-3900
Fax: (630) 961-2168
www.sourcebooks.com

Printed and bound in the United States of America
RRD 10 9 8 7 6 5 4 3

Chapter 1

FEELING USELESS, PAUL CUNNINGHAM PROPPED HIS broken leg on a few more pillows as he and Lori, his wolf mate and she-wolf leader of the pack, watched from the deck of their lakeside cabin. Their best friend, Allan Rappaport, was heading down the dock to practice diving with his new police dive partner Debbie Renaud. Allan had been partnered with Paul, who was now sidelined with his leg casted all the way up to his hip after a freak accident on a dive rescue mission.

"I still think Allan should ask the sheriff to make new assignments," Lori said. "You and Allan were raised as brothers, you're SEAL team members, although you've left the Navy, and you're used to working with other men, not women. And you're both wolves, not that anyone on the force knows that, but it makes it easier to work together. This business"—Lori motioned to Allan and Debbie as they talked to each other on the dock—"is bound to cause problems."

"Allan respects her work too much. Switching partners would look like he's having trouble with her on a professional level. He won't do anything that might jeopardize her career."

Looking cross, Lori folded her arms over her expanding belly. Paul reached over and she slipped her hand into his. "They'll be all right. Allan's smart enough to know the boundaries between *lupus garous* and humans," Paul said.

"I couldn't believe it when the sheriff assigned Allan to work with her after the accident. Are you sure Allan didn't ask to be teamed up with her?" Lori sounded like a guarded wolf.

Paul knew Lori was simply being a concerned pack leader and friend. "No. Allan and Debbie just both needed partners and were available to work together at the same time."

The ache in Paul's muscles and tendons kept reminding him how serious the compound fracture had been. The vehicle had rolled, pinning him on the bottom of a swiftly flowing river. He was fortunate to even be alive, due to Allan's heroic effort. Unfortunately, everyone there—rescue workers, ambulance crew, police—had witnessed the gruesome sight when Allan carried him out of the water.

With so many witnesses, Paul would have to pretend the knitting of the bones and the healing of the surrounding muscle and tissues took the same length of time as a human's injury, when their wolf kind actually recovered in half that time. Even so, because of the severity of his injuries, recovering was going to take three months as a *lupus garou*. It had been two weeks already and he still couldn't walk. Hell, Allan had to help him onto the chaise lounge. Paul hated being so incapacitated, though he had to be grateful he had survived. If it hadn't been for Allan, he would have drowned.

The problem was that Debbie's longtime dive partner had retired, the next one had moved to another state, and Allan had been without a dive partner because of the damnable accident. And the sheriff's department had needed Allan for some risky dive jobs.

"You needn't be concerned about them," he said. "Allan understands what he is and what she is, and he knows not to get involved with her." Paul hoped Lori was right. But where men and women were concerned, the waters became muddied.

Lori sat on the chair next to Paul's lounger and squeezed his hand. "Watch the way she looks up at him. They've been together for only two weeks and she is so enamored with him. All smiles and sweetness. She adores him. He's a SEAL, and women just fall all over themselves when they learn that."

Paul raised his brows at Lori.

She shook her head at him. "I know the two of you too well. Your SEAL status doesn't affect me in the least."

He chuckled. "Debbie is a smiley, sweet woman, Lori. You worry too much."

Lori frowned and settled back in her chair. "You're making light of this, but it's dangerous. He hasn't dated any of the eligible women in our pack, and we have several. Sure, he's nice and polite, but he's not interested in any of them. Look at the way he helps Debbie with her dive checks. They look like they're lovers."

Paul smiled. He knew Lori wanted Allan to care about a woman, but the woman *had* to be one of their kind, or the relationship would cause all kinds of complications they couldn't afford. "Come here."

"Your leg—"

"Come on the other side." She moved to his chaise lounge, and he snuggled with her. "He'll be okay. We're talking about Allan. In all our years of wolf longevity, how many times has he fallen for a human woman and not been able to let go of the notion?"

Lori relaxed then. "Never."

"Right. Never. So they're just working together, doing practice dives as a team so when they have risky dives to make, they'll be working in sync with each other. And look, they didn't have to dive here in front of us, knowing we're observing every move they make. He could have taken her anywhere to practice with her."

"True. But they won't always be here under our watchful supervision."

Paul chuckled. "Lori, you are a worrywart."

The day was nice and hot, perfect for practice dives, if that's all that was going on between Allan and Debbie. But Lori knew she wasn't just paranoid. She knew Debbie was interested in Allan and he returned the interest right back. What was not to like about Allan anyway? He was sexy and fit and loved to do what Debbie loved to do—dive. They had an easy way with each other, like they already knew each other intimately, not like people who had just started to work together. No formality between them. No getting to know each other.

Though Lori supposed he'd met Debbie on other occasions before she was partnered with him, like during monthly emergency rescue training.

There was just something about the two of them that seemed overly comfortable between new partners. Though Allan was careful not to be too friendly around Debbie when he was with Paul and Lori, she saw the way he cast Debbie looks. Intrigued looks. Not just on-the-job-training looks.

Paul was trying to calm her fears, but he was worried about Allan too. How could he not be?

Debbie was a lovely brunette and vivacious, something that totally appealed to Allan. She was definitely an alpha, ready for adventure. She loved the police work, loved saving people and animals, just like Allan. Worst of all, she was single.

Even if he hadn't been totally attracted to her at first, it would have been hard not to be when Debbie clearly admired him. She asked about his missions—that he could talk about—and wanted to know about his personal and family life. Any man would be flattered with the way she seemed to genuinely care about him, and Lori sensed that Debbie wasn't just intrigued with him because he was a hot SEAL.

As far as Lori was concerned, Debbie should be ultra-professional and just get the job done.

"You need to talk to him," Lori told Paul.

"He's a grown man and knows what he's doing."

"He's human, well, and wolf, and both are going to get him into trouble."

"I'll talk to him, but he's going to wonder what all the fuss is about."

Lori was certain Allan would know just why they were concerned.

—∾∾—

Allan was just as concerned about working with a human woman as Paul and Lori were, but he knew he could handle this. Going on dives with Debbie sure was a hell of a lot different than going with Paul.

He'd become so used to working with Paul over the

years that they did everything in perfect sync—the hand signals, the body movements, the awareness of their partner. Some signals were universal, but he and Paul, along with the other members of their SEAL wolf team, had developed some over the years that were distinctive to them.

Allan knew Paul and Lori were warily observing them. He had to admit watching Debbie swim was a hell of a lot more attention-grabbing than watching Paul. And when she smiled at him, she made him feel as though he was dating her and not just working a job. He had to remind himself to act professional and get the training done. On an assignment, they had to concentrate on the mission so they could get the results they needed—evidence from a crime scene, people or animals to safety—while ensuring they came out unscathed.

If he'd been assigned to a human male dive partner, no problem. But working with a single female, one who fascinated him like she did, was different. He could see it would take a lot of diligence on his part to keep his mind on business and not on Debbie. If he could just become interested in one of the new single females in the pack, that would solve all his problems.

But when he swam next to Debbie in the clear blue lake, she fired his testosterone sky-high. That didn't happen when he was around the single women in his pack. He hoped he could deal with this without getting them both into dangerous waters.

Chapter 2

Four months later

THE TIRES OF ALLAN'S HATCHBACK SLID ON A PATCH OF ice on the bridge just as he spied tires sticking up out of a deluge of water in a culvert. A rush of adrenaline poured through his veins, readying him for the frigid conditions and a rescue mission. In the cold of winter in northern Montana, he and his dive partner were the first to arrive on the scene of the accident and had to act quickly.

Debbie was requesting emergency backup and an ambulance as she held on to the dashboard, looking just as alarmed when the tires lost traction on the ice. He worried that they'd end up down the embankment, crashing into the upside-down SUV.

Frantically, a woman jerked at the back door of the SUV without success.

As soon as Allan saw who it was, his heart took a dive. It was Franny White, wife of the new chef at their wolf-run Italian restaurant, Fame del Lupo. She didn't go anywhere without her daughter. But the baby wasn't in her arms and Franny was trying so hard to get into the backseat, he knew little Stacy had to be buckled into her car seat and submerged underwater.

"Cancel the call for the ambulance!" he said to Debbie, knowing that this was a risk he had to take. "Call this number!" He gave her the number for the medical clinic that catered to his kind, though Debbie would be clueless. "I know the woman—her baby is in the car. Just...call it." He didn't have time to make up a cover story.

Debbie hesitated, and he knew she had to be thinking his request was a dangerous mistake. That precious time could be wasted. But lots more was at stake if the human-run hospital's ambulance picked up Franny and Stacy and they shifted. Debbie quickly called for the other ambulance and canceled the one for the main hospital in Bigfork.

As soon as he could safely brake the car and stop, Allan and Debbie were out of the vehicle, dashing down the steep incline on the crunchy snow and ice. Debbie had grabbed the emergency medical kit on the way out.

Seeing Allan and Debbie, Franny screamed, "My baby's in there! She's in a car seat in back." She was soaking wet, her tearful words were slurred, and she was stumbling around as if she were drunk. She was wearing just a sweater and jeans as she stood in the nearly waist-deep water. Allan was certain she was hypothermic. Confusion and the natural instinct to warm herself could cause her to shift. Between that and needing to rescue the baby, they were in a hell of a fix.

"She's only three months old!" Franny added, as if she didn't recognize Allan—another sign she had hypothermia.

"Get the mom out of the water," he said to Debbie as her boots crunched in the snow and ice behind him.

She slipped, her boot kicking the back of his. He swung around and grabbed her arm to keep her from falling.

"Thanks," she said, looking a little embarrassed.

"It's slippery." He was having a difficult time staying

on his own two feet, but with bigger boots and more weight than Debbie had, he was managing better.

When he reached the moving water, he waded right in. The icy cold sent a jolt of adrenaline straight through him, and he wished he were wearing a wet suit.

The driver's-side door was open where Franny had managed to get out. Allan pushed through the strong currents to the SUV, while Debbie went after Franny. When he reached the car, he tried to get the back door open but couldn't. He scrambled into the driver's seat and squeezed through the front seats to access the baby's carrier. Upside down and buckled firmly into her carrier, the baby was unconscious. The cold water covered her, and Allan feared the worst.

He shined his light inside the vehicle to give more illumination in the dark, though he could see well enough with his wolf night vision in most conditions. But this was so precarious, and with a life hanging in the balance, he didn't want to make any mistakes.

Praying he could revive the unconscious baby in time, he yanked out his knife. The icy water made his hands so stiff and numb, he feared he would drop it as he cut the straps to the car seat, careful not to injure Stacy. He yanked at the straps until they gave way. Pulling the baby free, he cradled her against his chest and backed out of the vehicle. He held the lifeless infant close as he waded through the icy water toward the snow-covered shore.

Debbie was still struggling to guide the mom out of the water. Franny was stumbling, shivering—though they all were—and instead of moving briskly out of the water like Debbie and he were doing, Franny kept stopping and turning. Debbie kept reassuring her that she was taking her to her baby, holding the woman close to share body heat and trying to rush her out of the water as fast as she could.

If he could have, Allan would have given Debbie the unresponsive baby and carried Franny from the water. But he had to resuscitate the baby pronto. Every second counted.

"I'll get the blankets," Debbie said as she left Franny on the shore and ran up the incline to the vehicle while Allan administered CPR on baby Stacy.

The infant suddenly coughed up water and let out a weak cry. Allan swore his stopped heart came back to life. She wasn't out of danger yet. She was lethargic, and her skin was bright red and cold.

Franny was trying to pull off her wet clothes in the frigid weather. Allan was afraid she was planning to turn into her wolf.

"Franny, hold on. We'll get you and Stacy to the clinic as soon as we can. The ambulance will be here any minute. Dr. Holt will take care of you both." He pressed the baby against his wet chest with one arm, while holding Franny close to him with the other and trying to keep her from stripping out of her wet clothes. She needed to, but not as a prelude to shifting. He moved them up toward the hatchback to get them out of the stiff, cold wind, but Franny was struggling to get free.

Slipping a bit, Debbie hurried as fast as she could back down the hill to reach them with blankets and some dry clothes.

"Let's get them up to the vehicle. You can remove the baby's clothes inside the car, and I'll take care of Franny," Allan said.

"Okay," Debbie replied, and Allan gave her the baby, then lifted Franny's trembling body into his arms and trudged up the hill.

"Need…to…turn," Franny bit out.

Yes, their double coat would help warm her, as would the shift itself, but then her baby would turn too. He could just see Debbie dropping the baby-turned-wolf-pup and screaming in fright.

"When you're in the ambulance, Franny. Just wait." He spoke firmly, like the pack sub-leader he was, encouraging her but at the same time commanding her to do his bidding.

At the car, Debbie climbed into the backseat, pulled off the baby's soaking-wet pink fleece jumpsuit, and wrapped her in a dry blanket, while Allan struggled to remove Franny's wet clothes. She was shaking badly from the cold, which was better than if she wasn't shivering at all, but her skin was ice white, her breathing abnormally slow.

Sirens in the distance told them the cavalry was coming. Thank God. He just hoped it was *their* ambulance and not the regular one.

"What happened?" Allan asked Franny. He had to keep her talking and alert, keep her from shifting unexpectedly.

"Red car—no accident."

Allan paused as he was trying to get a wool ski hat on her head, but she kept removing the blanket. She was either thoroughly confused or she really wanted to shift. Maybe a little of both.

Franny looked on the verge of collapse as he pulled the wool knit cap over her head and removed the rest of her wet clothes. Then he wrapped her tightly in the

blanket, lifted her into his arms, and set her inside the
hatchback. There she was at least protected from the
bitter wind. Debbie was holding the baby close. Both he
and Debbie were also suffering from hypothermia. He
felt his speech slurring, and he was having a hard time
concentrating on what *he* needed to do next. But he had
enough presence of mind to know not to shift.

"Your daughter's breathing and her heartbeat's
steady," Allan reassured Franny, though he couldn't
know for sure about the baby's overall condition until
the EMTs took her to the clinic and had her checked out.

Debbie frowned a little at him, and he realized he'd
made another mistake. The problem was that his wolf
senses were enhanced enough that he could hear, smell,
and see things that humans couldn't. Debbie probably
figured he was just soothing the mother with a story.
The truth was that he could hear the baby's heartbeat. It
was steady, which gave him a modicum of relief.

The ambulance pulled up and the medics took over
from there. Allan should have asked Franny more par-
ticulars about the accident, but he wasn't thinking as
clearly as he normally did in an emergency. Not that
Franny could have responded with any real mental clar-
ity, but it was something he should have done in a case
like this.

He and Debbie were shaking as hard as Franny from
the cold, but the EMTs had already given them blankets too.

"My...purse," Franny said, her teeth chattering.

"Anything else you need from the car?" Allan wished
he could put on his wolf coat or his wet suit. He was
afraid she had something damning in her purse with

regard to being *lupus garou*, though he couldn't imagine what. He didn't want to jeopardize their situation if anyone else went to get the bag for her later. So he made the decision to go after it, despite how chilled he was.

"Just…purse," she managed to get out. "Front…seat."

Then again, the hypothermia might be the reason she felt she had to have her purse. It might have nothing to do with keeping their secret safe. Just more of a concern about her money, credit cards, driver's license, and whatever else she might have in it. Hell, he knew of a case where a woman told her adult son to return to her burning house to retrieve her laptop. And then she was kicking herself for it afterward, wondering why she even had him do it. Irrational, sure, but people could do or say crazy things in a crisis.

Still, Allan felt it was safer if he went back for it—just in case. "I'll get it for you," he reassured Franny.

Debbie took hold of his arm. "You're already suffering from hypothermia. Let someone else do it."

"I'll be fine. I'm already wet. We'll get warm and dry real soon." Their wolf pack didn't have wolves working for the sheriff's department, except for Paul and Allan as contracted divers. So they had to take care of their own. Not that he could let on to Debbie why that was so.

At the edge of the culvert, he dropped the blanket on top of the snow.

Despite already being soaking wet and chilled to the marrow of his bones, he felt even colder when he entered the water. But his faster wolf healing abilities would help him overcome this more quickly than any human responder could.

He waded out, then dove into the submerged SUV,

glad Debbie had returned to the hatchback to protect herself from the chilling wind. He pulled his flashlight out in case he needed it and to make sure no one would question how he found the purse in the dark. He was certain Debbie would be watching to ensure he would return safely.

He located the black leather bag resting on the roof of the upside-down SUV and pulled it out. Fearful he wouldn't be able to hold on to the purse in the fast-moving water, he clutched it to his chest and waded to the shore. Once there, he grabbed the blanket and wrapped it around himself, then trudged slowly up the slope to the waiting ambulance. He felt as if he were wearing wet cement shoes.

"Thank you," Franny said, taking her sopping-wet bag and holding it tightly to her body, as if it were her baby too.

The EMTs shut the ambulance doors, but before the ambulance took off, a bark came from inside. Then with its lights flashing and siren blaring, the ambulance headed for the clinic as some of the sheriff's men arrived at the scene.

Debbie was staring at the ambulance as it drove away. "Did you hear a dog bark inside the ambulance?"

"No." A wolf, yes. Dog? No.

"You should have let someone else get her bag, Allan. You're not invincible," she said, shaking hard as they sat inside the vehicle with the heat blasting them, a cold north wind sweeping across the area as they waited to speak to the police officers who had just arrived.

"Well," said Rowdy Sanderson, a homicide detective, his blue eyes considering the two of them, "why don't you get into something warm and dry before both of you need hospitalization too. I'll handle this until you can file a report."

"What the hell are you doing here? No dead bodies," Allan said. He knew Rowdy was here because Debbie was.

"Could have been," Rowdy said, glancing at Debbie.

"Thanks. We're out of here," Allan replied. They had to get into dry clothes pronto.

Allan and Debbie were always on call if something came up. They had been finishing up some paperwork on the Van Lake murder case. A car had been found in one of the area lakes, and the driver had contusions that were probably not due to the car accident. More likely, the victim had been beaten and the accident had been staged. Allan and Debbie had been on their way to get lunch at the pizzeria when they saw Franny's SUV upside down in the culvert.

He still couldn't believe it had been one of his wolf pack members. He would have contacted Paul and Lori with the news right away, but he knew the EMTs would let them know what had happened. He figured it was safer that way, rather than calling them in front of Debbie.

"Why did you want them to go there instead of to the big hospital?" Debbie asked.

"Franny's baby was born at the clinic. The doctor there is Franny's and the baby's doctor."

"She doesn't have a pediatrician for the baby?"

"No. Dr. Holt is board certified in family medicine and pediatrics. Franny trusts her."

"Okay, but I don't think we should have canceled

the first ambulance. I want to drop by the clinic as soon as we can change and get warmed up." Debbie leaned down to pull off a boot, and then the other. She slid off a wet sock, dropping it on the floor, then struggled to get the other off.

"Agreed. I can drop you off at your place, let you get a hot shower, dry your hair, and dress. I'll pick you up, and we'll head on over there."

The clinic took only *lupus garous* for long-term care. In an emergency, they would provide care for humans, stabilizing the patient so he or she could be sent off to the hospital in Bigfork. That meant human visitors rarely came to the clinic. The staff would have to be on alert when Debbie dropped by to see Franny and her baby.

"Thanks, sounds like a good plan," Debbie said.

She pulled off her sopping-wet sweater and dumped it on the floor. This was the first time in the four and a half months they'd worked together that they'd had a situation like this—where they needed to get warm and dry pronto, and were too far from anywhere to do it quickly. He hadn't expected Debbie to start stripping though. It was a good idea, but he just hadn't predicted it.

Next, came her black turtleneck. He was trying to concentrate on the ice- and snow-covered road, but out of the corner of his eye, he saw that her bra was purple-and-white polka-dotted silk. He smiled a little, never having thought of her wearing bright and fanciful underwear.

She unfastened her bra and dropped it on the floor. He nearly missed the turn to the main road that would take him to Whitefish where Debbie lived. He *really* was trying to be a gentleman, but, hell, he'd worked with her for months, and lots of times when she was wearing a skintight diving suit, he'd envisioned what she would look like naked. Now she was stripping next to him?

Not that this wasn't essential to their—well, *her*—good health, but it was wreaking havoc on his libido, despite how cold and wet he was. He was a wolf, after all. But he was going to have a damn accident if he wasn't careful.

She used one of the towels they kept in the car when they went diving to cover her waist and another to dry herself off.

Thankfully, she was concentrating on pulling on a dry turtleneck and then a sweater, too cold to notice him glancing at her. They always kept a couple pairs of clothes in backpacks in the car for diving and emergencies. She struggled to get her jeans off next and then wiggled out of her panties, which matched her bra.

As soon as she'd pulled on the rest of her dry clothes, zipped her parka up to her throat, and tugged her ski hat on, she said, "Pull over. You've got to get out of your wet things too."

"I bet you say that to all the guys you dive with." He pulled onto the shoulder and they switched places, the cold outdoors feeling even icier.

She laughed. "If I were diving with Lou Messer, probably not. His brand-new wife told the sheriff if he paired Lou up with me, he'd be leaving the police dive force."

Allan smiled. "I heard she checks up on him all the time, wanting to know where he is, what he's doing, and if he's safe. I'm glad I don't have to deal with her. If I did, I'd probably say something and get myself in trouble."

"Yeah, but everyone needs your expertise, so they're stuck with you."

He laughed. "Stuck with me, eh?"

"It can be a good thing. I still can't believe you went back for Franny's purse. The crew could have gotten it when they pulled her SUV out of the culvert."

"You know how women are. She was probably afraid of losing her credit cards, cash, driver's license, no telling what. Maybe a special keepsake she was afraid might be lost."

Then it was Allan's turn to remove his wet clothes. He moved the passenger seat as far back as he could to give himself more leg room and began the tedious project, his fingers numb with cold and the shivering impeding his progress.

"Well, it was sweet of you, but too risky."

After he got a dry flannel shirt and wool sweater on and had yanked a wool ski hat over his head, he finally felt relief. Then he tugged at his boots, socks, and jeans. When he got down to his black boxers, Debbie said, "I figured you for white briefs."

"I figured you'd wear a white lacy bra and matching bikini panties."

"You looked!" But she was smiling when she said it.

He chuckled and pulled on a pair of blue briefs, jeans, socks, and a pair of dry boots.

All dry now, he was feeling a hell of a lot better. His hair was cut short, but Debbie's was long. He was certain her wet hair was still making her cold, but the hat she wore would keep the heat from escaping in the meantime.

He got a call on his cell and fumbled to get it out of

the console, realizing then he was still feeling some of the effects of the hypothermia. The call was from Paul. He and the rest of the SEAL wolf team members still did contract missions together, but they'd put that part of their life mostly on hold while they raised families. The shared responsibility of raising *lupus garou* pups was all too important to a pack like theirs.

Now wasn't the best time to call because Allan was with Debbie, but Paul would know that. Which meant Allan was probably needed for a pack-related emergency. He worried that it had to do with Franny and her claim that the SUV sliding down the embankment hadn't been an accident. With Paul's broken leg still incapacitating him, Allan was taking up the slack.

"Allan, we've got a problem."

"Okay. Just a sec. Debbie and I were just on a case, and we're suffering from a mild case of hypothermia." Which Paul would be aware of, because the EMTs who rescued Franny would have told him. But Allan couldn't let Debbie know that Paul was aware of it. "We're dropping by her place so she can dry her hair and get warmed up a bit and then I'm headed over to my cabin. Can I call you back?" Allan didn't want to have to watch what he was saying.

"Call me as soon as you can. We have a minor emergency."

"Will do." Allan was dying to know what the emergency was—if it was related to Franny or something else—but he didn't want to ask in front of Debbie and then have to make up some story about it later.

They ended the call and he phoned the clinic. "How are Franny and Stacy doing?" he asked Dr. Christine

Holt, glad Lori had found her to help establish a clinic for them. When Dr. Holt had delivered Franny's baby, the whole pack had come out to see the new mother and cub. His sister, Rose, was pregnant with triplets, and they had thought she would be the first pack member to give birth. But then Franny and Gary had joined the pack. It was good to see new blood in the pack.

"They're in stable condition. Your partner didn't suspect anything?" Christine asked him.

"No."

"Good. Are you all right? The EMTs said that you went back in the water after her purse."

"Yeah, in case she had something important in there."

"Well, she pulled a piece of paper out of her purse, sopping wet, the ink all gone, but she said it wasn't important anyway. She was so out of it, she just knew she had to have her purse with her. Both Franny and her baby will be fine. Her husband is here with them now."

"Good to hear. Debbie and I will be dropping by as soon as we can get dry and warm."

"Give us a heads-up when you're on your way. We don't have any other patients at the moment, but you never know when we might, and we need to make sure that Franny remains human."

"Will do."

"Take care."

Allan told Debbie about the condition of mom and baby, but not about the purse. He didn't want her reminding him how he shouldn't have gone after it.

He was tasked with ensuring that all the new wolf pack members worked well together, but he also helped with any trouble the pack was having.

He should have been interested in one of the lovely single she-wolves, but he couldn't get his thoughts off a certain sexy, kick-ass human. Some of it was because they worked together, but they also had a lot in common. They both loved to dive as a hobby, liked thrillers and Italian food, and read some of the same fantasy books.

They had been on a number of missions together already—rescue diving for underwater casualties and search-and-recovery diving for evidence and bodies. And they were still trying to find clues in the Van Lake case.

"I'm glad to hear Franny and her baby are doing well. Is there a problem at home?" Debbie asked.

"Not sure. Probably some minor family issue." This was the part Allan hated. He'd told her about his family, as far as he could say. That his mother and sister had taken Paul in. That he was like a brother to them. But Allan hadn't been able to say much more than that. Certainly nothing about their wolf pack and their increased longevity. That had changed though. They were aging nearly the same as humans now, but they hadn't figured out why. He and his family had lived for many years, although they didn't look it.

Trying to explain how eons ago he had run through a forest that once was on dry land and now was buried underwater in Lake MacDonald—and other such things—wasn't an option. He had gone diving with her there just for fun and wished he could have told her about the time Paul and he had had a very close call with a bear, when the forest *wasn't* underwater. She would never have believed him.

"Hope everything's all right," she said, sounding genuinely concerned.

The problem was that she had a cop's way of thinking. She was curious and had good instincts. She could tell something was going on. He knew the longer they worked together, the dicier it would get. Paul had warned him, but what could Allan do? He didn't want to ask for another partner when he really loved working with her, and how would he explain why he couldn't work with her any longer?

Anything he said might hurt her career. And he wasn't about to do that.

He sighed. Somehow he would just have to keep up the facade. That meant not letting on that he could smell things that humans couldn't. She'd already commented on his remarkable eyesight when it was getting to be dusk and dawn.

Yeah, working with her was great…and dangerous. Not only because of what he was, but because he totally had the hots for her. And that was a no go in this business. He told himself it would be easy because partners didn't normally date. If he just kept it on a professional basis, he should have no problem.

His focus turned to Paul's phone call. He knew the situation wouldn't be a minor issue. He was anxious to learn what the trouble was this time.

Chapter 3

DEBBIE REALLY LOVED WORKING WITH ALLAN, THOUGH he was…different. Maybe that's why she loved working with him so much. She could tell he really wanted to see her after hours, and he did sometimes—to talk more about a case. But she believed he wanted more. She wanted more. And yet he was clearly reluctant, probably because of his work ethics. Which was another reason she really liked him.

They would keep working on cases no matter the hour, have dinner together, and work on them some more. Get up early, start on it again. This month, they'd rescued four people who had fallen through the ice while ice fishing, saved a baby moose that had fallen through ice, and rescued two victims of accidents due to icy road conditions. Not only that, but they'd been working on this murder case, and though the vehicle and body had already been removed from the lake, she and Allan planned to see if they could find anything else in the water around the site of the accident.

She glanced at him, trying to read his expression. He had one of those faces that made her think of a really nice guy—sweet, cherublike—but she'd seen him arrest a man high on PCP and knew Allan could be all business when it came to taking someone in hand. He used military moves that she wanted him to teach her in case she ever needed to take a guy down like that. Allan's hair was a rich, dark brown, and his dark-green eyes seemed to see right through her. It should have been disquieting, but she really found it amazing.

He appreciated her training and often remarked on what a great partner she was. She knew he wasn't saying it just to be nice. He truly meant what he said, and she really respected him for it. She felt the same way about him.

"Are we still on for pizza?" she asked. She wanted to check on the baby and mom at the clinic to see for herself they were okay, but she was also dying to have a pizza. She hadn't had one in ages, and it would be a nice way to take a break once she dried her wet clothes and her hair. At least the car heater was warming her up now.

"You bet." His eyes always lit up when his gaze caught hers. He was seriously sexy, muscular, and in great shape, and that appealed too.

She always wanted to hear his SEAL stories, the ones that he could share with her. He'd told her about a couple of rescues he and his team had performed for private contracts. They'd been in the Amazon a number of times on dangerous missions. She found him to be the most fascinating man she'd ever met.

Some of her fascination was because his family was so important to him. She was estranged from her own. Her father had been the town drunk and her mother the perfect enabler. Good thing Debbie was an only child so she was the only one who had to suffer the consequences of a dysfunctional family like theirs.

When Allan had asked her about her family, she really hadn't wanted to say anything about them. On the other hand, she appreciated how thoughtful he had been in asking. Not too many police officers she knew cared anything about their partners' families. Maybe about a husband or wife and kids, but not about parents and siblings, unless they lived in town. But Allan seemed really family-oriented.

"While you were getting Franny's purse, she told me a red car had nearly hit hers and slid on the ice, and she turned to avoid it. That's how she ended up careening down the hill and sailing into the culvert. She said he did it on purpose, but she doesn't remember the SUV being upside down. Just that somehow she managed to get out and then couldn't get to her baby. So I suspect she just imagined the driver had caused the accident on purpose."

"Hell, I thought she was mistaken," Allan said. "The driver didn't stop to help? Call it in or anything?"

"It wasn't technically a hit-and-run, and he might have been afraid that if he tried to brake on the ice, he'd be where she was."

"If it was a woman or someone elderly, I'd give the driver the benefit of the doubt, but her baby could have died. And Franny could have too."

"Agreed. She said he was wearing a camo cap and his hair was cut short, but that's all she could see before she swerved to avoid him. He was about our age."

"Then he should be strung up."

She wasn't surprised at the way Allan felt. She had thought the same thing, though she had tried to see it from the other driver's point of view too. But she had to agree with Allan.

"We can eat at the pizzeria for lunch, unless there's

a problem at home," she said, giving Allan an out. She didn't want him to think she would be upset if he couldn't make it because of family obligations. His sister was pregnant with triplets and Paul's wife with twins, so maybe one of them was having some difficulty. She sure hoped not.

When he drove into her duplex driveway, he finally said, "Uh, about lunch, yeah. I'll give you a call in just a bit."

Then he dropped her off, and she knew, as distracted as he was, that whatever was the matter had to be really important.

Allan pulled out of her driveway, a frown on his face as he talked to someone on his cell. She wondered again just what the trouble was and if she would be going alone to the clinic.

She realized she really wanted to be part of his life, to be there for him if he needed someone to talk to about family stuff. Not in a boyfriend-girlfriend relationship particularly, but just as a friend. That had been something she'd had trouble with growing up. She hadn't had anyone to talk to about her parents. Better to just leave home and stay away. As a kid, that had meant spending hours at the library after school and immersing herself in books until it closed for the night. Often a police officer would drive her home.

She'd gotten to know nearly everyone on the police force that way. One of the officers had rescued her father from his submerged truck when he'd gotten drunk and crashed it through the bridge. The officer had only delayed the inevitable though. Her dad killed himself a year later in another accident, one with a concrete bridge column. But the officer's dedication as a diver, and her love of the water and subsequent scuba diving certification, had made her career decision for her. She had become a contracted police diver just like Officer Hardy Monroe.

She knew Allan had chosen to be one so he could work closer to home and spend more time with his family, though he had told her that when he was needed for a mission, he would have to take a leave of absence and deal with it. She was surprised he would continue to do missions away from home, considering how close he was to his family. In the four and a half months he'd been working with her, he hadn't gone on any. She was glad because she really enjoyed working with him. Trying to train with a new dive partner would mean learning his or her idiosyncrasies all over again.

Paul Cunningham also was continuing to do contract work out of country, though he'd set aside that business because his wife was pregnant. Debbie had felt bad when he'd broken his leg and hoped it would mend just fine. He was out of the cast now, but he was still using a cane. When he was fully recovered, would he go back to being partnered with Allan?

That made her feel a little blue.

After washing up, getting dressed, and drying her hair, she was hopeful she could have lunch with Allan and head over to the clinic. But when she checked her phone, she saw that Allan had texted his regrets: Need to deal with some family issues. Talk to you soon. Allan.

No "sorry about lunch." No "wish I could see Franny and the baby." Debbie knew those family issues had to be bad news or Allan would have said something more.

He was always good about that. And he was always conscientious about personally seeing the victims they'd rescued to learn how they were faring.

She wished she could help in some way. She put in a call to the clinic as she headed over there, hoping when she saw Allan again, he'd feel comfortable sharing with her.

---~~~---

"We don't know who she is?" Allan asked Paul, angered that a *lupus garou* had come into their territory, maybe looking for protection, and had been murdered.

His countenance stormy, Paul stared out the window of his cabin overlooking the lake, his arms folded across his chest. "No. Since she was naked and one of our kind, we presume she was trapped and killed as a wolf. Your sister and my mate were out running as wolves before dawn's first light and came across her body in the woods near the cabin.

"Whoever did it caught her in an animal trap and shot her. The ladies saw burn marks on the bullet wounds. Though ballistics haven't come back to confirm it yet, the rounds had to have been silver. The ladies smelled the sweet, subtle scent of pure silver. She had lots of defensive wounds from trying to get loose from the trap and bite her attacker."

"Did she actually bite him?"

"Yes."

"What about DNA samples from his blood? Skin?" Allan considered the ramifications further. "What if her bites transferred the *lupus garou* genetics into his bloodstream and he turns into a wolf? He won't have much control over it for some time. He won't be able to shift for another week since it's the phase of the new moon right now."

"The forensics lab is testing the blood and tissue samples. But you know it takes a while for the results of the lab work to come in. If he hasn't committed any crimes, or even if he has, he might not be in the database. An autopsy is being done as we speak. If we find the bastard soon, he'll be wearing some hefty bite marks and scratches. But if he's been turned, that's another story. That means we have a week to catch him before the half moon appears. What's worse is someone anonymously reported the murder. If he was a wolf, we'd have to handle it on our own. But now the police are involved."

"The killer reported it?"

"Possibly." Paul let out his breath. "Probably. Neither Lori nor Rose saw, smelled, or heard anyone. The killer had to have been wearing hunter spray while in hunting mode. Rowdy Sanderson is the homicide detective in charge of the investigation. Because the killer used silver rounds, whoever murdered the wolf had to have known she was a *lupus garou*. Even if he wasn't certain, once she shifted into her human form after she died, that would have confirmed it."

"He didn't try to remove her body to claim he'd killed a werewolf?"

"No. I'm declaring that no one in the pack shifts until we can learn who did this and take him down."

"Good idea. Any clues?"

Paul shook his head. "I suspect the woman was coming here to meet with us so she could join the pack. But why was she running as a wolf? I want you to check out the crime scene. I've got Everett trying to track down who she was. I've asked Lori's grandma to find out if the woman had any contact with any member of our pack, since Emma and your mother have been involved the most in asking single female wolves to join the pack."

Thinking in a purely police-procedural way, Allan said, "Often the killer is actually someone who knew the victim. It's a family member or a close friend or an acquaintance. Random killings are more unusual. But in the case of someone using silver rounds to kill a wolf?" Allan didn't even want to think they might have a self-professed werewolf hunter in the area. "Sounds like we have a werewolf hunter on our hands, don't you agree?" In all the years of their existence, they had never had to deal with such an issue.

"It sure as hell sounds like it. On the other hand, what if it is a *lupus garou*, and he covered his tracks by making it *look* like a werewolf hunter was after her? If that's the case, his victim wouldn't have turned him."

"Yeah, I was just thinking that too. And if he's not recently turned, that can be good and bad. Good, because he won't shift unexpectedly around humans and give our kind away. And bad because he'll be harder to track down."

"Either way, we have to stop him. But if he hasn't been turned, we need the police to handle this." Paul headed into the kitchen and got them each a bottled water. Then they moved to the living room and took seats on the couches.

"Agreed." Allan noticed Paul's cane leaning next to the couch, but he wasn't using it today. "How's your leg?"

"It's fine. If one more person asks…"

Allan nodded. He knew how much that had to bother Paul. "But you're getting around without the cane, and I don't see you limping."

"Inside buildings I'm fine. Plowing through snow-drifts or walking on ice…" Paul shook his head. "Besides, I get enough coddling from Lori, Mom, Rose, and Grandma. I don't need it from you too."

"*Me* coddle *you*? When have I ever done that? It's not in my SEAL or wolf nature. Hell, any of us, broken leg or not, can have trouble on ice unless we're in our wolf form and have better traction. It'll get better."

Paul grunted, then took a swig from his water bottle. "There was a *lupus garou* pack that had to deal with a werewolf-hunter group. They successfully turned one of the men, and he works for the pack. The others had to be put down. The pack members couldn't have the men arrested and tried for murder, but they had to deal with the threat permanently. Otherwise the men wouldn't give up their quest to destroy the wolves and convert new wolf hunters.

"They hadn't even been looking for werewolves initially. They were searching for Bigfoot but saw a *lupus garou* shift. The same could have happened with this case. I could be mistaken, but I suspect the shooter is someone who had prior military service or is a hunter. I can't imagine the average man taking up a gun to hunt werewolves."

"All right, so that's a possibility," Allan said. "That the hunter didn't know about our kind until the woman shifted and he saw her. I would agree with you about him being a hunter or prior military." Allan set his bottle on the table.

"Here's another thought, though it's even more far-fetched," Paul said. "After seeing the murdered woman, Rose told Lori that while we were away on a mission, she had looked into one of those live-action role-playing — LARP — groups in southern Montana: werewolf versus villager werewolf hunters. She wanted to see if it was just a game or if any of the players were real wolves."

"Hell, Paul. Why would she even do that?"

"She had been corresponding with one of the players online, thinking he was one of us. She had no one to date in the area, and she had discovered his website where he talked about werewolves and being one."

"Which should have clued her in that he wasn't."

"I agree. But no *lupus garous* had passed through our area in months, and she was lonely. When she began to talk to him, she convinced herself he really was a *lupus garou*. So she went down to see him. This was a month before she met Everett. Which shows we were right to stay here and take over the pack."

"Sounds like it." Allan couldn't believe his sister had done that. "I'm surprised Mom wasn't upset about her doing something like that." Rose was way too curious for her own good.

"She told Catherine she was going on a shopping trip to pick up leather-crafting supplies to make some things for her shop. Catherine never knew the real purpose of her visit because Rose brought back leather-working materials. When Rose arrived in Helena, she had lunch with the man, Guy Lamb, and discovered he really was a wolf."

Allan's jaw dropped, then he shook his head. "I never would have believed it. And by the name of Lamb?"

"Yeah, it was his parents' idea. Everyone teased him about being a lamb when he was a kid, so he had fun with saying he was a werewolf on his website."

"A wolf in sheep's clothing."

"Right. Anyway, he liked Rose, but once she met him, she wasn't interested in getting to know him further. She said he was too weird for her. Loved horror stories, music she didn't care for, books she wouldn't read. He was such a big horror fan that he loved to act in plays of that nature and visit horror conventions. They just didn't have anything in common. But she wanted to check out the game for curiosity's sake, in case one of the other players was also a real wolf. Someone she might connect with more.

"Rose did manage to meet with the group, which had eight werewolf hunters, one seer, and two wolves. Though who was playing which roles was a mystery. She said no one smelled like a wolf. But when she and Lori came across the woman's body, Rose was pretty rattled and told us about the group, in case it had any bearing on this situation."

"Okay," Allan said. "I can't think of any other scenario offhand. The notion the killer saw the *lupus garou* shift and then eliminated her has my vote."

"I agree. Even so, just to be thorough because we certainly don't want any more surprises like this one, I checked to see if any LARP groups were listed online. I didn't see anything like that in our area. If it is a local group whose members don't share about it on the Internet, then we wouldn't know about it."

Allan rose from his seat and paced across the living room floor. "It doesn't sound like someone who was just playing a game. The business with silver rounds and luring a wolf into a leghold trap first…"

Paul finished his bottle of water and set the empty container on the coffee table. "After viewing the wounds inflicted on the woman, I really think something deeper was going on. The murderer attacked her in a rage. It wasn't just a case of killing a random person. Passion was involved—anger."

"Maybe he was a former lover and discovered what she was?"

"Now that could be."

"Why would he leave her like that? Why not hide the body?"

"Lori and Rose's arrival might have stopped him."

"Why would he call the police to warn them about the killing, if he was the one who called in anonymously?" Allan asked.

"Because he's proud of the kill? Maybe he thought the coroner could prove she's a werewolf through DNA. Then he could brag about killing a werewolf."

"Then he had to know or believe the woman *was* a werewolf. She had to have known him, probably trusted him." Thinking of an even worse-case scenario, Allan ran his hands through his hair. "What if he was watching when Rose and Lori arrived? And when they left, he followed them?"

"That's what I'm worried about. The police were at the crime scene while you were at work this morning. I told the homicide detective in charge that you'll also be looking into it since it happened so close to our cabin and we're concerned about more trouble for the two ladies who found the victim."

"Good. What were the police told about how Lori and Rose located her?"

"They were taking a hike through the woods. There's a trail near there. They were headed up to the lookout over the lake. Anyway, that's the story. In truth, they smelled blood—and lots of it. So they headed that way to locate the wounded wolf and help if they could. When they discovered the woman and realized she was one of us, they hated to have to leave her body behind, but they didn't have any choice. They went to the cabin, shifted, dressed, called me, and then headed back to the killing site to 'find' her as humans."

"They didn't wait for you though?"

"No. It would have taken me too long to get there. I was at Lori's dojo, working out some of the stiffness in my leg. Lori called me to make sure she and Rose were doing the right thing. Of course, I didn't want them returning to the scene in case the bastard was still in the area. But understandably, they wanted to call it in before the body happened to vanish, if the murderer decided to dispose of it."

Allan swore under his breath. "Rose is too far along to be running as a wolf, and both she and Lori could have been in real trouble. Still could be."

"Rose said it was her last time to run. They didn't expect to find the dead woman."

"Hell. If the killer was watching the women arrive as wolves and then return as humans, he could have put two and two together, tracked them back to your cabin, learned you're Lori's mate, and well, hell, about everyone related to them—Lori's grandmother, Mom, Rose's mate, and his mother and sister. And that's just the few of us from the original pack."

"You and me. Yes, very possibly. Which means we have to catch this bastard pronto. Rose contacted everyone on the pack roster to let them know they need to avoid seeing any of us for the time being. We don't know if this guy has any way to track the rest of the pack members, but if we cut off seeing them in person, that might help." Paul pointed to a map on the wall showing the whole area: lakes, parks, trails, even elevations. "Here's where the woman was found."

"I'll let you know if I discover anything further."

His blood cold with anger, Allan left the cabin and drove to the logging road closest to the location of the crime scene. Even if the murderer had witnessed Rose and Lori discovering the body as wolves, then returning later as humans, Allan knew they would have pretended they had suddenly come across this horrific scene, screaming and calling Paul on his cell, maybe pretending to be calling 911. So if the murderer was watching, he might not have made the connection between them and the wolves. But they still couldn't chance it.

On the way to the site, Allan made a call to Debbie, wanting to know how she was doing and how Franny and her baby were faring. He had already called ahead to let the staff know that Debbie would be arriving to check on them on her own, but he had learned from them that she had called ahead. He felt bad that he hadn't been able to go with her, that he hadn't been able to see to Franny and the baby, that he'd had to break his lunch engagement with Debbie, and that he hadn't been able to discuss this other business with her.

"How are the baby and Franny doing?" he asked.

"I'm still at the clinic and the doc is keeping them overnight. They're going to be just fine. Thanks to you."

"And you. Hell, you saw the vehicle first."

He mentioned that only because she'd commented on his keen vision too many times to count, and he didn't want her to find that odd. "I'm sorry about lunch. I'll make it up to you later."

"No problem at all, Allan, but I'll certainly take you up on it. Is everything all right?"

He couldn't lie to her and say everything was fine. Everything wouldn't be all right until they caught this maniac. "It's a small family crisis." Which was the truth. Anything that affected *lupus garous* in their territory affected them. So it *was* a family crisis. But small? Not really. Especially if the man was a newly turned wolf who had shifted and was wholly out of control. "I'll be back tomorrow to help investigate the Van Lake accident scene." It was located fifty-three miles from where Allan lived, so not too far.

"Can I help in any way?"

"No, thanks. I'll...I'll call you later tonight." He hated this part of their relationship, where he couldn't be completely honest with her. He could imagine just how well telling her the truth would go over. That he even considered such a notion bothered him. Normally, he never gave it any thought when he was around humans. He and his kind were what they were and that was their own business.

"All right. I'll fill out the accident report on the mother and baby. I'll...talk to you later."

He knew she wasn't happy with the way he always shut down about his family when there were issues.

She'd told him about her alcoholic father, and he suspected it bothered her that he wouldn't come clean with *his* family "issues."

"Talk to you later, Debbie." He hung up as he reached the area where the killing had taken place.

He hated that tens of thousands of leghold traps and snares were legally set up on Montana's public lands and along waterways. Reportedly, fifty thousand wild animals were trapped a year, but trappers weren't required to check traps regularly or report numbers. People and pets could be the victims, as well as any other animal the hunter wasn't interested in capturing. One of the former vice presidents of the Montana Trappers Association had agreed that trappers cause pain and suffering to animals, but would apologize to no one. Really a sad state of affairs.

Allan reached the murder scene and found yellow police tape roping it off. He left his vehicle, smelling around the area for the scent of the trapper who had set the leghold trap. Allan was careful not to look like he was trying to breathe in scents in case the killer was in the area observing.

He found the victim's blood splattered all over the fresh snow. Tracks were everywhere from the wolves who found the victim and the humans who had come to retrieve her body. He looked around at the thick pine forest and where the trap had been set near a tree, buried by the snow. He tried to sense if the murderer was in the area. The trappers were a danger to them all. But this guy, even more so.

So many people had been in the area, it was hard to say who might have done this. Allan followed boot tracks in the snow for over a mile, then went back and followed another set of tracks. None of them led him to anything suspicious. Tons of tire tracks were on an old logging trail nearby too—the ambulance and police vehicles for sure. So again, nothing that could help him.

Once he climbed back into his vehicle and shut the door, he called Paul. "I didn't find anything that stood out to me."

"I just got the preliminary report on the autopsy. She was shot five times, and all the rounds were silver."

"He has to be a werewolf hunter then."

"You know, we've been thinking it's a he, but it might have been a she. Some of the murdered woman's wolf fur was stuck to the blood on the jaws of the trap, though the coroner believes that a wolf had been caught earlier. Rose and Lori identified it as the woman's fur by its smell. So the victim couldn't have been a new wolf or she couldn't have been in her wolf form."

"We need to put this guy down."

"I'd like to, but as long as the killer might be human and the police are involved, we have to let the homicide detectives working the case deal with it. We've got to catch the guy before they do to determine if he's one of our kind now. If we catch him and he's still human, we turn him over to the police. I've let everyone know to be extra vigilant if they think they're being followed. I don't want anyone to see our families except for you and me. I don't want him to identify anyone else as a pack member so no one else will be put in harm's way."

"Agreed." Allan couldn't believe what a nightmare this could be for all of them.

"We have another situation that arose. Lori went to

see Franny and she wants to speak with you about her car crash. Lori thought maybe she was confused, but Franny was adamant it wasn't an accident."

"That's what she told me. She talked to Debbie about it too."

"Franny knows you're the only one in the pack available to investigate it right now, but I think there's something else she's hiding."

"From Lori?"

"Yeah. If you're going to investigate this, she'll have to tell you what she knows."

"All right. I'll drop by the clinic next." What *else* could go wrong?

"Hey, Debbie," Rowdy said, meeting up with her as she headed to the clinic lobby. She was ready to get takeout somewhere close by and then work on the accident report back at the sheriff's office. She was relieved Franny and baby Stacy were doing well.

She was surprised to see Rowdy here, since he was a *homicide* detective.

"Hey," she said, disliking the speculative gleam in his eyes.

He glanced around the lobby and, seeing it was empty, said to her, "I heard you were here by yourself and wondered where your partner had gone."

She shrugged it off. "He had a minor family crisis."

Rowdy raised his brows.

She suspected then that he knew something she didn't and that it wasn't good news. *Especially* since he was a homicide detective. But if someone in Allan's family had been murdered, she was certain Allan would have told her. "Well, spill."

"Allan's twin sister and Paul's wife were hiking in the woods when they came across a body near Paul's cabin. Didn't he tell you?"

Chapter 4

DEBBIE COULDN'T BELIEVE ALLAN HADN'T TOLD HER what had happened to his sister and her friend. Was Allan so upset that he felt he couldn't discuss it with her? She knew whatever he'd been worried about had to be bad, the way that he had been so distracted. Allan had to know she would hear about it eventually.

"Thanks, Rowdy. Can you fill me in on the details?" Debbie asked him.

After he did, he told her about an earlier case that he hadn't worked—bank robbers found dead at the scene—but he had reviewed it and found it disquieting. "One man was found floating in the lake, naked, dead, near the jumping cliff. And another man had been torn up by a wild animal—confirmed wolf saliva. Not only that, but the tires of one of their vehicles had been bitten into."

"By...? Wait, the wolf did it."

Rowdy shrugged. "Any canine could have done it. Since one man had been bitten by a wolf, I assume a wolf also tore up the tires at the crime scene. I read about a case where car tires were regularly being punctured along a stretch of street in front of a housing development. Police tried to catch the culprit for months and finally put up cameras to see who the vandals were, figuring they were kids. But a dog? No one in a million years would have believed it. Seems the owners would walk the dog off leash, and the dog would bite into the tires and puncture them."

"That's weird."

"A couple of months earlier, the dog had been hit by a car."

Debbie was glad the dog was fine after being hit and could hardly believe it had been attacking tires in revenge. She didn't blame the dog, and she imagined how the police had felt when they discovered the culprit. "So why would a dog—or should I say, wolf—do that to the perp's vehicle?"

"To keep the criminals from escaping."

"So the wolf had been trained to sabotage tires." She couldn't believe what Rowdy could come up with. "Wolves don't normally attack humans."

"Not usually."

"Okay, so another scenario?"

"The wolf wasn't a wolf. And that same wolf or part of its pack killed the one bank robber."

"Wolves don't do that. Not normally," she repeated.

"You're right. They don't. But what if they were werewolves?"

"Ah, come on, Rowdy. So the naked man was a werewolf too?" She knew he loved paranormal shows, but this was going a bit far.

"Makes sense. Too many unanswered questions in the case. I would have figured okay, so wolves were involved in this other case too, but a lot of shooting went on."

"No silver rounds, right?" She wasn't buying this werewolf business, but if silver bullets had been used, then, yes, she would believe a connection existed between the two cases.

"Correct. No silver rounds. But guess who was involved in the shoot-out."

"Lori and Rose?" Debbie asked, unable to keep the surprise from her voice. Now *that* would be a weird coincidence.

"Lori, Paul, Everett, and Allan."

"They weren't involved in the killing of this woman." No way did she believe anything bad about Allan and his friends.

"No, I doubt it. But don't you think it's a bit odd that two strange cases that have some similarities come up only a few months apart? First, some of the same people were involved in both, but in any case, they're all related in one way or another. And second, we have two unexplained naked bodies."

Debbie folded her arms. "But there were silver bullets in this one and none in the other." She had been known to come up with some fairly far-fetched notions herself in trying to solve crimes, but this line of reasoning was going way out of the ballpark.

"True enough. So what if in this case, we have werewolf hunters armed with silver rounds, and in the other, they were all wolves, so no one was using silver rounds."

"Okay, so if they're all werewolves, why wouldn't they use silver? They can't be killed by regular bullets, can they?"

"Maybe they can. And the only ones that don't know that are the werewolf hunters."

Debbie shook her head and patted Rowdy on the chest in an appeasing way. "You need to be working with the detectives on *The X-Files*."

"I'm just saying you need to watch yourself."

"Wait. You're saying that Allan, Paul, and the rest of their family could be werewolves?"

Rowdy glanced at the receptionist, then turned his attention to Debbie again. "You never know. Just… keep your eyes open, consider what I've said, and if anything seems…unusual, let me know. I've got to run. Take care."

Werewolves.

Debbie couldn't believe how Rowdy teased her, though she suspected that making light of something dark sometimes helped him keep from becoming totally numb to the killings he investigated.

Now she had a choice: call Allan and ask if she could do anything for him or his family after learning the horrific news, or let it go and give him time to deal with this on his own.

She still couldn't believe it. To think poor Rose and Lori had found the dead body when Lori was pregnant with twins and Rose with triplets. And Rose was near term, Debbie thought. They had to have been terrified that the maniac might still be in the woods. She frowned as she got into her Escort. She hoped Allan wouldn't try to locate the guy and take him down on his own.

Before she hit the road, she punched in Allan's number.

"Yeah?" Allan answered right away, sounding concerned.

Which she appreciated, considering the frame of mind he had to be in. "I heard about the murder near Paul's cabin. Are your sister and Lori all right?" She wanted to ask if *he* was all right. He had to be distressed over the whole situation, but she suspected he wouldn't appreciate her asking him that.

"Yeah, thanks, Debbie. I really didn't want to talk about it."

"I understand. Were you digging around at the crime scene?"

"Yeah, but I didn't find anything else."

"The guy has to be some sick bastard."

"I agree."

"Can I do anything for Rose and Lori? I'd like to help, if you think they'd appreciate it."

"No, thanks. We're good."

Well, maybe Allan was "good" with it, but Debbie had met both ladies and really liked them. She would have to see what she could do to make them feel better. She'd had all kinds of police psychology training on dealing with issues like this. Paul and Allan probably had some training, but they were too close to the situation. She could imagine how upset they both were.

"Do you have any plans for supper?" Allan asked out of the blue.

Debbie didn't say anything for a moment because she was so surprised. "Um, no. Do you want to grab some of that pizza?"

He chuckled. "You really had your heart set on having some, didn't you?"

"Yeah, I did. Would six be too early?"

"That'll be fine. Can we meet at the pizzeria?"

She hesitated to respond. If he was trying to tell her this wasn't a date, she wanted him to know she hadn't viewed it as such, as much as she wouldn't mind if the dynamics changed between them. Maybe he was worried that his family might need him, and he wanted to be free to run off and take care of them without worrying about taking her along.

She shouldn't be overanalyzing this so much. If she were a guy, just a partner, she wouldn't be. Which made her realize how much she wanted to be more than just his partner.

"Okay, sure. Works for me." In the meantime, she would check on Lori and Rose. They had to be more than distraught over the whole business. If they didn't want to talk about it, that was fine, but she wasn't letting Allan speak for them.

As soon as they ended the call, she headed over to the ranching community of Cottage Grove where Rose's house, a new two-story log home, had been recently built on an acre of her mother's property behind her home. Rose's husband, Everett Johnston, had actually built it and Debbie loved how beautiful and remarkable it was.

She really liked how much the family stayed together. She imagined how helpful it would be for Rose's mom to live right there. When Rose needed help with the triplets, she would have it.

On the drive to Rose's place, Debbie mulled over all that Rowdy had told her, wondering what really had happened.

Allan was glad to learn from the receptionist at the clinic that Debbie had left twenty minutes earlier. He needed to speak with Franny in private and didn't want to have to make excuses about that to Debbie.

At the reception desk, Yvonne Messner frowned

at him when he arrived, and he wondered what was
wrong now.

"That homicide detective, Rowdy Sanderson, was
here, talking to your dive partner in private. She seemed
surprised and then upset. I tried to listen in, but I was
fielding calls about Franny and the baby and missed out
on it. I did overhear him telling her about Lori and Rose
discovering the body."

"Thanks, Yvonne. She just told me." Allan liked
Rowdy. He was a friendly sort, but Rowdy really liked
Debbie. Allan couldn't help feeling a little possessive
about her in a wolf way, which he had no right feeling.

"Franny is with her baby in room three. She's expect-
ing you."

"Thanks."

When he reached the room, he found Franny lying in
bed with Stacy, both sound asleep. He hated to disturb
them, but being a wolf, Franny instantly smelled his
scent and opened her eyes.

"You'll keep what I have to say private?" she asked
before he could inquire about how she was feeling.

"If the person who forced you into the culvert did so
on purpose and I'm investigating it, I can't guarantee the
word won't get out. I'll be discreet, and Lori and Paul
will have to be kept informed, but otherwise, we'll try
to keep it between ourselves."

"I…I don't want my husband knowing."

Allan raised his brows marginally, then took a seat
next to the hospital bed so he didn't tower over her and
appear intimidating.

"We can have lovers—human lovers, I mean—before
we're mated to a wolf, you know," Franny said. "So I saw

this guy for a while, too long really. Not just for a few times, but we dated seriously for a couple of months. I even had the notion of turning him. I know it was foolish. His name is Cleveland Hawkins. Then I met my mate and knew he was the one for me. That was about a year and a half ago. We found your pack and the perfect job opportunity for Gary as the chef at the new Italian restaurant. And we wanted to raise our baby with the pack.

"Cleveland was angry when I called it quits with him and started stalking me. He threatened Gary. He drove a red Camaro. I mean, I can't be one hundred percent positive, but it looked like his car. I saw the guy's camo cap. I really couldn't get a good look at more than that, but I'm fairly certain it was him. My gut reaction when I saw the car was that it *was* him."

"And he swerved his vehicle at yours, causing you to lose control?"

"Yeah. If I'd hit him, I probably would have totaled his car, but I automatically swerved to miss his vehicle and lost control."

"Are you certain the driver's car didn't just slip on ice? When I was in the vicinity, my hatchback did."

Franny took a deep breath and nodded. "It's possible. But what if it is him?"

"I'll definitely check into it. When was the last time you saw him?"

"Stalking me? Before we moved here, which was four months ago. I thought that was the end of seeing him."

"And you came here from Boise, Idaho?"

"Yes."

"Did you ever meet his family?"

"No."

"Friends?"

"Just one. Some guy who was a hunter like him. They'd been in the military and were best friends. The two of them loved playing paintball, and they both loved to hunt and fish."

"Job?"

"He worked in a pawn shop. I don't want Gary to know about it because he'd kill him. And then get himself into all kinds of hot water."

"If this truly is a case of Cleveland Hawkins stalking you, then Gary and everyone in the pack needs to know—for your protection, Gary's, and Stacy's. We'll talk to Gary. Make sure he knows how important it is for us to handle matters the best we can. But if this guy comes after you, Gary needs to be there to protect you and the baby too."

Looking sad, Franny nodded.

"We'll call a meeting between you, Gary, Paul, Lori, and me. We'll all come up with some plans to handle different scenarios."

"Okay."

After reassuring Franny that they'd take care of this if the guy was still stalking her, Allan left the clinic and called Lori to tell her what was up.

"I'll make arrangements for a meeting as soon as she and the baby are released from the clinic," Lori said. "We need to get on this right away if what she suspects is true."

"Agreed." Allan couldn't believe all the trouble their pack was having with the new members who had joined them, but he was glad he and the original pack members could help out.

He hoped Franny was wrong and the other driver had just slipped on ice and was an ass for not checking her and the baby's welfare. But he was prepared to take harsher measures against the guy if what Franny suspected was really true.

———

When Debbie arrived at Rose's house, she saw someone peek through the blinds. Debbie got out of the car and headed for the door.

Rose opened the front door with her mother, Catherine Rappaport, standing just behind her. Debbie was glad Rose's mother was there for her. Rose's face was so pale, she had to still be reeling from the frightening experience. "Hi, it's me, Debbie Renaud. I came to see you after hearing what you witnessed. Can we talk?"

"Thanks for dropping by." Rose quickly ushered Debbie inside.

Catherine looked just as shaken.

"Listen, I know Allan and Paul are here for you, but I want you to know that I'm also available to talk or assist with anything else. Whatever you need," Debbie said as they led her into the living room. Sometimes women just needed other women to talk to.

"I was just fixing hot chocolate for us. Would you like some too?" Catherine asked.

"Um, sure. That would be really nice. Thank you," Debbie said, glad they seemed to appreciate her dropping by.

Rose motioned for her to have a seat on a chair across from the couch where she sat.

"I'm so sorry about what happened to you. Allan

didn't tell me or I would have come sooner. I had to hear it from the homicide detective in charge of the case, who happens to be a friend. Is there anything I can do for you?"

"No, thank you for asking though," Rose said.

Catherine brought in mugs of cocoa on a tray that she set on the glass-topped coffee table. She sat next to her daughter and motioned to the mugs. "Please, have one. And thanks for coming by. It was awful. Who would have done something so ugly?" She shook her head. "Too many sick people in the world."

"I agree. From what Rowdy said, everybody's looking into this around their own workloads." Debbie wanted to mention how concerned everyone was, but she didn't want to get into it any more than that. "How are you feeling, Rose?" Allan's sister was petite, so carrying triplets made her look as though she was due any second.

"Oh, just fine. The babies are kicking away, especially at night. Thankfully, Everett gives the best foot and back massages. What I can't get used to is my protruding belly." Rose rubbed her hand over her stomach. "I keep forgetting it's there despite how big it is, and when I go to open doors, especially the fridge door, it's in the way."

Debbie laughed. She was glad to hear Rose seemed to be all right. It was good she had such a supportive network to help her through this, and she seemed to be in good spirits, if a little pale. Her mother still looked anxious.

They talked about the recent snow, and Rose wanted to know all about the baby Allan had saved earlier from the flooded SUV in the culvert. He had said Debbie played a major part in the rescue, which was sweet of him. She wanted to deny it was true, but didn't want to contradict him.

"How do you like working with Allan?" Catherine suddenly asked.

Debbie couldn't help her reaction. Her cheeks heated with embarrassment. Did his mom know how much she loved working with Allan? That she hoped more than a friendship could develop?

"He's great to work with. He treats me like a partner should." Though all the men on the diving team were really great sports.

Rose and Catherine exchanged glances, but Debbie—despite all her police training—couldn't read their feelings in that shared instant.

"Well, I'd better be getting back to the office. I still need to write up that report, dig a little more into another case, and then share a pizza with Allan later."

"You're having a pizza," Catherine said, frowning.

"Oh sure, I know it's not the most nutritious food, but I've been craving one ever since he mentioned going out to have one." Not that Debbie believed his mother was concerned about nutrition. She couldn't put her finger on it, but his family seemed to be acting a little oddly about the fact that she and Allan were now partners.

"Allan did?" Catherine said, as if she had thought it was all Debbie's idea to go out together.

Debbie sighed dramatically, then rose from her seat. "Yeah. Before my previous partner retired, we used to go out every Friday night for pizza. He was a widower, a fatherly type, and we enjoyed letting our hair down after work. I haven't done that in about a year. So I mentioned it to Allan, and he suggested we go out for pizza. We meant to do it for lunch, but…" She stopped speaking. She didn't want to bring up the murder again.

The ladies really didn't need to know all her and Allan's business, especially if they didn't approve for whatever reason. But some small part of her did care what his family thought about her. Since the family was so close knit, she thought they'd probably want to approve of her if things between her and Allan got serious. Maybe they were worried that she might hurt Allan if things didn't work out.

She wasn't even sure if she could handle being that close with family. She'd never had anything like that growing up. Not that there was anything going on between her and Allan, but…

"Thanks so much for dropping by. Some of the other police officers said they'd drive by here at different times, just to ensure there's no trouble," Catherine said.

"Good. I'm glad to hear it."

"Thanks, Debbie," Rose added. "I really appreciate you coming by."

"It was good to see you again," Catherine said, and both ladies walked her to the door.

"I hope my coming here wasn't too much of an intrusion. I just wanted to offer my services. Call me anytime if you need anything at all."

With final thanks and good-byes, Debbie headed back to the office, wishing she'd further clarified that she and Allan were *not* dating.

As she always did when she was driving, she watched traffic around her, behind her, in front of her, and pulling out of roads on either side of the main one she was driving on. She did so because of her police training, watching for any misdeeds, but when she glanced at her rearview mirror again, she swore a black sedan had followed her from somewhere close to Rose's house all the way to the town where Debbie worked. That was forty miles away.

When she parked at the sheriff's office, the vehicle turned off on a street two blocks away. She had planned to get the driver's license plate number when he went past her. She admitted she was probably being paranoid. But on the other hand, if she saw a car like that following her again, she'd call in his license plate to have him checked out—just in case she *wasn't* being paranoid.

Chapter 5

ALLAN GOT A CALL FROM ROSE AND PICKED UP IMMEDI-
ately, concerned that something was seriously wrong.
He'd been worried his sister or Lori might go into pre-
mature labor over this whole murder business.

"Allan, just a quick heads-up. We had an unexpected
visitor," Rose said. "Debbie Renaud came by the house
to offer assistance if I needed it."

Now that was one scenario he'd never expected.
"Hell, I told her everything was fine when she asked me.
What did she say?" Allan didn't want Debbie having
anything to do with the family, in the event some nutcase was looking to take down werewolves and thought
she might be one too.

"She didn't say anything about the case, and we just
let on that it was awful, which it was. Then we talked
about other subjects. What could Mom and I tell her?
No, we couldn't talk to her? She was really sweet and
making sure I was okay. She also assured me she'd help
us out anytime we wanted her to. But what's this business with you taking her out for pizza?"

"*That's* what this call is all about? It's not a date.
We're partners, remember?"

"You're not a widowed, fatherly type, unlike the
retired partner she used to have pizza with on Friday
nights," Rose told him.

"Hell, Rose, it's not a date. She's been missing her

old partner. He was her mentor, and I do things a little differently so it's taken some getting used to. I just thought it would be a nice thing to do."

"If you say so."

"She's human. I have no intention of being anything more than her dive partner on the job." And why was he explaining himself to his sister?

"You haven't dated any of the single wolves in our pack." Rose had brought that fact up more times than he cared to think about. Some of it was because the women thought that if they talked to his sister, she could convince him to start dating one of them.

He hadn't wanted to. The truth of the matter was that he really liked Debbie, even though he knew nothing could come of it. She and he loved to dive, for one thing. And with the criminal investigations and rescue missions, they both were really into their jobs. As for any of the new she-wolves in the pack, he had no real connection with any of them, except that they were *lupus garous* like him. There had to be more to a relationship that would last a lifetime if they mated.

"Got to go, Sis."

"All right. But remember… If this maniac comes after us, and he sees her with you too much, he might also go after her."

"We work together. She's a police diver. And we're fairly new partners. So if he knows about the family, that's one thing. If he's watching us, I don't want her around the rest of the family."

"I know. I'm just saying this business with you taking her out for pizza…"

He let out his breath, annoyed with this discussion,

but then remembered what a shock she and Lori had had
earlier today. "Are you really all right?"

"Yeah, Everett's here. Mom's here too. We're fine.
Just…be careful with her."

Like Rose had been careful with Everett? Even
though Everett was a wolf, she'd gotten into a mess
with him all on her own, so Allan really didn't think she
should be offering him advice on relationships. "Talk
to you later."

When he arrived at the pizzeria, the parking lot was
packed. He spied Debbie's blue Ford Escort parked out
front. Allan also recognized Rowdy's bright red sedan
parked nearby. Frowning, but not wanting to make
anything of Rowdy's presence—it was a Friday and
the pizza place was really popular with locals—Allan
headed inside the busy restaurant.

The jukebox was playing golden oldies and the lights
were dimmed. Three cooks stood at butcher-block tables
behind glass windows, tossing pizzas in the air as they
put on a show while making them.

Allan loved the atmosphere in the place. Long, dark
wooden tables and benches filled the center of the restaurant. A mix of booths, some small for more intimate
parties and others larger for family and friend gatherings, were situated along three of the walls. A long bar
accommodated a dozen patrons as they sat on red vinyl
seats, drinking and conversing. The place was a mix of
old world, mountain view, and rustic. The ceiling fans,
green crystal lanterns, and drink glasses lining the dark,
smoky mirror all added to the ambience.

He glanced around the room to see if he could
locate Debbie and spotted her talking to Rowdy, who

was standing next to the jukebox and making a selection. Allan shouldn't have cared, but he didn't like that Rowdy was talking to Debbie, smiling and laughing along with her as if *they* were on a date.

"Only You" by the Platters began to play.

Why should it matter that the two of them were enjoying each other's company? They all worked for law enforcement in some capacity. Allan couldn't get involved with Debbie. Yet he felt all growly in that instant, wanting to show his alpha posturing and let Rowdy know to back off. What would Debbie think of that? And Rowdy? He'd probably get a kick out of it.

But the warier side of his nature kicked in. What were the odds Rowdy just happened to be here alone at the same time as Debbie was here? Allan thought back to how Rowdy just happened to drop in at the clinic at the same time Debbie was there. Hell, was he stalking her?

Getting his annoyance under control, Allan headed toward them. Rowdy saw him first. He smiled a little, as if he knew it would bother Allan that he was having fun with Debbie when she was here to have dinner with Allan.

As soon as Allan joined them, Rowdy said, "Debbie asked if I'd have pizza with the two of you. So what do you like on yours?"

Surprised as hell that she would invite Rowdy to join them, Allan glanced at Debbie, wondering if she had felt obligated to be polite since Rowdy appeared to be alone. She was all smiles, which showed just how pretty she was, her long dark hair pulled back, her brown eyes sparkling. She seemed to be thrilled to be here, and

Allan was glad he had offered to join her. But if he'd picked her up, he wouldn't have had to deal with Rowdy joining the party.

"I love double cheese and mushrooms, if that's good with everyone," Debbie said.

Allan snapped his mouth shut. Okay, he reminded himself, this wasn't a date. She was just his partner, and they were just having a pizza. And Rowdy wasn't dating her either. Just three people that had work in common and now were having a dinner out. So why did Allan feel like telling Rowdy to get lost? Or interrogating him about why he seemed to be at the same places Debbie was today?

"Yeah, sure, whatever everyone else wants." Allan really tried not to show his growlier wolf nature, but he was having a hard time keeping his feelings hidden. He figured at this rate, they might as well sit at one of the long tables, but Rowdy steered them to a booth and maneuvered it so that he was sitting next to Debbie on one side.

She didn't seem to mind. In fact, Allan thought she looked pleased with the arrangement. Was she miffed at Allan because he had wanted to take separate vehicles? He'd wanted to be able to leave at a moment's notice if any of his family called to tell him there was more trouble. And he didn't want it to look like he was dating her if a werewolf killer was on the loose.

"So, what do you make of this latest case?" Rowdy asked.

"I'd say the person was crazy," Debbie said. "Who traps a naked woman like that and then shoots her several times?"

The waitress came and took their orders. She brought back a pitcher of beer and mugs, then headed for another table.

"The only thing I can come up with is some lunatic thought the woman was a werewolf. I thought of vampires, but hunters kill them with wooden stakes." Rowdy poured everyone a mug of beer.

Allan had heard Rowdy watched the TV series *Supernatural* and several other paranormal series, so he wasn't surprised when Rowdy came up with that scenario as a lighthearted approach to his ongoing murder investigations.

"Werewolf? Right." Debbie sipped her beer.

As far as Allan knew, Debbie loved the epic, more historical kind of fantasy, but wasn't into the urban fantasy stuff—like vampires and werewolves.

"We still don't have a clue who she was?" Allan wasn't about to get pulled into a discussion about werewolves or any other paranormal creatures.

"No word yet," Rowdy said. "And the victim didn't have any wolf DNA."

Debbie rolled her eyes. "They did *not* test for wolf DNA."

Rowdy smiled and winked at her. "I asked the county coroner to look for it, and she said she always checked blood work, as a matter of course. No wolf DNA. Just plain old human blood."

"She did *not* check for wolf DNA," Debbie said.

Rowdy laughed. "If she'd found some when she did the other tests, wouldn't you have been surprised?"

Allan couldn't help but be amused at the way the conversation was going. He wouldn't have been surprised if Rowdy had asked the coroner to check the blood for wolf DNA.

Thankfully, *lupus garous* were all wolf in appearance, DNA included, when in wolf form and totally human when they were in human form. So if anyone ran any kind of tests on them, they wouldn't show both in any of their systems.

The three of them finally got on to other subjects, and despite disliking that Rowdy was here with Debbie to begin with, Allan liked the guy and found his company agreeable. He was a good homicide detective with a sterling reputation and a great success rate in solving murder cases and getting convictions. If Allan hadn't loved diving so much, he wouldn't have minded working with Rowdy in his field of expertise.

Debbie sipped more of her beer, then set her mug down. "I have a confession to make. You guys are a lot of fun." Her eyes were bright and glistened a bit in the ambient lights in the restaurant.

Allan raised his brows a little. Was she slightly... drunk? After only a beer?

Rowdy smiled.

"No, really. You know I've been working with Allan for nearly five months and I've known you, Rowdy, for what? About the same? Maybe a little less. This is the first time I've had a chance to just" — she pulled off the clasp holding her hair up, and the dark-brown curls cascaded over her shoulders — "let my hair down a bit."

Allan had never seen her hair loose. Silky, rich, and thick. He could just imagine running his hands through the soft strands.

Rowdy saluted her, still smiling. "Here's to letting your hair down."

She looked like she was feeling a bit tipsy. But after one beer? Granted, the mugs were big, but... He frowned. She'd told him her dad had been an alcoholic. Had she never taken a drink before?

"Do you want a soda? Water? Coffee?" Allan asked.

"Nah, I'm fine." She pointed a slice of pizza at him. "I dropped by your sister's place to offer my shoulder if she ever needs it."

"I heard."

She frowned at him. "I don't think they—your mom and sister—liked that we were going out on a date."

He opened his mouth to object, but she quickly added, "Oh, don't misunderstand. *I* didn't say we were going on a date. But for whatever reason, I believe that's what they concluded. Should I have repeated that this wasn't a date? That's why I asked old Rowdy here if he'd like to join us—because we aren't on a date." She grinned, then took a bite of the cheese pizza.

Rowdy laughed. "How often do you go out drinking?"

"Me?" Debbie's eyes were wide. "Oh, heavens. Never. It's just been a rough day, and I thought for a date...well, not a date, just a pizza get-together where everyone drinks beer...well, it would seem antisocial of me if I didn't join in on the fun." She finished her pizza and looked from Allan to Rowdy. "What?"

"Do you think you can drive home okay?" Allan asked. He wasn't going to let her, but it was better if she thought it was her idea. "If not, we'll drop you off at home, and we can leave your car at your place."

"No, thanks. I can drive." Then she chewed on her bottom lip. "You don't think I'm that bad, do you?"

"We'll take you home," Allan said. Even if she was fine, he didn't want her to risk getting in an accident on the way to Whitefish thirty miles away that would get her into trouble with the sheriff's department. He doubted her blood alcohol level would be that high. Even so, the beer definitely had affected her.

"Okay. But I'm really feeling great."

That's what Allan was worried about. That she was feeling *too* great. After they finished the pizza, they walked outside and found it had been snowing the whole time they were eating. Because of the weather conditions, Allan was glad they were taking Debbie home. He drove his own vehicle, and Rowdy drove Debbie's. She sat in the passenger's seat, leaning her head against the window of her car. Allan wondered if she'd gone to sleep.

Halfway to her place, Allan noticed a black sedan following him through the traffic lights. The car continued to follow until Allan turned right at a street that would take him out of his way. The sedan continued on past.

Once Allan had turned around and gotten back on the main road to Debbie's home, he saw the black sedan turn down the next street. When Allan passed the street, he expected to see the sedan still driving along, but it had vanished. Other than a number of businesses closed for the night, there wasn't anywhere for the sedan to go, except to turn down the next street. He had to have been flying at that point to make the corner before Allan reached the intersection.

On the rest of the drive to Debbie's house, Allan kept

watching for the black sedan. It probably meant nothing sinister, but working for law enforcement, he was wary.

When he pulled into Debbie's driveway, Rowdy was just parking. "What happened to you back there? I thought you'd gotten lost," Rowdy said, getting out of Debbie's car.

Allan went to the passenger door when Debbie didn't get out. "I thought I…" He didn't want to sound paranoid and changed his mind about saying anything. He shrugged. "Is Debbie asleep?"

"The whole way here," Rowdy said.

Allan was glad they had driven her home, given the circumstances. He opened her door, but she stirred and smiled up at him. "Ohmigod, I've never fallen asleep on a date. Well, it wasn't a date. But you know what I mean."

Allan helped her out of the car, and she was boneless. He noticed she'd left her purse on the seat and seized it. But she managed to walk on her own. "Are you going to be all right tonight?"

"Yeah, sure. Long day. Missed lunch and breakfast— meant to have both, but never got around to either. I had some hot chocolate at your sister's house to tide me over, but I think the beer got to me. A little."

Allan smiled and held the door to her duplex for her. She didn't move out of the doorway, but waited for him to hand over her purse. "Thanks. I had a lovely time. Next time, I'll have water. It would be safer that way." She waved at Rowdy, who was standing beside Allan's hatchback. "Night. That was fun. We'll have to do it again sometime."

"Next Friday?" Rowdy asked in a hurry.

She glanced up at Allan, her dark-brown eyes wide with expectation.

"Sure." What the hell. If the three of them were going to have pizza, maybe on a regular Friday-night basis, no one would get the notion he was dating Debbie. *Himself* included.

"Night, Debbie. See you tomorrow." Even though it was Saturday, they were diving to Van Lake again to see if they could find more clues.

Rowdy waved good-bye. "Night, Debbie."

"Night, all." She closed her door and Allan waited until he heard the lock snick closed.

"I sure admire you for the work you do," Rowdy said as they climbed into Allan's car. "I wanted to be a police diver. I thought it sounded really glamorous and more fun than regular police work. Then Debbie's retired partner told me about diving in murky waters, with swift moving currents, under ice, in frigid water, and at night or other times when there is zero visibility. The worst was the idea of diving in intake pipes and sewer water. So I decided I liked my job just fine. I guess with your SEAL training, diving suits you. Still can't figure out why Debbie would want a job like that."

Allan nodded. He wasn't about to explain what she had told him if she hadn't mentioned it to Rowdy.

"So sorry about your kinfolk seeing that murder scene today. I can imagine how horrified they must have been. With both being pregnant, I worried about miscarriages."

"They were shook up, sure. After witnessing such a thing, they're wary now, of course. Until we catch the murderer, it's a big concern for everyone."

"I agree. I hope that I didn't mess things up by butting

in on your pizza night with Debbie. She was just so adamant, I couldn't say no."

Allan shook his head. "Like Debbie said, it was
nice getting to know a little more about each other off
duty. After such a harrowing day, the evening went
well, I thought."

"It did, but I can bow out next time. I didn't want to
say anything in front of Debbie, but I can make excuses."

"I don't have any problem with you having pizza
with us."

"She said you weren't on a date."

"No, we weren't."

"Then you wouldn't have any objection if I ask her
out sometime?" Rowdy asked.

"Not at all." Allan told himself she *should* go out with
other guys. They could be work colleagues and maybe
even friends, but nothing serious could happen between
them. And if she were dating a police officer, that might
deter any lunatic wanting to kill werewolves.

So why was he so annoyed with the idea?

He dropped Rowdy off at the pizzeria so he could
get his car and then headed back to the site of the
woman's murder. The location was two miles from
Paul and Lori's cabin, but he didn't intend to disturb
them tonight. Not unless he found something important
related to the case.

When he arrived as close to the scene as he could
get, he parked on the logging trail and hiked to the
killing site. He sniffed around the area in the dark,
though he could see somewhat. He was mostly relying on his sense of smell. To his surprise, he smelled
another wolf.

Maybe a real wolf attracted to the blood? If it was a *lupus garou*, it was a male and unknown to Allan. And it was recent. The male hadn't scent-marked the area, but his wolf scent was in the air. Allan would have shifted to see if the wolf had left a scent from his paw pads, but he couldn't do it if the wolf killer was watching.

Allan texted Paul with the news.

Paul texted him right back: You're at the site now?

Yeah, just got here.

Drop by the cabin when you're through.

Allan hadn't wanted to alarm Lori, but he texted back: Sure.

Lori was the pack leader too. She had to know everything going on with regard to the pack.

Allan tracked the wolf's scent trail for two miles into the wilderness. Snow covered the tracks, so Allan couldn't tell if the wolf had been in human form or was a wolf. He thought if it had been a *lupus garou*, he would have headed for a vehicle parked on the logging road. But he hadn't. He tracked it for another four miles and got another text. He checked it out.

Paul had texted him: Where are you?

Just tracking the wolf trail. I'm coming in. Be there in about two hours.

I'm coming for you if you're not back in two.

I hear you.

Allan headed in the direction of his car, his boots crunching in the snow. He told himself the trail had to be a wolf's. Why would a *lupus garou* be running through their territory in the vicinity of a crime scene?

He reached his car and paused, listening to the wind howling through the snow-covered branches. Then he got in and drove to Paul and Lori's cabin. As soon as he parked, Paul opened the door. He was bundled up, looking as though he intended to search for Allan, which Allan hadn't wanted. Not with Paul still on the mend. On a summer's day, he probably could take a short hike. But in these snowdrifts and with his leg muscles and tendons still healing, no.

"Sorry it took me so long."

"Verdict?" Paul asked as he pulled off his gloves and coat while Allan shut the door.

The place was quiet, and except for the living room, the rest of the house was dark. "Is Lori asleep?" Allan asked, his voice hushed.

"Yeah. She knew you were on your way. She hasn't been sleeping well, so she wanted to go to bed early. I'll let her know the news tomorrow." Paul got them some beers. "So what's going on?"

"No prints. Too much snow had fallen for me to tell if it was a wolf or a wolf shifter. But it was male and he didn't mark the territory, just moved through it. He could have been attracted to the blood, thinking it was a fresh kill. We have a number of real wolf packs in the forests here, so that's reasonable."

"Your gut instinct?"

"My gut instinct is it's a pure wolf. Why would a *lupus garou* be up here at the crime scene otherwise?"

"He's related to the woman who was murdered?"

"I hadn't considered that. Or maybe the killer was a *lupus garou*, but the first time he came through the area, he used a hunter's spray to conceal that he was a wolf."

"I don't buy it."

"I thought someone was tailing me today. Well, not me, but Debbie. I swore a black sedan was following me after we left the pizzeria, so I turned off on another street, then came back around, and the black sedan continued to trail Debbie's car."

"Why were you following Debbie's car?" Paul sounded a tad suspicious of Allan's motives.

Allan stiffened a bit. "She'd had a little too much to drink." Before Paul could ask why he allowed her to drive home, he quickly said, "Rowdy met us at the pizza place and he drove her home. I gave him a ride back to the pizzeria."

Paul visibly relaxed.

"I wouldn't let her drive home like that."

"I understand."

But Allan thought it was more than that. Paul was glad Rowdy was with them sharing pizza, and *he* had driven her home.

"So how long did the sedan follow her vehicle?"

"As soon as I was behind him, he made a quick turn onto the next street. By the time I reached the street, there was no sign of him. There wasn't anything really suspicious about him, but with this situation with Lori and Rose, and Debbie dropping by to see Rose today…I just feel the need to be more vigilant."

"Agreed. I take it you didn't get his license number?"

"No. I planned to when I was behind him, but I didn't get close enough."

"Okay, so we'll have everyone watching for a black sedan and be on the alert for a male *lupus garou* stranger. And a red Camaro, if Franny's ex-lover has found her and is stalking her. I'm glad to hear that there's nothing serious going on between you and Debbie. Rose and Catherine were worried about you."

"Rowdy is asking her out. I'm not dating her, Paul. I know the rules. We just shared some pizza and beer. Next week, we're planning to do the same thing, the three of us, unless Rowdy starts dating her. Then it's strictly just work and she's all his."

"Okay, glad to hear it. I know it's tough, and if you're not interested in any of the females in the pack, that makes it tougher. But getting involved with a human is too dangerous."

"Yeah, don't I know it." Allan finished his beer. "Well, I'm calling it a night. Debbie and I have an early dive tomorrow on that Van Lake investigation we're looking into."

"Any leads?"

"Only that it looks like a murder set up to look like an accident."

"Okay, Allan. I'm working a case tomorrow..."

Allan couldn't conceal his look of surprise.

"From home. Hell, I can't dive. I can walk, but not on this damn ice without risking breaking my leg again or tearing up ligaments or something. I'll be home."

Allan took a relieved breath. "You'll be as good as new soon." They healed in half the time it took humans, so Paul must have injured himself worse than they had first thought.

"Right. I'll be busy, but if you learn anything, let me know."

Allan said good night and headed home. He kept watching for signs of car lights following him. It was late, the snow was still falling, and traffic was light on the lake road he took to get back to his mountain cabin. When he arrived, he headed inside, shucking his winter coat and gloves and tossing them on the sofa. He stripped off his clothes in the bedroom, then took a shower. But in the middle of the hot, steamy shower, he heard his phone ring.

Now what? He turned off the water and jerked a towel off the bar, drying himself as he went to get his phone.

The caller ID said it was Debbie. At once, he worried something was wrong. "Debbie, are you all right?"

"Rowdy called me for a date. Did you put him up to it?" She sounded pissed.

Chapter 6

DEBBIE FELT BETTER AFTER SHOWERING AND FALLING asleep on the sofa for a couple of hours. Note to self: no more drinking when out with the guys. She couldn't imagine how her dad could drink so much and then pass out. She'd barely finished a beer.

When Rowdy had called, she couldn't believe it. No way did she want to go out with him on a date. The problem was Allan. She had to admit he did something to her deep inside. Had her wanting to impress him on the job and as a woman. With Rowdy, she didn't care. But with Allan, she did.

So when Rowdy called to ask her on a date and told her he had cleared it with Allan, she was ticked off. Rowdy didn't need to get permission from Allan. Just from *her*.

She didn't think there was a way to let a guy down gently either. Even though Rowdy acted as though he was fine with the rejection, she knew he wasn't. No one liked to be turned down in the romance department. He probably thought she was hung up on Allan, who wasn't hung up on her. She knew Allan wasn't married or seeing anyone. She'd seen some women show interest in him when they had coffee at the local diner one morning before work. But he hadn't shown any interest back. He just was polite and offered a casual good morning, nothing more.

"He asked me if he could ask you out. I said sure.

What else was I to say? No, you can't ask her? Sorry, Debbie, but you invited him to have pizza with us. I guess he thought you were more interested in him." Allan almost sounded a little smug about it.

She pursed her lips. "Great."

"Just tell him no."

"I did. I think I hurt his ego."

"He'll get over it. How are you feeling?"

This was the Allan she knew. He was always so considerate. Rowdy hadn't asked at all. But Allan? She really liked that about him. "Better. I showered and napped. I guess that's it for drinking for me."

He chuckled. "You're not used to it."

"Sorry I was kind of a party pooper."

"No problem. We've got to get up tomorrow early to dive anyway."

"Yeah. I had fun. I'm not sure what's going to happen with pizza night next week, but Rowdy might not join us now." She wanted to ask Allan if that would be a problem. She purposely had asked Rowdy to eat with them because of the way Allan's family had acted about Allan "dating" her. But she hadn't expected Rowdy to ask her out on a date.

"Well, it's his loss. If he's man enough, he'll join us. Or if he's interested enough, he'll keep trying."

She sighed. "I don't want him to keep asking me for a date. Well, since we have such an early day tomorrow, I need to say good night."

"Same here. I'll see you in the morning."

They ended the call and she was glad Allan *hadn't* suggested to Rowdy that he date her, but she was still annoyed Rowdy would seek Allan's permission.

Tucked under her covers in bed, she began thinking about the case of the dead man in the car. She didn't count sheep. She counted key pieces of evidence, working them over in her mind. And then she recalled something from the police report. Two eyewitnesses had seen a black sedan leaving the scene right after the victim's car went into the lake.

Coincidence? Or the killer?

She grabbed her phone and called Allan. Before he could even say hello, she said, "Do you remember that a couple of eyewitnesses said they saw a black sedan speed off after the victim's car ended up in the lake?"

"Black sedan," Allan said, his voice darker than she thought it would be.

It could mean absolutely nothing, but Allan sounded like he believed it might.

"One followed me when I was headed in to work earlier."

"One was following you after we left the pizza parlor." Bedcovers began to rustle. "I'm coming over."

"What? You're kidding. Why didn't you arrest him?"

"He gave me the slip. Besides, I wasn't certain he was really following either of us."

"I'm fine," Debbie said, not wanting to cause further speculation about why Allan would be staying the night at her place. "I'm armed and dangerous."

For a moment, he didn't say anything. She would have liked it if he came over, truth be told. She had a guest room, and if someone was after her next, at least she'd have backup. But Allan seemed to believe she could handle it on her own. She had wanted to give him an out, hadn't she? Besides, she *was* armed.

"I'm coming over. Be there in a half hour."

Relieved to the max, she sighed. She knew he'd be rushing if it only took him half an hour, especially in winter when it was snowing again. "Take your time. I'll be fine." But she truly was glad he was coming to stay the night.

"Okay, I'll be on my way to your place in a few minutes."

They said good-bye and ended the call.

She wondered what his log cabin on the mountain was like. The family had owned it forever, he had said, and she bet it was really nice no matter what the season.

She considered getting dressed in a pair of jeans and a sweater before he arrived. But it seemed silly when she was just going to put on her thermal pajamas again once he was settled in. She threw on a robe instead and slipped on a pair of boot slippers. They were pink, and so was her fluffy robe. Her pajama top sported a teddy bear wearing a ski hat with earflaps and braided ties. At least her pajamas were gray, so she didn't look too girly.

She realized that whenever she saw anyone, she wore somber colors. She thought it made her appear more professional. But with her nightwear and underwear, she loved being frivolous. Maybe she should wear her jeans and the sweater. Then in the privacy of her bedroom, she could be herself.

She glanced around at all the pastel colors—light green, light blue with navy accents. Oh, well, there was no escaping her love of all things colorful.

She brushed out her hair again to remove all signs of having been in bed and then straightened up the place, though it was already fairly neat. Living by herself with reading as her only hobby meant she didn't make messes often.

She checked her watch again. Twenty minutes before he would arrive. She went into the guest bedroom and checked it out. She wanted to turn down the bed, to do something to thank him for coming over to help watch her back.

He was her dive partner, she told herself. This was nothing personal; he was just concerned. She turned off all the lights in the duplex and peered out the windows, moving from one room to the next to see if she could catch sight of a black sedan. Security lights and streetlights in her complex cast a strange orange glow on the misty snow. It looked like the perfect night for a murder.

Before he hit the road, Allan called Paul, hating to wake him but needing to tell his pack leader where he was going. He knew Paul wouldn't like it, but Debbie was his partner and he had to watch her back.

Paul answered with, "Hell, Allan."

"Can't be helped," he told Paul.

"Yeah, I know, but you're digging yourself deeper on this one."

"I'm not turning her, and I'm not mating her. I'm just protecting her." Allan threw his bag in the car and slammed the door.

"Yeah, you remember what happened between Hunter and Tessa?"

Their SEAL wolf team leader had gotten into a real mess with Tessa, a human with wolf roots. This was different. Debbie didn't have any connection to the wolves. That would make it even worse if Allan turned her. Which he had no plan to do, no matter what.

"Yeah, yeah. This isn't the same."

"Isn't it? Hunter had to protect Tessa and look what happened then."

"They're happily mated wolves," Allan reminded Paul, pulling out his ice scraper.

"Right, but she had wolf ties. Your partner doesn't."

"Which I'm well aware of."

"You need to find a mate. That would be the end of this…infatuation you have for her."

"We mate for life, and I'm not going there with just any she-wolf so that everyone will get off my case about my partner. I'm not infatuated with her. I enjoy working with her, that's all. Got to go. I'll let you know if anything else happens."

"All right, buddy. Just be careful."

He knew Paul wasn't talking about the driver of the black sedan. Allan couldn't believe the sedan had also followed Debbie earlier in the day.

He called Debbie back as he scraped the snow off his windshield. "When did the black sedan follow you, and to where? Your home?"

"I picked him up somewhere around Cottage Grove. I noticed him sometime after I left your sister's house."

Allan swore under his breath. This was so not good. "Why didn't you say something earlier?"

"I didn't think of it in relationship to our case. I figured if I saw the car again, I'd try to get his license plate number. Why didn't you mention the guy following you?"

"Same thing. We'll keep a watch out for the car. I've alerted Paul about what's going on."

She didn't say anything for a moment, and he suspected she wondered why he had to run this by Paul.

"How did Paul react?"

Not good. "Concerned we might have some trouble with this guy." Allan couldn't tell her how Paul really felt about the situation.

"Just take it easy and I'll see you when you get here."

Allan drove through the misty snow on the slippery roads. His vehicle was equipped with snow tires, but he still slid a bit coming down off the mountain. The roads were sanded, even though the accumulating snow was hampering road crews.

When he finally arrived at Debbie's brick duplex, he pulled into the carport in back and got out of the vehicle. The back porch light was on, and she opened the door. Standing there in the halo of light in her pink fluffy robe and slipper boots, she looked like a pink sugar cone, sweet and soft—not an image he wanted to remember every time they were working an assignment together.

He grabbed his overnight bag. He'd need a shave in the morning—no way did he want to show up for work looking like he'd been out partying all night.

"Hey," he said, and she opened the door wider for him.

"I'm so sorry you had to go to all this trouble."

"No trouble at all. I didn't see anyone suspicious around the neighborhood. If the guy is the murderer of the drowned man in the car, why would he follow you? Not both of us? At first, I thought he was following me, but then when I turned off and came back around, he was driving behind you. So I assumed he was really following you all along."

She shook her head. "If a couple of eyewitnesses hadn't seen him—if it's the same vehicle—I would have thought I was being suspicious without any good reason." She led him to a bedroom. "Here's the guest room. Bathroom is down the hall. Make yourself at home. If you need anything in the kitchen, it's yours."

"Thanks. I know you felt I didn't need to come over and stay the night, but I wouldn't have slept a wink if I hadn't checked the area out. Get some rest. We'll be up and out of here before we know it."

"Agreed. And thanks. I really appreciate it. I doubt I would have gotten much sleep either. Night, Allan. Thanks." She padded off to the bedroom at the end of the hall.

He walked into the guest room all done in lilac and pink. He smiled a little. This was a side to Debbie he'd never known. He heard her door close, but he didn't shut his. He wanted to be able to hear if anyone made the mistake of breaking into her home in the middle of the night.

With that final thought, he stripped down to his boxer briefs and settled into the comfy bed, pulling the purple and pink floral comforter under his chin and wondering what Paul would say if he saw him now.

Chapter 7

"HMM," LORI SAID, TRYING TO GET COMFORTABLE IN Paul's arms that night. "I think these babies are starting their martial arts lessons early. Here I thought I'd have to train them when they got to be about three or so."

Paul wrapped his arms around her, not believing they were having their own set of twins in just a few months. But he was worried about everything that was going on: a possible killer on the loose, Franny's possible stalker, and Allan's fixation with Debbie. "Allan said a black sedan had been following Debbie. We need to put out the word for all of our pack members to be on the lookout."

"Black sedan? I swore one followed me to the grocery store this morning. But when I came out, it was gone."

Paul didn't say anything for a minute, wondering if the guy was a werewolf killer. But if he had been spotted at Van Lake after the murder there, that confused the issue. The dead man hadn't been a werewolf. So what was going on?

"I've got to let Allan know the guy tracked you. Maybe others in the pack too."

Lori groaned. "I was just getting comfortable."

"I'll give you another back rub. I want Allan to know the guy has been sighted more than once."

"If it's the same black sedan. Grandma has one that's similar. That's why I noticed."

Paul hesitated.

"It wasn't hers."

"Okay, I'm calling Allan." Paul made the call.

Allan picked up right away. "Yeah, what's up?"

"The black sedan followed Lori to the grocery store too."

"Damn it to hell."

"Yeah, agreed. We need to learn what he's up to as soon as we can. If any of us see him, we need to get his license plate number and run a check on it at once."

"Gotcha."

Silence.

"Are...you alone?" Paul asked.

Allan hung up on him.

Paul sighed, put his cell on the table, and began to give Lori a back rub.

"Well?" Lori asked, her voice sounding sleepy.

"Well what?"

"You know Allan better than any of us. *Was* he sleeping with her?"

Paul smiled and shook his head. "No, he wasn't."

"How do you know for sure?"

"I know Allan better than any of you. He hung up mad."

Lori chuckled. "That's our Allan."

"Yeah." But Paul still worried that Allan was getting way over his head in this situation with Debbie.

In the middle of the night, Debbie thought she heard Allan in the kitchen, opening a cabinet door. At least, she hoped it was just him. She turned on her lamp, grabbed her Glock, and headed down the hallway. She saw the guest bedroom door was open, no sign of Allan, and she sighed a little with relief. He must have just needed something from the kitchen.

She heard the water dispenser in the fridge door running. "Hey, just me," she announced as she walked toward the kitchen.

"Got thirsty. Pizza always does that to me," he apologized. He looked so damned sexy in a pair of black silk boxer briefs, she stared as if she was starved for a man. Which, when he looked like Allan—buff, tan, mostly naked—she had to admit she was. "Did I wake you?" he asked.

"Really light sleeper." She realized she wasn't wearing her robe now. In the chilly kitchen, her nipples had to be showing through her lightweight, clingy pajama top. "Just making sure it was you."

Allan motioned to the kitchen counter behind him where he'd placed his Glock. "Better to be safe than sorry, in case anyone had tried to break in."

"Agreed. Can you sleep now?" She glanced at the clock on her oven. Three thirty in the morning. Ugh. She'd gotten up at that time on occasion, but it wasn't her preferred hour of waking.

He hesitated to say if he could get back to sleep.

"Feel free to…well, if you're hungry…"

He smiled.

She felt her cheeks warm, and the heat just slid all the way down her body. "I don't think I can. Get back to sleep, I mean." She moved to the fridge, opened the door, and grabbed the milk jug. "Do you want some hot cocoa? That always helps me."

"Sure. Thanks. What can I do?"

"Grab mugs up there?" She pointed to the cabinet.

He pulled out a couple of mugs while she warmed up the cocoa. He chuckled. She turned to see what was funny and nearly had a heart attack.

He was holding one hot-pink-and-white mug while reading it, the other sitting on the counter: *Men should be like my curtains, easy to pull and well hung.*

Her lips parted, and she flushed and turned away quickly before she burned the cocoa. Now what? Explain that a friend had given them to her when her last boyfriend and she had parted company? Or just ignore the fact that they were drinking out of those cups?

He brought the mugs over. "Anything else?"

"There's a can of whipped cream in the fridge, if you want some."

"Real cream," he said, eyeing the can. "Looks good." He gave it to her and lifted the mugs.

She shook the can and pointed it at the right mug and pushed the nozzle. The cream dripped and fizzled. Not to be thwarted, she shook the can again, hoping it wasn't defective. And then the whipped cream swirled around with perfect ridges in a twirl with a cute, little pointy peak. Perfect.

Then she turned to the other mug, shook the can again, and pushed the nozzle. It was working great until halfway through her little mountain of whipped cream twirling to perfection, when the nozzle malfunctioned again and spewed whipped cream everywhere.

In horror, she stared at the white cream that had splattered all over Allan's chest and dotted his boxer briefs. Her mouth agape, she glanced up at him.

His eyes sparkled with mirth and he laughed.

"Oh, oh, let me get something to wipe it up," she said belatedly, and she set the can of whipped cream on the counter.

She grabbed some paper towels and dampened them, then rushed back to wipe the mess up. Allan was still holding both hot-pink mugs of cocoa. She had every intention of taking one and letting him clean himself, but he just moved his arms apart, as if to say she had made the mess, so she could wash it up.

She thought she was going to die. Yes, he was totally hot. And yes, she'd fantasized about making love to him—since they were both unattached and she truly liked him. But in her wildest dreams she would never have imagined making him cocoa in the middle of the night while he stood in sexy silk boxer briefs, nice and formfitting, and then proceeding to splatter him with whipped cream. All over his tanned chest and those black briefs.

She quickly wiped his chest down and glanced at his briefs. His erection was straining against the black fabric, and no way was she going there.

"Here, let me," she said, and hastily took one of the mugs from him while handing off the wet paper towels.

He was still smiling, the rogue, as he wiped off his briefs.

"Should we sit down to drink these?" That way her gaze wouldn't keep drifting lower. "I'm so sorry. I should have known that might happen."

He just laughed and leaned against her kitchen counter and drank his cocoa. "This is really good. Thanks for thinking of it. The whipped cream adds that special touch."

She didn't think he was talking about the whipped cream on top of his cocoa.

She finished hers in record time. After he set his mug
down on the counter, he drew close, placed his hands on
her shoulders, and kissed her mouth. Gently, sweetly—
even more so because his mouth and hers tasted like
sweet whipped cream and cocoa.

"Are you ready for bed now?" he asked.

She laughed. "Uh, yeah, and you're probably ready
for a shower."

He smiled back, and they walked down the hall to the
guest room where he said good night.

"Night," she said and hurried off to her room. She
wouldn't be able to sleep a wink after this.

———

After a hearty breakfast of ham-and-cheese omelets,
precooked pork sausages, and slices of cantaloupe the
next morning, they were on their way to the scene at the
lake. She was glad Allan knew how to prepare meals,
although he had admitted his mother finally got after
him about making Rose do all the meal preparations
when his mother wasn't around.

The snow had stopped and everything was as pristine
as before. They saw that the edges of the lake had frozen
over as they headed into the water. Despite the suits providing insulation from the chilliness, it was always cold
for a bit until their bodies warmed the water filling their
suits. Debbie hoped they'd find something in the lake that
would make all the effort worthwhile. She and Allan had
both been quiet this morning. She normally didn't have
company at her place, so having someone to talk to wasn't
part of her morning routine. Allan was also alone most of
the time, so maybe he was quiet for the same reason.

On the drive to the lake, more silence. Maybe they were both just tired. Maybe he wasn't a morning person. It took her a while to wake up in the morning. Three cups of coffee and another hour, and she'd be more awake. It had taken her forever last night to quit thinking about the whipped cream incident.

Of course, once she took a dip in the icy water, she'd instantly wake up.

Still, she couldn't stand the silence between them. They'd barely said anything other than "Good morning," and "Sugar or cream in the coffee?" or "Ham and cheese in the omelet?" She did worry that maybe he was concerned he shouldn't have kissed her. Allan had always been sensitive about others' feelings, so maybe he was worried about her.

Truth was, she didn't know how to feel. One part of her really wanted more between them. The other part was waffling about whether that was such a good idea. If things didn't work out, then their diving partnership would be over, and what would they do then? Wouldn't it look unprofessional for both of them if they suddenly said they couldn't work together? She wanted to clear the air between them if he was bothered by what had happened between them last night.

"So, not a morning person?" she finally asked.

He smiled and glanced at her. "Sorry. Gathering wool. Just running over several scenarios in my mind."

"Any that you care to share with me?"

He turned off on the road to the lake and shook his head. "Nothing earth-shattering. Same stuff we've been pondering since we started this investigation."

"Why would the sedan follow me? We're both

working the case. Why would the driver follow me and not someone else who's investigating it? Doesn't make any sense to me."

"Not sure. If he was a serial killer and you fit the description of the victim—a beautiful brunette, petite— then maybe we would see a similarity. Or if you knew the victim, which you didn't. So I really don't know where this is leading."

A beautiful brunette? That made her feel a little better. "Are you a morning person?" She had to know. It seemed everyone she knew married opposites. Not that she was thinking in those terms, but she was just curious.

"I love the dawn and dusk and every moment in between."

She smiled at that. "That's nice. I guess the case just has you bothered." And the one involving his sister and friend's wife too. No matter what, Debbie didn't want a little kiss to come between them.

Chapter 8

ALLAN REALIZED DEBBIE WAS BOTHERED BY HIS distant behavior this morning. He really shouldn't have kissed her. He hadn't planned to. Not until he saw her funny mugs and her face turn fifty shades of red, and then she had sprayed him with whipped cream and washed him down. He'd thought the cocoa would help him sleep, but after all that?

Hell, all he could think of was how much he wished he could have joined her in bed.

"Yeah, sorry. I'm usually much chattier in the morning when someone's around. Like Paul," Allan said quickly, not wanting Debbie to think he had been shacking up with all kinds of women. Why he felt compelled to explain himself, he had no idea.

He generally talked to Paul in the mornings when they were staying together on assignments. But this morning, he kept pondering the cases. Not to mention the situation between him and Debbie. He was perturbed with himself over it. He knew better than to get intimately involved with a human woman he really cared about, even if they'd only shared the sweetest of kisses. He hadn't wanted to stop at that and had to use the utmost restraint not to pull her into his arms, hold her close, and kiss her the way he had really wanted. That was the problem. Not what they had done, but what he had wanted to do—and ensuring it didn't happen.

"Ah, well, if you begin talking to me like that in the morning, I'll hear you, but it might take a while to process and respond."

He chuckled. "Truly? I noticed." On a couple of other assignments when he'd run ideas past her and she had to be asked two or three times, he had been certain she wasn't a morning person. After the beer last night, he believed she wasn't a night person either. He knew it took Debbie a while to wake up in the morning, so he really didn't think she'd notice he was being so quiet. He guessed then that he must normally talk more to her when they met to work on the day's activities than he realized.

She sighed. "Sorry."

"I don't mind. As long as you're not ticked off with me about something, I'm good."

She laughed. "Okay. Same here."

They'd already suited up before they arrived because it was too cold to put their wet suits on next to the lake. But when they got out of the lake, they would be in a rush to undress. They both had water parkas—long coats with soft fleece inside and a windproof and waterproof outer fabric that would keep the snow and frigid wind from cooling them down too much on the trek from the car to and from the lake.

This morning, it was a brisk seventeen degrees with snow showers on the way.

Off in the distance, a couple of men were getting ready to ice fish on the frozen lake. No longer was the venture like the old days when Paul and Allan would catch fish in the winter, sitting atop a fish bucket, hoping the trout would swim by and take the bait. Now the guys who were setting up had power augers—often used to dig postholes in the earth—to drill a hole through the ice. And they had brightly colored yellow-and-red portable shelters, underwater cameras, and sonar fish finders.

"Did you ever ice fish?" Debbie asked, making her pre-dive safety checks.

"Yeah, but not quite like that. Much more primitive."

She nodded. "Me too, in the old-fashioned way. Did we catch anything? Sure. Once I caught a trout. Another time, a yellow perch."

"Who did you fish with?" he asked. From what she'd told him, her dad hadn't been there for her when she was growing up.

"My dive partner and mentor. I told you. He was like a father to me. Man, was it cold. I decided fishing in the summer was the only way to go."

"Maybe we can go fishing sometime. In the summer." He knew he really couldn't do it and keep their relationship impersonal.

"Sounds good to me. But, hey, if you're up to it, there's a charity Penguin Plunge at the Winter Carnival in Whitefish in February. A hole is cut into the ice at Whitefish Lake and then participants take a dip to raise money for a great cause. Sounds like a Navy SEAL job to me."

He laughed. "Are you doing it?"

"Every year."

"If I don't have anything else going on, I guess I could risk it." He should have said he would be busy. Hell, he might be if Rose was having the babies and ran into trouble.

Debbie smiled at him, her cheeks and nose rosy

from the cold, looking so pleased that unless he had something really pressing going on, he knew he'd be taking the Penguin Plunge with her. But maybe he could convince Rowdy to go along with them, just to stay out of trouble.

They finished their dive checks, then walked out on the ice to where the car had broken through. The ice had been so clear when the accident first happened, it was like walking on glass. They could see the vegetation on the bottom of the lake in the shallower parts. But now snow covered the ice.

They dove around the bottom of the lake where the car had rested, searching for any other evidence they could find.

Debbie pointed to some thick vegetation. Allan joined her as she took pictures of the location of a 9 mm gun buried in the plants. She bagged it as evidence and slipped it into her mesh diving bag. After looking for as long as they could and not finding anything else of importance, they returned to the surface. But Allan was glad they had found that much. Once they removed their face masks, tanks, and flippers, they threw on their parkas and headed back to the car.

"Good find," Allan said. "What I don't understand is how the gun was outside the vehicle if it belonged to the dead man."

"The driver's window was broken. Maybe the pressure of the water filling the car caused the gun to float out or be pushed out. Or maybe it didn't belong to this guy. Maybe it was there already. But it looks like it hasn't been down there for long."

Allan looked it over. "I agree. No rust on it."

"Considering the location of the gun, I assume it moved a bit in the soil and vegetation when they dragged the car out of there."

"Probably."

They began the task of removing their wet suits—gloves, hoods, and booties first. Then the parkas had to come off so they could pull off one sleeve, then the next. They were both wearing long-sleeved rash guards, and she looked sexy as hell in hers. It was a royal blue and fit all her curves. Which she had in abundance.

Allan tried damn hard not to look when she was stripping out of her clothes. He didn't want her to feel like he was ogling her, although he was having a hard time not doing that. If she were a wolf, it would be different. They were used to stripping out of their clothes in front of each other, for the most part, unless it was a single wolf without a pack. And if he had wanted to show interest in her, he could. Just like a she-wolf could with him. But with Debbie being human and him being wolf, he really had to curb the natural wolfish inclination. It wouldn't be considered politically correct among humans.

He peeled out of the top half of his wet suit and then his rash guard. He grabbed a towel out of the hatchback and rubbed his chest, back, and arms vigorously before he noticed Debbie watching him. He smiled a little.

He tugged on a flannel shirt and then his wool sweater. "We'll have to turn the weapon in at the station and see if they can get a ballistic match with any other crimes in the area. And see if this guy had a registered handgun."

"Agreed." Debbie shivered. "I *really* like diving in warm weather better." She pulled a blue changing robe over her head. It was a long-sleeved toga affair that allowed her to slip out of her rash guard without the fear of losing a towel.

The idea she was naked underneath the changing robe sure had his attention, again.

"Yeah, warm weather definitely has its advantages." He tucked his towel around his waist and began removing the bottom half of his wet suit.

Now that seemed to have *her* attention.

His phone jingled that he had received a text, but he had to get changed first. When he and Debbie were in the car with the heat on full, he pulled out his cell. The message was from Paul.

Allan said to Debbie, "Paul sent a text about the autopsy report. He said, 'Got news on the Van Lake murder investigation. The vic didn't have any water in his lungs. He died from a blow to the head before the car entered the water. No ID on him yet. The vehicle was stolen from a man in Helena, Montana.'"

"He died before he was submerged in the lake," Debbie said. "We assumed that he had been murdered, but that just confirms it. But the part about driving a stolen vehicle? Any leads on that? If he were a regular criminal, he'd be in the database. Well, if he'd been caught before."

"No. Apparently, if he was in a local database, they haven't found him yet."

"Do you want me to drive so you can call Paul?"

"Yeah. Sounds good to me."

They switched places and then Allan made the call. "We found a 9 mm. We can't be sure it belonged to the vic, but it might give us some clues."

"That's good to hear. We've got some bad news. Two more wolves were trapped and shot with silver rounds. Except they were just plain wolves."

"So then the guy is randomly killing wolves, hoping he'll get—" Allan paused. This was what he hated about having pack conversations around humans.

"A *lupus garou*, yeah. I believe he must have known the woman was one and he tracked her here. And the wolves were near the location, probably drawn by the blood. So he shoots them, thinking they're werewolves too."

"Right. Which means he's still in the area and still a real threat to our…a wolf pack. I'm surprised he didn't shoot any of us when we were investigating the scene."

"You were in your human form. He might not be willing to shoot humans until he knows for certain. At least, that's my guess. And you're on contract work with the sheriff's department. Just think if he'd killed a bunch of police officers working the case out there. So I think he's being careful as far as that goes."

"Except that Lori and Rose arrived at the scene… first." Allan was going to say as wolves. Paul would know just what he was going to say.

"He might not have been there when the ladies arrived. At least, I'm hoping that's the case."

"All right. I'll keep you posted if I learn anything more. Talk to you later, Paul."

"Same here."

When Allan put his phone away, Debbie cleared her throat, then said very seriously, "You know, Rowdy thinks you and the rest of your family are part of a werewolf pack."

Allan found her comment disquieting. "He does, does he? You know what they say. It takes one to know one."

She laughed.

"So how did he come by that notion?" He pretended to take the news in a lighthearted, humorous way, even though he felt anything but.

She explained about the shootings near the jumping cliff. "You have to admit it sounds rather peculiar."

Allan was quiet for some time, but then he let out his breath as if relieved. "He didn't see me shift then."

Debbie chuckled, loving that Allan could play along. "Besides, *you* are the one with close family ties. Rowdy has none. So he couldn't be a wolf. But he told me to watch out where you're concerned."

"All that means is that he's a lone wolf and not associated with a pack."

"I'll tell him what you said next time."

"So what do *you* think?"

"Oh, you're a wolf all right."

He smiled.

"He told me about the shoot-out you had with bank robbers. Rowdy thought a pack of wolves was involved. But wolves don't go after humans like that. Unless they were rabid, maybe, but then the victims would have tested positive for rabies. He said you witnessed that attack."

"No, I was shot and couldn't do a whole lot."

"Where were you shot?" she asked, surprised. She didn't remember seeing any mark on his beautiful skin, except for some cute freckles on his shoulders. But she hadn't witnessed any scars due to a bullet wound.

"Minor scratch, and it's all healed up. No scar even."

"You must have been in a bad way. They took you away in an ambulance, Rowdy said."

"Just as a precautionary measure."

"You wouldn't have been lying around when armed men were shooting at you and the others." Then she frowned a little. "Do wolves heal miraculously like vampires? No wounds left behind?"

"Absolutely."

"Thought so. I'll have to let Rowdy know. Did Paul see any of the 'wolves'?"

"He was too busy trying to rescue Lori. She'd struggled with one robber and then both fell off the cliff. You know she was pregnant at the time, right? So Paul was concerned about her condition and was trying to reach her right away."

"Yes, that was so awful. I was glad to hear she was fine. I realize she knows martial arts, but she's seen these two bad criminal cases that must have really shaken her up. So in the bank robber case, she had been struggling with a naked man?"

"The police found his clothes in his vehicle. Maybe he was planning to dump them, afraid he'd been identified, or maybe he had blood splatter on them from shooting me. Anyway, we thought maybe he was high on something, but nothing showed up in his system during the autopsy."

"That leaves only one real plausible explanation. He removed his clothes, shifted, and chased after Lori as a wolf."

"She wouldn't have been able to fight off a wolf."

"Unless she had been a wolf too."

"A female fighting against a male?" Allan shook his

head. "I doubt a female would have survived a vicious male's attack."

"Unless Paul came to rescue her as a wolf. And then there would have been two wolves against one."

"I see you have all this well thought out. Have you asked Paul about his role as a wolf?"

"Heavens no. I figure you and I are friends, and you'll keep the others from turning me."

Allan raised his brows a little. "What if I wanted to turn you to make you my mate?"

She smiled as if she rather liked the idea. "I might just bite you right back."

"That's all part of being a wolf." Then he let out his breath. "About tonight…"

She knew before he said it that he wasn't staying with her tonight. He was backing off from getting too involved, and she couldn't help but be disappointed. "Yeah?"

"I need to stay closer to home, but I'm calling the sheriff's office to make sure someone drives by to check on you every once in a while."

"I'll be fine, Allan. Really." But she knew he'd call it in anyway. And she had to like that he still worried about her, even if things were cooling off between them again.

<hr />

After ensuring some of his law enforcement friends would check on Debbie periodically, Allan drove to Paul and Lori's cabin on the lake. He really hated leaving Debbie alone, partly because he wanted to be the one protecting her and partly because he wanted to just plain be with her. But despite how he wanted it, he knew this was the best for all concerned.

When he arrived at Paul and Lori's cabin, Lori fixed them dinner.

"Rowdy told Debbie we were part of a werewolf pack," Allan told them.

"How did he come to that conclusion?" Lori asked.

Allan knew Paul and Lori would take Rowdy's claim seriously, even if most people would think he was just having some lighthearted, storytelling fun. If Rowdy mentioned it to the police, they'd rib him mercilessly. But it was still a concern for the pack. Allan explained all that Debbie had told him.

"He told Debbie, not you though," Paul said thoughtfully, setting the table.

"Maybe he thought I'd turn all wolf and that would be the end of him." Not that Allan was being serious about it.

"He had to know she'd tell you. He must have figured she'd get a kick out of it," Paul said.

"Right, just what I had assumed. Which means he wants to see how we react to Debbie's claim."

"I wonder if he's armed with silver bullets." Lori served up the rolls while Paul dished up the bowls of chicken and dumplings.

Allan stoked the fire, thinking how nice it would be to have one going at his place while Debbie sat with him on the couch. "Ah, but he believes any bullets will kill us."

Paul set beers on the table for him and Allan, then returned to the kitchen to get a glass of milk for Lori. "True. Just like silver bullets can kill humans. Your reaction to Debbie was fine. As far as Rowdy goes, I'd just ignore it. Just be your normal self around him and Debbie. There's not much else we can do for now."

Allan joined them at the table. "I agree. I was just a little surprised. Not often does someone believe the evidence points to werewolves."

"I'm sure he's just pulling our legs. Coming up with bizarre explanations for bizarre circumstances. But even if he did believe we're werewolves, I'm sure he realizes we're some of the good guys." Lori took a roll and passed around the platter.

"True. I just wanted to make you aware of it to alert the pack members, in case we have any trouble with him. I can see him putting surveillance on us." Allan eyed the roll. "Fresh baked."

"Only for you," Lori said.

Paul grunted and began to coat his roll with gobs of butter. "She made them for me."

She was watching Paul, then pointed her knife at his roll. "Do you have enough butter on your roll?"

When Allan had shared meals with Paul, they always had to get an extra tub of butter—the large variety.

"He'd have us under surveillance during the full moon especially." Lori peered into the empty butter container.

Before she got up from the table, Allan said, "Do you have another tub of butter?"

"In the fridge, thanks."

He went to get it. "Wouldn't Rowdy be surprised to learn we don't have to shift during the full moon but can do it at any time."

Lori shook her head. "He may be rethinking the lore, if he truly does believe we're wolves."

"So if he truly believes, what then?" Allan set the new tub of butter on the table in front of Lori.

She opened the lid, giving Paul a look that said this

tub was hers, and he smiled back. "We'll take care of Rowdy if it becomes a problem."

"Turn him, right? We could use someone like him on the force and on our side." Allan thought it could work, particularly since Rowdy had no family to speak of.

"Yes. I agree." Paul winked at Lori, and she relented, giving him the new tub of butter. At least it was for his second roll.

Chapter 9

FOR THREE WEEKS, NOTHING HAPPENED. IT WAS AS IF nothing had *ever* happened. No black sedan had been spotted. No more wolf killings. Maybe the killer had been disconcerted when he killed the wolves and they hadn't turned into humans. Maybe he hadn't realized the Cunningham wolf pack was located here and had just followed the dead woman.

As to the business with the man driving the red Camaro, no sign of it either, though everyone had been diligent about watching for it.

Allan was trying to be careful around Debbie, and he didn't like it. He couldn't tell her why he was backing away. Despite his behavior, Debbie was being really upbeat and good-natured about it, and trying to show it was no big deal. And that made the situation all the harder to deal with.

He could tell it did bother her, as evidenced by the way she averted her gaze at times when he caught her watching him, or when their hands touched or their bodies brushed against each other, and she'd pull away as if he'd burned her. It was killing him to treat her like she wasn't important to him, except as a partner. He knew kissing her had been a mistake, because that little kiss and everything that had led up to it had made him fantasize more than once about what becoming intimately involved would be like.

She'd invited him over a few times and he'd skillfully declined, sometimes because he had other commitments and sometimes because he was trying to put some distance between them. The problem was that he couldn't see her as just his partner or a human that he had no business getting involved with. He'd been short-tempered with Paul and his family too. They had tried to reassure him it was for the best, but he didn't need them telling him anything where Debbie was concerned.

It was time to meet her and Rowdy at the pizzeria for another Friday night "date." For three weeks, they'd done this, and he'd hoped to dispel any notion that he and Debbie were an item.

He tried to think about the case, but the way this was going, he was afraid it would end up in the cold-case files before long. Unless the killer struck again. Although they certainly didn't want that either.

When Allan arrived at the pizzeria, he saw both Debbie's and Rowdy's vehicles. He had to remind himself they'd had fun every time they had met for dinner, though after the first time, Debbie had water to drink. Rowdy had asked her to go out with him a couple more times, but she still said no, to Allan's relief. The more he saw her and got to know her, the more he wanted to know her even better. He genuinely loved her company, her smiles, and her teasing nature, and he loved to tease her right back. He'd grown more lax around her, allowing more of his wolfish nature to show—the possessiveness, the playfulness, and the sexual overtures—although he shouldn't have. But she brought it out in him, and he had a hard time keeping his wolfishness under wraps around her.

That was the trouble when a wolf began to really
get interested in a good prospect for a mate and the
female wasn't a *lupus garou*. He'd even allowed
himself to envision her being turned, of him doing
the deed. That was a dark road he had to turn back
from now.

Then right in the middle of refilling Allan's mug with
beer, Rowdy asked Debbie out to dinner for Saturday
night. And, hell, she looked at Allan, as if waiting for
him to approve or get her out of it this time!

"We have a date tomorrow night at Captain
O'Keefe's Seafood Restaurant," Allan said, smiling
a little at Rowdy and hoping Debbie wouldn't be
annoyed with him for saying so. Of course he'd take
her out, but that would just stir up things between
the two of them again. Allan told himself he was
just doing it to rescue her from Rowdy since he was
trying to wear her down and she looked ready to fold.
Or maybe she was playing her woman's intuition—
women could be tricky like that—and forcing Allan
to take a stand.

Rowdy lifted his mug of beer in a salute to Allan.

Allan raised his to Rowdy. He ventured a look in
Debbie's direction. She'd folded her arms and was
frowning at him.

Well, maybe they wouldn't really go out to dinner.

"I'll call you about tomorrow night," he said.

Allan and Debbie had continued to arrive separately
at the pizzeria. He thought she was trying to flirt with
other dive team members who were single, but he could
tell her heart wasn't really in it. He felt like a real heel,
but what could he do about it? Nothing.

Rowdy shook his head. "See you all next week, if we're still on."

"Sure," Debbie said, smiling.

"Right. Next week," Allan agreed.

Then he left and headed home. When he arrived at his cabin, he got a call from Debbie. "Listen, about tomorrow night—"

"When did you want me to pick you up?"

"I...don't want you to feel obligated."

"I'd like to go out, if you'd like to."

"Sure. Thanks for rescuing me from Rowdy. I don't think he believes you've had a change of heart about us, but I appreciate that you made the offer."

Allan couldn't share how he really felt. How much he wanted to take her out. How much he wanted to stay with her afterward. She was like a drug to him, an addiction he couldn't give up.

"Would six be good?"

"Okay, see you then."

Allan knew he shouldn't be doing this. He knew it, but he told himself there would be no harm in a little dinner date.

Late the next afternoon, Allan got a call from Rose. Every time he did, he worried she was going into labor. "I was looking over the applications—"

"You're not going into labor," he blurted out.

Pause. Then Rose chuckled. "No. I guess every time I call, I need to preface the conversation with, 'I'm not going into labor yet.' Every time I call anyone, I get the same panicked comment."

Allan breathed a sigh of relief. "Okay, you were going over applications from potential new members who want to join our pack and...?"

"I found one from around the time Lori and I discovered the dead woman. We've either met and accepted or rejected everyone else who sent one. Or they rejected us. I didn't think she could be the woman because she said she would check us out in a few weeks. But we found the dead woman only a few days after this was sent. So I didn't make the connection, thinking this Sarah Engle was still coming to see us in a few weeks. A few weeks have passed. Allan, I think...I think she might have been part of that LARP group in southern Montana that I went to check out."

He sure hoped this was the break in the case that they so desperately needed. "Is that where she was from?"

"On her application, she said she was. I didn't see her with the group when I went down there, but under hobbies she said that she loves theater production and mentions LARP—not that particular group, just listed the acronym. So I'm thinking she could have been with Zeta's group. I told Paul and Lori, but he wanted me to call you and tell you everything I knew. He wants you to speak with Zeta Johansson, the woman who runs the group. I'd go because I've already met her before and she seemed to like me but—"

"You're due any day now. I'll go."

Rose gave him the address. "Let us know what you find, all right?"

"I will." Then he ended the call and looked at the clock. It was three already and it would take three hours in good weather to reach Helena. He'd have to see if he could schedule a meeting with Zeta for Sunday because of the lateness of the hour, the worsening weather, and his date with Debbie.

But then the name of the place jogged a memory. The dead man in the car submerged in the lake had stolen the car in Helena, Montana. What were the odds that two people from there weren't related somehow? Both murdered near Bigfork. Both from Helena. And murdered only a day apart. What if the murdered man had also been a member of the LARP group?

"Paul," Allan said, giving him a call right away. "You're not going to believe this, but..."

Chapter 10

THIS WAS IT! ALLAN WAS FINALLY TAKING THE BULL by the horns and asking her out. This would be their first real date, and Debbie couldn't have been happier and more excited about it. She spent the day doing laundry and cleaning the duplex, just in case Allan stayed the night. Not that she thought he would. But then again, she wanted to be prepared.

During the day, she'd gone over her wardrobe a million times. Nothing suited the occasion. Too flashy, like she was ready for a New Year's Eve party, or too dark and businesslike, as if she were a female detective on a TV series. Or too casual—soft, million times washed jeans. One dress looked too frumpy. Another like she was going to a church social. Maybe slacks. One pair was too baggy. Another too short-legged and tight. When had they shrunk?

She eyed her black jeans and a jade sweater that was so soft and cuddly. That would do. She threw them on and then considered her hair. Up and sexy, or was that too much like the way she wore it all day on the job?

Down and soft and curling about her shoulders? Despite how tipsy she had been the night she'd had the beer at the pizzeria, she had seen the look on Allan's face when she'd let her hair down—admiration. But was it sexier if he removed the barrette? That if they started kissing, she would go from polished to ready for some fun loving?

She never thought about her clothes or hair this much for a date. A little, sure, because she didn't want to be underdressed or overdressed for the occasion. But never all day, trying on clothes, taking them off. Trying her hair up, then down. Then up. Then down.

She groaned as she considered herself in the mirror. She wasn't going to the church to get married today. No one was going to take pictures of the date, capturing what she looked like for all time. And really? She didn't believe Allan would care. He'd seen her in frumpy and casual and nice, and he seemed to enjoy being with her no matter how she looked.

A knock at her door made her jump. She glanced at her watch. Either Allan was half an hour early, or someone else was knocking at her door. She hurried into the bedroom and grabbed her Glock from her bedside table drawer, then stalked toward the door.

When she reached it, she peered out. Rowdy was standing there. She frowned, worried he had bad news about the case. He couldn't be thinking of joining her on her date with Allan tonight. Maybe he had bad news about Allan.

Trying not to overreact, she opened the door and Rowdy smiled appreciably at her. "Now I *really* wish you had gone out with *me* on a date."

"What are you doing here?" She hadn't meant to sound so annoyed, but she really didn't want Allan to see Rowdy here when he arrived.

"Allan said he might be late coming to pick you up. There's a massive pileup on the road he has to take after he leaves the mountain. Since I live in Whitefish, he called in a favor and asked if I'd pick you up and take you to the restaurant. He knew your car was in the shop, and he didn't want you out driving in this weather anyway."

She wanted to groan out loud, but instead, she showed Rowdy in.

"I don't intend to join you for dinner, so you can't twist my arm or anything." He smiled at her.

"Thanks, Rowdy. I…well, I—" She felt terrible that he continued to ask her out and she kept saying no, but then he would rescue her tonight. She felt she owed him a dinner.

"Would you like something to drink? Water? Coffee?"

"Coffee would be good. I came early because I wanted to make sure I got you to the restaurant on time. I'll hang around until Allan makes it."

"Thanks, Rowdy. I really appreciate it." She started a pot of coffee, then turned to face him. "Why didn't Allan call me or text or something?"

"He did. Or he said he did. You weren't answering."

She patted her pocket, realizing at once that her phone was on vibrate and in the jeans she wore earlier today. "Oh, damn. Sorry." She headed for her bedroom, pulled out the cell, and found she had ten missed calls and five text messages, all from Allan. She shook her head at herself, felt bad that she'd probably worried him, and called him right back.

"Hey," he said. "I worried about you. Rowdy will be there to pick you up and take you to the restaurant. I'm on my way now, but I might be about five to ten minutes late."

"He's here now. My phone was in another pair of pants. I'm so sorry, Allan."

"No problem. He was happy to check on you and take you over there."

"Should we invite him to join us for dinner?"

Allan didn't answer right away.

"It's up to you," she added.

"Yeah, hell, sure." But Allan sounded disappointed to have to make the offer. "It would be the right thing to do."

"Okay. I'll tell him. See you in a bit." Feeling horribly disappointed the way things were working out, Debbie ended the call and tucked the phone into her pocket, then returned to the kitchen where Rowdy was pouring himself a cup of coffee.

"Cream?" he asked.

"Uh, yeah." She went to get the cream. "Allan is on his way. He said he might be five to ten minutes late, and he wanted me to ask if you'd like to join us for dinner for all the trouble you've gone through to come and get me." She handed Rowdy the creamer.

He poured the cream into his coffee. "Think nothing of it. I hope he'd do the same for me if the situation was reversed, and I definitely wouldn't barge in on a date. Besides, when you didn't answer your phone, he worried about you. Why didn't you tell me someone driving a black sedan had been following you? I'd have every one of them pulled over and the driver investigated."

"It hasn't happened again. I think he must have left the area. And it might not have been anything. Thanks for coming by to check on me."

"Any time. About the case, we'll get whoever was

involved in both murders. I really thought we'd have more leads and have them wrapped up by now, but we'll learn the truth before we know it."

"Do you still think the murderer of the woman was a werewolf hunter?"

"Yeah. And the other guy in the stolen car. Why else would they have guns loaded with silver rounds?"

"They were both crazy."

Rowdy glanced at his watch. "It'll take me ten minutes to get you to the restaurant, and we'll make sure you get your table. Captain O'Keefe's is always busy on Saturday nights. I was surprised Allan could get a reservation at that late a date."

"Why do you think that?"

"I'm a homicide detective. I saw the surprised, then relieved look on your face when he said he was taking you out. He hadn't planned it, just winged it, hoping you'd agree."

"I…"

"When I say 'relieved,' I mean that you were glad he finally asked you out. Hell, why do you think I keep asking you? Not that I don't want to take you out, but I've been attempting to give him an incentive to quit delaying the inevitable."

"Even if he's a wolf with a wolf pack."

"As many cases as Paul and Allan have solved, and people and animals they've rescued, they're some of the good guys. So if he's intent on making you his mate and you're intent on wanting the same thing, who am I to say what is right or wrong?"

She smiled and shook her head at Rowdy. "You're a good detective. And not bad at making up stories either."

"The best when it comes to murder investigations," he admitted freely. "But I don't mind saying I had hoped you'd dump him and start seeing reason and date me. Still, if you ever change your mind…"

"Thanks, Rowdy." If she hadn't been so hung up on Allan, she might have been interested in dating Rowdy.

When they arrived at the restaurant, Rowdy was the perfect gentleman and waited with her at the table until Allan got there. He was fifteen minutes late, and she'd already ordered stuffed mushrooms as an appetizer and glasses of water to appease the waiter.

Rowdy didn't eat any of the mushrooms, though she'd offered. She felt uncomfortable eating in front of him when he wasn't even her dinner date. Allan called twice to let her know his progress. Two more accidents had caused massive slowdowns on the highway.

"Listen, if you get hungry, just go ahead and eat. Or if they're getting antsy about needing the table, go ahead and order me a salmon and—"

"I ordered stuffed mushrooms. We're good. I don't want to order your dinner and then have it get cold before you arrive. The waiter's been fine," she assured him.

"All right. I'll be there as soon as I can."

Then five minutes later, Allan arrived looking like a SEAL on a mission, his expression dark until he spied her. Instantly he smiled, casting a glance at Rowdy. But he also took in the table arrangement—the glasses of water, hers half-empty, the other filled to the top. The one uneaten stuffed mushroom, her plate showing she'd used hers, the other completely clean.

Rowdy got up from the booth and shook Allan's hand. "Hey, you owe me."

Allan shook his hand. "Thanks, Rowdy. I'm in your debt."

"Thanks, Rowdy," Debbie said. "Are you sure you don't want to eat with us?"

"Are you kidding?" Rowdy motioned to Allan. "He's a SEAL and knows more killer moves than I do, I'm certain. See you around."

When he left, Allan took Rowdy's seat. "I'm so sorry. The weather has been so bad, there was a third pileup on the way here and cars sliding on ice everywhere. I was fortunate I made it."

"We should have rescheduled once you had the first trouble near your house."

"Are you kidding? Not when I'd gotten all dressed up to take you out. Do you know how hard it was for me to figure out what to wear?" He was wearing a pretty blue sweater and his usual blue jeans.

"I thought only women had that problem." She figured he was teasing her as usual. She couldn't imagine he really had been indecisive about what to wear. "Rowdy was great about keeping me company. I'm just glad you got here safe and sound. I left you a mushroom, just in case you'd like one."

Allan laughed. "One, eh? No one can eat just one."

They both had roasted salmon and oysters, and Allan was glad he'd made the effort to get there, despite the road conditions. He kept looking at Debbie and thinking how truly beautiful she was, wearing the softest jade sweater, her dark hair curling about her shoulders. He planned to enjoy having dinner with her. He really was starving, and it had nothing to do with the oysters.

He was glad Rowdy had kept her company, and

gladder still that he had left when Allan arrived. And yet Allan told himself this was really all wrong. He should have insisted that Rowdy stay and dine with them. He shouldn't have a first real date alone with Debbie. They were discussing the usual pleasantries, so the problem wasn't exactly the date, but what came next.

"Is your car still in the shop?" he asked.

"Yeah, bad alternator. I can pick it up Monday."

It was probably good that she lived so far away. The thirty-minute drive meant he wasn't going to drop everything and run by her place because he was in the area, as much as he had wanted to on numerous occasions.

But now he had a new dilemma. He was probably going to stay the night with her, but he had made arrangements for late tomorrow afternoon to see Zeta about her LARP group. She had confirmed that Sarah Engle had been part of the group but was missing. Not only that, but when he showed a picture of the Van Lake murder victim to Rose, she acknowledged he'd been one of the players in the same LARP group. She didn't remember his name though. Was the one who had murdered the woman in the group too? They didn't have a photo of him that they could share with Zeta for confirmation.

After a great dinner, Allan drove Debbie home. On the way there, Debbie was watching out the window as the snowflakes hit the glass and the windshield wipers wiped them away. Out of nowhere she said, "I don't understand about the silver rounds. I mean, I do."

He was surprised she was mentioning that now when they hadn't talked about the bullets in over a week.

"The nutcase is a werewolf hunter—has to be, because he killed a woman he thought was one, and he killed two wolves, all three riddled with silver rounds," she continued. "And the bullets were all from the same gun. As for the dead guy in the lake—if the unregistered gun was his, what does that mean? He can't be the woman's killer because we found him before the woman was murdered. And the ballistics for the murdered woman and the dead wolves didn't match the gun in the lake. But it was also filled with silver rounds."

Allan took a deep breath and let it out. "Right. What if there are two werewolf hunters?" He figured there wasn't any sense in trying to treat this like a normal case because it was anything but—even for *lupus garous*. So he might as well play along for a bit, fill her story full of holes, and hope they still could find the murderer soon. But initially, he hadn't considered the possibility of two hunters and the Van Lake murder being connected to the leghold trap murder.

"Okay. So a werewolf killed the hunter before he could kill any more werewolves. But the werewolf didn't want to take him down as a wolf, because that would prove they exist," Debbie said.

"That's assuming that werewolves exist and the wolf that killed him wasn't a genuine wolf."

She gave him a small smile as if she thought he was teasing her. "Right. But a wolf couldn't stage a car accident. Or"—Debbie paused dramatically—"he wasn't his mad-wolf self when he went to kill the werewolf hunter."

"A werewolf has a mad-wolf self?" Now Allan was amused.

"Sure. In some of the old horror movies I watched, the werewolf would go on a rampage. He no longer could have any thoughts as a human and was a total beast of prey. And then he wanted to die because he didn't want to hurt the ones he loved."

"So a werewolf couldn't have a conscience when he's a wolf," Allan said. That kind of thinking was one reason why *lupus garous* never wanted to expose what they were to the human population. Even if some humans accepted them for what they were, lots more would be afraid of them—afraid because of the fictional myths and legends perpetuating the evil wolf and werewolf scenarios—and want them dead.

"Well, not according to legend. Or at least one of the legends," Debbie replied. "I guess for the sake of argument, one could say they still had their human awareness when they were a wolf." She took a moment to gather her thoughts on where she was going with this. "Oh, and there was no full moon when the man in the submerged car died, so the werewolf probably couldn't even turn into a wolf. So he had to take down the hunter before the full moon was out because he wouldn't have any control over his wolf half after that. And the werewolves have to hide their wolf half or people would think real wolves were on the attack and kill every wolf they saw."

"So you're saying the man in the car was a werewolf hunter—that the gun with the silver bullets were his—only the werewolf killed him first."

"Right. A werewolf wouldn't have a gun with silver bullets. The werewolf's concern would be to protect his werewolf pack. All of them would be running as wolves during the full moon, so the pack leader would want to ensure they remained safe. The werewolf discovers this guy is hunting his pack and kills him, then stages an accident."

Which sounded damn plausible, Allan was thinking. Except that no one in his pack had killed the man in the lake. "We have a problem with that scenario. If the woman was supposed to be a werewolf that the other man killed, there was no full moon then either." At least that could be a problem in Debbie's werewolf world.

"Right. She wasn't a *real* werewolf, Allan. Just work with me here. But he *suspected* she was. Maybe she was into werewolves, like she was part of a pretend pack online. I checked to see if anyone was professing to be a werewolf hunter. What I found was a website run by a blogger who claims to have spotted a werewolf. A lot of people chimed in to claim they were part of werewolf packs—all in good fun. Some responded that they would join the packs; others that they'd shoot a werewolf on sight.

"Maybe our guy was following a thread like that. A real nutcase, he believes one of the 'werewolves' is truly a werewolf, gets to talking to her off the loop, and he tells her he's a wolf too. She is so into playing the game that she convinces him she really is a wolf. He wants to meet her. Of course, he might not be a werewolf hunter, per se, but just some predator that lures women online to his lair and he's acting out this werewolf hunter fantasy.

"So our werewolf hunter chases her into the trap and waits for her to turn into a wolf. But then he realizes his mistake. She can't shift because the full moon isn't out yet. So he shoots her with silver rounds and that's the end of her—which would be the end of anyone—but he's convinced that the rounds have to be silver to kill a werewolf. Then when real wolves visit the crime scene, he's confident they are part of her pack. He shoots them with silver rounds, but they turn out to be bona fide wolves. No human genetics at all."

"So you're saying he really believes werewolves exist?" Allan asked, trying to sound incredulous. Two werewolf hunters, and one werewolf hunting *them*. So was the man in the black sedan a werewolf who killed the hunter and then the other hunter found his friend dead?

"Of course werewolves aren't real. Sure, he believes this, but the 'werewolf' who came after him wasn't *really* a werewolf. He probably was a relative or friend of someone else who was murdered by one of these men and was trying to take them down. So he got one of the purported werewolf hunters, but before he could locate and kill the other, the hunter murdered another supposed werewolf. The woman. Then the hunter killed two regular wolves by accident, thinking they were werewolves. But why would the killer of the werewolf hunter in Van Lake—if that's what he turns out to be—not hide the evidence of killing him better?" she asked.

"Because he wants the other hunter to know that he's onto him? If he's an alpha, he wouldn't be sneaky about it. Yes, to cover it up a bit for the police. But for the hunter? No."

"Okay, wait. So you're saying the murderer was alpha-like, not that he really was a werewolf. But just a take-charge kind of guy."

"Yeah."

"That makes sense. But then the werewolf hunter killer could get tripped up and sent up for murder."

"Often criminals make mistakes. We see that all the time. The foolproof murder turns out not to be so foolproof after all." But if the killer of the man in the submerged car was a *lupus garou*, Allan hoped he didn't get caught. Their kind couldn't go to prison.

"True." Debbie leaned back comfortably against the seat, as if she felt they'd solved some of the mystery.

He was beginning to wonder if they had. "Paul and I were wondering if it was a role-play group and some of the members began to take the game seriously."

"You mean like some were playing the roles of werewolves and others the hunters? In one of those live-action games?"

"Yeah, only it got out of hand."

"Have you checked into it?"

"We have, but we couldn't find anything for this area online. But if they began to do this for real, they probably would have taken the site down, if they had one."

He was still pondering if he should take her with him to see the woman in charge of the LARP in Helena. He was trying to come up with a plausible reason for believing the murdered woman might be Sarah Engle and a member of the LARP there. He couldn't tell Debbie the truth.

Debbie glanced out the side window. "Okay, so then we have the man driving the black sedan."

"That we haven't seen any sign of lately."

"Right and no more murders or wolf killings. So that could mean the driver was the murderer of the woman and he found his hunter friend in the lake."

"Exactly."

"Or...he killed the man in the lake and the murderer of the woman left the area, and he's after him."

"Could be. Or he murdered both the man in the lake and the woman."

"No, couldn't be because the woman was supposed to be a werewolf, and the man in the lake, a werewolf hunter."

"Okay." Allan had hoped they'd find both men and learn the truth, because the hunter could definitely be after other wolf packs if he'd learned how to identify and locate which ones were *lupus garous*. The newly turned wolf scenario was as much of a problem as the other. Allan and his pack wouldn't have any peace of mind until this was resolved. "Rose called me and told me about a woman who was going to stop in and see her about joining a LARP in Helena. But she never came to see her."

"Why in the world would Rose want to join a group like that? That's three hours from her home. And with triplets on the way?"

"This was before she met Everett. And she thought it would be a fun lark."

"Oh, okay. So the woman never got in touch with Rose and…?"

"Rose was thinking about it and said what if Sarah Engle was playing a wolf, and she—"

"Ohmigod, and she's the woman Lori and Rose found murdered?"

"Yeah. It might be a really far-out notion, but—"

"We don't have any other leads." Debbie glanced at her watch.

"I was planning on running down there and talking with the woman who runs the group in Helena."

"Did Rose or you try calling Sarah?"

"Yeah. There's no answer on her phone. I called Zeta

Johansson, the moderator of the LARP group, and she said Sarah's been missing."

Debbie frowned at him. "It's her then."

"The far-out scenario began to look not so far-out when I learned that. She hadn't lived there for all that long, and anything else could be possible."

"Did Zeta call the police and report Sarah missing?"

"Yeah, she did."

"And they said?"

"They didn't believe she had enough evidence to prove the woman didn't leave of her own free will with her lover."

"Let me guess. He's also missing."

"Right. But it's still a hunch and nothing more. There's no real evidence of foul play. Sarah didn't have a job yet, so no one reported she was not at work. She'd paid her rent up for two months, required by the management, so no alarm bells went off there."

"And the lover?" Debbie asked.

"Lloyd Bates. I ran a check on him, but he didn't come up in any databases."

"Now that sounds like alarm bells to me."

"Right, but without anything to go on—no evidence of foul play or dead bodies, at least that we can confirm—you know the rest. They didn't feel they had a case. But we have another clue. Rose went to see the group and met a bunch of the players. Sarah wasn't at the group meeting that night, but a man was that Rose said looked a lot like the man murdered at Van Lake. She couldn't be a hundred percent sure because the man in the lake was bearded, and the one she met had been clean-shaven."

"Did you tell Rowdy?"

"Not yet. If we learn this man is still with the group and not missing, then we don't have the right man. I wanted to show Zeta the photos in person to see if she could identify the dead man and woman."

Debbie was quiet after that as Allan pulled up to her back door.

"I had such a lovely time tonight," she said. "I hope you don't mind me talking about this case. I can't stop thinking about it."

"Not at all." He shook his head. "Truth is, I can't either. I wake in the middle of the night thinking about it. I hate cases that grow cold."

"Me too. But maybe this is the lead we needed."

Chapter 11

WHEN DEBBIE AND ALLAN PARKED AT HER DUPLEX, she invited him in. Since this was the first time they'd had a real date, though he had been careful not to call it that, she wanted to end it with something special after all the trouble he'd had getting there in the bad weather.

She hadn't planned on anything other than having some hot cocoa, although she'd picked up some beer in case he wanted one. It was probably safer for him to have a beer rather than cocoa and whipped cream again.

She knew he was holding back, wanting something more, but for some reason believing they should keep their relationship on more of a professional basis. Yet, tonight, the dynamics had changed some. He'd been more relaxed, and she wondered if that had anything to do with Rowdy not being at dinner with them.

She was also thrilled to think they might have a lead on the dead woman's identity and maybe something about who murdered her.

Whatever the reason, Debbie felt less stressed tonight with Allan and just wanted to finish the evening with something nice. "Would you like to come in?"

He hesitated.

She thought of just dismissing him. Just telling him, "Maybe some other time." But she wasn't sure she'd give him another chance. A woman had to have some pride. Then she smiled sweetly and was about to say,

"Okay, well, see you tomorrow then," but it never got to that. He moved into her space, capturing the door and locking it behind him, while never taking his eyes off her.

Just as before, she felt his raw, primal need as he pulled her into his arms and looked down at her. "What did you have in mind?"

Oh…my…God. He was already kissing her before she could answer. But this…this was what she'd hoped for, except she hadn't expected it right this minute. Not that she was complaining.

Nor had she imagined what kissing would be like if he really let go of his reserve. He was one hot kisser, his mouth on hers, and then their tongues were tangling, his hands unzipping her coat as she tried to get to his. The living room was way too warm for parkas, especially when he began to kiss her like he was going to die if he didn't have her this very instant.

He pulled her parka off her shoulders, their mouths still fused. Her parka hit the floor, and she held his face with her hands, kissing him back.

He yanked his parka off, tossed it aside, and pulled her into his arms, breaking free from the kiss for a moment. "We shouldn't be doing this."

His eyes were dark with lust, his sensuous lips enticing her to kiss them again, and she did, ignoring whatever he was going to say. Why? Because they were working together? She wasn't buying it.

Another police dive-team couple had ended up getting married, so getting involved wasn't off-limits. Maybe Allan thought it was wrong somehow, but she didn't have a problem with it.

They took the kiss slower this time, and she relished the way his tongue felt sliding against hers, so eager, the way he brushed his mouth against hers in a hot and sexy manner. Then he pressed his mouth tighter against hers again, conquering, demanding, passionate.

He groaned a little and pulled his mouth free, pressing it against her forehead, then her cheeks.

"I was going to start a fire—"

He smiled down at her. "You did."

She chuckled. "In the fireplace. Just to put a nice ending on this snowy, wintry night. Sharing a mug of piping hot cocoa and chocolate chip cookies. Playing something we both might like on the CD player. Or maybe putting a movie on."

He didn't let go of her, and she wanted to say, "Or we could just continue this." But she couldn't quite read him. He seemed reluctant to let go of her, like he really wanted to keep kissing her. But he didn't, and she was afraid he was thinking about why he shouldn't be staying.

He combed his fingers through the strands of her hair, surprising her. His touch felt so sensuously divine.

"You don't have your car," he said quite practically.

"I don't," she agreed.

"I'd have to drive all the way home in the snow in the dead of night and then come all the way back here in the morning to pick you up so we can interview Zeta in Helena."

"You would," she said, trying not to smile.

"So unless you object to my staying overnight again…"

"I'd be the worst kind of partner if I sent you home tonight, considering how bad the weather is."

He smiled. "Okay, so where are those chocolate chip cookies? Homemade?"

"You bet." She snagged his hand and led him into the kitchen. "They were freshly baked this morning. I couldn't sleep and baking helps me in that regard. And they're double chocolate chip. It's not a chocolate chip cookie if it doesn't have a chocolate chip in every bite."

He laughed. "I could smell them." He wrapped his arm around her shoulder and walked with her into the kitchen, smiling when he saw the tray piled high with chocolate chip cookies.

"All for you?" he asked, his brows raised a little.

"I was going to drop some by the police station, but they never made it because I had car trouble."

"We can do that tomorrow, *if* there are any left over by then."

She grinned. She couldn't help it. She was always pleased when someone loved her cookies. Of course, she'd better reserve judgment. After he took a bite, he might not care for them at all.

She realized then that he didn't have an overnight bag. Although he always carried a change of clothes or two for emergencies. Maybe he had a shaving kit in his bag. She had some spare toothbrushes and toothpaste. If he didn't have a razor, she might have some spare throwaways. They would be pink though.

"Music or a movie?" she asked as she made the hot cocoa and he carried the tray of cookies into the living room.

"Movie. We can get our mind off work that way."

"Okay. Just pick out whatever you'd like."

Allan had rationalized that driving back and forth

from his home to hers on the snowy and icy road would be unsafe when they were going to do the interview together tomorrow anyway. And further, with her car in the garage, they didn't have any other choice but for him to pick her up. The kiss? That was harder to rationalize. He told himself that the situation between them wasn't going anywhere. But as soon as he kissed her and she kissed him back—just like a hot alpha she-wolf would—he knew he was going to have trouble stepping away from any further relationship with her.

Wolves could have flings with humans, no mating for life allowed. So a brief relationship—a couple of dates and maybe a little sex—could work. As long as they both knew this wasn't going anywhere. But if Debbie wanted this to go somewhere further with him, she wouldn't understand why he couldn't. That was the trouble. She would be hurt in the end, and he didn't want that.

He sifted through her movies and found the *Underworld* series, all about werewolves and vampires, and tons of other paranormal movies. Maybe she was more into the paranormal than he'd suspected.

"Anything you would prefer to watch?" Allan asked.

"*Jingle all the Way*."

"In January?"

"Yeah, I want to watch something funny and light-hearted. Or whatever else you'd like."

He saw she had *Game of Thrones* and *The White Queen* and other historical fiction series he'd heard had a lot of sex in them. He smiled. He'd always seen Debbie as very sexy. She had a natural appeal. Her movie selection was an interesting side to her that he hadn't known about.

He figured it was safer sticking with humorous stories like *Jingle all the Way*. He could just imagine snuggling with her on the couch, watching something with sexual overtones, and wanting to take her to bed.

She joined him with two steaming mugs of cocoa, this time in bright green mugs. She'd already topped the cocoa with whipped cream, which was for the best, since he was fully dressed this time. He thought the night couldn't get any better.

At least he didn't think things could get any better, until he wrapped his arms around her while they watched the movie. She was warm, soft, and cuddly, and smelled like lilacs and spring, while the winter storm covered everything outside with a fresh coating of snow.

One last night of staying at her place with her like this, he told himself. One last night, and he could never do it again. Making love to her could lead to trouble in their work relationship—which up until now had been the best.

"Have you ever done that?" Debbie asked, feeling so good in his arms. In a way, he wished she was a wolf, but then again, he loved her just the way she was. But if she was a wolf, he'd love to go for runs with her and tackle her in the powdery snow.

"Forgotten someone's Christmas gift and it was too late to buy it? Nah. My family is really laid back. They're happy with whatever I get them. We always share a Christmas list way before Thanksgiving so everyone knows what we'd like to have, and we don't get a bunch of duplicate gifts that way."

Debbie smiled. "That sounds nice."

"What about you?"

"Not buying a popular gift in time? No. Not me. I think that's why I enjoy the story so much. I can just imagine having my own kid someday who hears about something everyone else in school wants, and then not ordering it in time because it's a limited edition. Actually, that happened to me once. On the receiving end. I wanted a doll all the kids were talking about. But"—Debbie shrugged—"only a couple of the girls in school got them, so it wasn't like I was the only one who didn't." She looked up at Allan. "Don't tell anyone else I played with dolls."

He laughed. "Your secret is safe with me. My sister loved playing with dolls. Lori was more of a tomboy. I don't see anything wrong with either."

"I bet you were hunting things when you were a kid, playing tactical maneuvers with Paul…"

"Fishing, ice skating, swimming, hiking, you name it. But yeah, hunting and playing tactical maneuvers too."

"Me too, except for the hunting and tactical maneuvers. But I also liked to play with dolls."

They watched the movie and had a really nice time—laughing, cuddling, and enjoying way too many cookies. Now the time had come to retire to bed.

"Ready to go to bed?" she asked.

"Yeah. Let me grab a bag out of my car."

"Okay. I'm going to get ready for bed."

―⁂―

When Allan returned to the house and locked up, Debbie was in the kitchen in her pajamas putting away their cocoa mugs.

She wasn't one to jump any man's bones. Not even

Allan's. Though she really was going to make an exception in his case if he was all for it. Not because she was so needy—well, maybe a little needy—but because she really, really liked him. What could be wrong in that?

His smile broadened.

It had been a long time for her. Her last relationship had ended over a year ago, and it hadn't ended well. He hadn't been ready to settle down, and he especially hadn't been interested in her diving sport. He hadn't liked when she wanted to take trips to places where she could dive and he couldn't join in on the fun. But if she was going to invest all that time and money, she wanted to do what she loved most: dive. Diving was such a big part of her life, it didn't make sense to have a boyfriend who disliked it.

In that regard, Allan seemed like perfect boyfriend material. He loved to dive with her, either on the job or off.

He set the empty glass in the sink, grabbed his Glock, snagged her free hand with his, and then headed for her bedroom. She took that as a hot damn, yes!

"No commitment," she said when they reached her bedroom and she set her gun on the bedside table. Not that she wasn't interested in having one with the hot SEAL, but she wanted him to know that she understood if he wasn't ready for anything like that and maybe wouldn't ever be.

"Right," he said.

She climbed under the covers, pulled off her pajama top and then her bottoms, and dropped them on the floor.

He set his Glock on the other bedside table, then slipped out of his clothes before coming to bed, smiling.

Judging by how erect he was, he appeared every bit as willing.

Feeling self-conscious, she explained about stripping underneath the covers. "You don't want to see my appendectomy scar." She didn't want him to see the *other* scars, in truth. She'd managed to hide them with the towel when she had changed in the car after they rescued Franny and her baby. She didn't want him to see her as anything but as gorgeous as she saw him, and she didn't want to explain why she had the scars either.

"You're beautiful," Allan said simply, and then all sexy six feet of him climbed into her bed.

But then he paused.

"Condoms?" she asked. "In the left bedside table. My ex-boyfriend had some in there." Too much information, she scolded herself. But Allan was already hard— could a man be built any more perfectly than that?—and ready, and she didn't want to stop in the middle of the action so she could mention all of that.

"I like a woman who is prepared," he said, smiling again.

She was glad he didn't seem to mind.

He was so gloriously good at kissing, and his hands were so gloriously good at touching, she felt she would come undone within a matter of minutes. Her body was so ready for him. The heat flared between them, making her wet and driving her to satisfy this incredible want.

The teasing, the heated looks. All a prelude to this moment.

His kisses were slow and tender and loving, and then they turned passionate and hot and pressuring. She loved his kisses and matched them with just as much heat and

SEAL WOLF IN TOO DEEP   133

enthusiasm, their tongues caressing in a sensuous dance. Her blood was on fire as he rubbed his erection against her, tantalizing her. She slid the palm of her hand over it, molding to him, loving the rigid feel of him. His hands caressed her skin all over, his tongue stroking hers as his hand slid over her breast, his fingers playing with her aroused nipples.

He moved his hand lower, tracing her appendectomy scar with a whisper-soft touch that tickled. He found another scar and then the last, before his fingers continued lower, searching for her nub, then stroking it and coaxing her into climax.

Her skin sizzled with his touch as he nuzzled her cheek and then her neck. He bit playfully at her chin and throat. She was reminded of how primal and intense he seemed at times, but playful and gentle too.

He kept rubbing her bud while kissing her breasts and throat and mouth. She felt the wave building, felt the anticipation climbing, and when the climax hit, she cried out with pleasure. She expected him to enter her then, but he didn't. He continued to touch her and kiss her like he wanted something more between them. That it wasn't all just sex.

Or maybe he was unsure whether he should proceed. Whether she would hate herself in the morning. If she would be unhappy with him for taking this too far and hurting their work relationship.

She didn't want to force him to do anything he didn't want to do, to regret it if he wasn't feeling ready for this. She wasn't used to a man waiting at this juncture. She wondered if he was afraid she was thinking this was forever, which she wasn't. Really.

Ah hell. She pulled him down for more kissing so he could make up his mind, and they started out nice and slow and began to build the tension, the raw passion between them spiraling upward. The next thing she knew, he was fumbling in the drawer for a condom, pulling it on before she could help.

He went slowly at first, filling her to the max, and then began to thrust. He was so powerful and perfect. She loved every moment as if it were her last with him. Because, for all she knew where Allan was concerned, it could very well be, and she wanted to enjoy it.

—◆◆◆—

Allan had never had sex with a woman who was this willing and then stripped naked privately underneath the covers. He wanted to toss them aside and prove to her that he thought she was beautiful and perfect, even if she had a ton of scars.

He loved the way she knew what she wanted and took it, the way she kissed him back just as thoroughly, seeming just as needy as he was. He kept reminding himself as he'd nuzzled her face and kissed her and stroked her that this was a momentary bit of enjoyment between a man and a woman. Nothing permanent.

Now she held him in her wet, warm embrace while he thrust inside her. He kissed her again, then continued to thrust deep inside her. When he came, he felt the intense exhilaration, and then a sense of peace descended over him. He kissed her thoroughly again, and then pulled out and left the bed to dispose of the condom, wash up, and return to her.

He slipped back under the covers and pulled her

into his arms. She seemed a little surprised at first, but then she eagerly cuddled against him. This was the way wolves slept, nestled together, even if she wasn't a wolf. He shouldn't have stayed with her for that reason alone.

Still, Allan thought he could do this. Have sex with Debbie a time or two, and then give it up. He told himself he just had to get it out of his system. That once they did it, they would relieve the sexual tension that seemed to be hovering between them.

He kept telling himself he could control his urges better after that. Like eating a sweet slice of cake and satisfying that need. Afterward, he'd realize—and she would too—that sex between them wasn't that big a deal. So why the hell did he want to do this again after they got some shut-eye?

After more hot loving a couple of hours later, Debbie said, "I need more dessert."

Allan chuckled. "Okay. More cookies?"

She smiled back. "Yeah, unless you want something else."

"I could eat the whole batch." He pulled on his briefs while she slipped her robe on and tied it, and then they headed for the kitchen.

While they were having milk and cookies in the living room, she began thinking about the case again. "Okay, so the case of the dead woman looked personal. I really believe the killer didn't murder her randomly. That he targeted her specifically."

"Right."

"Okay, so here's another far-out theory. We're

assuming the guy in the car was a werewolf hunter because the gun in the lake had silver rounds. But what if he was a werewolf? The hunter lost the gun in the lake, so maybe the werewolf disarmed him and threw it in the lake. Then the hunter had to kill the werewolf using other means. He beat him to death, then staged the car accident as a way to disguise the murder."

"But if silver is the only way to kill the werewolf…"

She shook her head. "Of course the victim wasn't a werewolf. The hunter only thought he was. So he died by regular human methods. Werewolves don't exist. I'm just trying to get into the head of the killer."

But a shadow crossed over Allan's face, and she swore he thought something she'd said had merit.

"What do you think?"

He smiled as if he wasn't thinking anything about the case and snatched up another cookie. "One more for the road."

Back in the bedroom when she made a move to slip beneath the covers before she pulled off her robe, Allan began kissing her, untying her robe and then slipping it off her shoulders. He wanted to show her in the worst way that she was beautiful to him. He wanted to see every glorious inch of her and revel in her. He didn't want her feeling self-conscious about her scars.

As soon as her robe hit the floor, she tried to slip away to the security of the bed.

He held her face and kissed her again to show her she didn't have to hide from him. With his lips pressed against her sweet, warm mouth, he began to pull off his briefs and dropped them on the floor.

He glanced down at the scars marring her milky

skin—the small appendectomy one and two others. They had healed up years ago, but the two were long and wicked looking, not the work of a surgeon's knife. He suspected that was the reason she had hidden them from him.

He leaned down to kiss a breast, his hand molding to the other. She was beautiful and perfect just the way she was, her dusky pink nipples growing rigid, her breathing turning rapid. He ran his tongue over a nipple and then sucked on it, moving over to the other to do the same thing.

"You're beautiful," he said, admiring her lovely breasts, her toned body, and even her pink toenails. Then he swept her up in his arms and carried her to bed.

In one fluid movement, he laid her down on the mattress and covered her body with his. He loved the feel of her hot, soft skin against his and the way he rested between her legs, his arousal nestled between them.

They began to kiss again, his tongue stroking inside her mouth, slowly and deeply, his body sliding along hers as she moved against him, making him all the harder.

I want you, he wanted desperately to say. He craved her now and forever. Did he want her because she was human and he couldn't fully commit to her?

She began stroking his back and he rubbed his cock between her legs, feeling her moisten for him, smelling her pheromones, and wishing she could smell his like a wolf could.

He dipped his hand between them and began to stroke her to bring her to climax while he kissed and licked her neck, then nipped at her chin. Her breath was nearly suspended, shallow, her heartbeat rapid as he stroked her into ecstasy. But his thoughts were moving to the dark side—he wanted to bite her and turn her.

She breathed deeply, held her breath, and let it out in a big sigh.

He began kissing her again, so eager to push into her, he almost forgot to grab a condom. As soon as he'd sheathed himself, he pushed inside her, filling her, enjoying the way she closed around him in a heated, tight embrace.

Driving home, he thrust deep inside her until he came, cognizant of her hands stroking his back and buttocks, the way she met his thrusts with eagerness, the way she gloried in the feel of him inside her. Spent, hating that this had to come to an end, he sank down on top of her. He wished she was a wolf and all his.

But after their late-night discussion, he had a new concern. What if she was right about the dead man in the lake being a werewolf? When Allan had helped pull the man from the car, he'd had his face mask on and couldn't smell anything. Once they had deposited the man on the shore for the coroner to handle, he and Debbie had returned to the car, searching for any other clues and taking more photographs. Before they resurfaced, the body had been removed. He would never have considered that the dead man might have been a wolf. Allan had to get word to Paul as soon as he could and have someone run down to the morgue to check it out.

Chapter 12

DEBBIE SWORE ALLAN HAD BEEN FIGHTING WITH himself over making love to her. She couldn't pinpoint why it appeared to give him such trouble when he seemed to enjoy it as much as she did. But she sensed disquiet in him. She was probably overanalyzing the situation, but he just seemed worried somehow. And yet he didn't just have sex with her and leave. He always treated her as though he truly did care for her.

Every time he left the bed to dispose of a condom, she worried he wouldn't come back to her. Yet every time he did, pulling her into his arms and holding her close the night through, as if he truly didn't want to lose her while they slept. She couldn't understand what he seemed to be concerned about.

He'd stroke her arm or back as if he liked to continue to show how much pleasure he took in being with her. And then they'd sleep and wake to more lovemaking.

She thought he'd go to sleep after a while, but this time he asked, "Where did you get the other scars?"

She hated talking about this. She let out her breath. She hated that she still felt responsible to some extent, despite receiving them in her youth.

Allan continued to caress her arm gently, not pressuring her to talk.

She let out her breath in exasperation. "My father was drunk most of the time or sleeping it off. He could barely hold a job. He'd have blackouts and night terrors and think he saw demons. I must have heard something, got scared, and went in to see my mother. He thought I was something evil. He had a hunting knife by the bed and cut me. Mom rushed me to the hospital and made up some story that I was making myself a sandwich, slipped on water on the kitchen floor, and cut myself."

"And they believed it?" he asked, his voice incredulous.

"Social services were called in. But either I was a good actor, or they didn't have enough proof to go on because I wouldn't tell them the truth."

"Nor would your mother."

"She was an enabler extraordinaire. Anyway, Dad's dead, so"—she shrugged—"it's over."

"And your mother?"

"We don't speak. How could she not protect her daughter better? She's in denial that he ever did anything harmful to me. Sometimes I think she actually believes the story she made up."

Allan shook his head. "You shouldn't have had to suffer through that. But you have nothing to be ashamed of."

"I shouldn't have gone into their bedroom…"

"You were a kid and scared. It wasn't your fault." He caressed her skin with a light touch. "You're beautiful."

She wrapped his arms around her, glad he was in her life but wishing he wanted more, like she did.

That morning, they made love one more time and then had a light breakfast before hitting the road for Helena. They stopped for hamburgers at a fast-food restaurant for a quick lunch, since Debbie wanted to get on with the investigation concerning the shooter, pronto. She was so glad they might finally have a lead in the two cases.

Zeta was the organizer of the Wolf Zone LARP game and was happy to meet with them when they told her they worked for the sheriff's department. When they walked into her apartment, they saw playbills of small-town theater productions posted all over her walls. She looked like Little Orphan Annie with bright orange curls, her lipstick the same color as her hair.

Debbie studied the posters while Zeta offered seats in her living room on the brown velour wraparound sofa.

"Another man came asking about Sarah Engle and Lloyd Bates. Otis Lister too. They're all members of the Wolf Zone but have disappeared. I was afraid something bad might have happened to them." She handed Debbie and Allan photos of each of the three people. "I take pictures of the players, and then we pass them around so that everyone can decide who the wolves are. Oh, and when a person dies, as in a werewolf kills a hunter or a hunter kills a werewolf, then everyone knows and that person no longer plays the game. They can watch but not participate. They're dead for the purposes of the game."

"Another man was questioning you? A police officer, you mean?" Debbie asked, glancing at the photos. She immediately recognized the woman from the morgue and the man they had found dead in the car. She looked to see if Allan had too.

He nodded to her.

"No, he wasn't a police officer. He said he was a

private investigator looking into a friend's request to find Sarah and make sure she was safe. I assumed he might actually find her when the police felt their hands were tied in the case."

"Okay, so this man," Allan said, pointing at the one that featured the Van Lake murder victim, "is Lloyd?"

"Yes. Sarah's lover."

Was the man in the black sedan Otis? Following Debbie because he thought she might know something about the case? But why would he not just go to the sheriff's office and ask them? Or follow anyone who was working on the case?

Debbie chewed on her bottom lip. "What was the PI's name?"

"Vaughn Greystoke."

No one Debbie knew. "Who was he working for?"

"He said it was a man named Devlyn Greystoke, so I assumed they were related. He said they were cousins."

Allan stiffened a little beside Debbie, and she glanced at him. Allan quickly pulled his gaze from hers and again looked at the photos. "What about the man who was her lover?"

"Mr. Greystoke wanted to know about him too, afraid that he might have had something to do with her disappearance. He said he was a private investigator, but I think he was more than that. He seemed really protective of her and angry her lover had disappeared too. Like he believed Lloyd had something to do with her disappearance in a bad way."

"Where was Mr. Greystoke from?" Allan asked.

"Somewhere in Colorado. Can't remember the exact location. I don't remember Sarah ever mentioning being from there. Then again, I don't recall her saying where she was from, nor did I think to ask."

"Are you sure the man who disappeared also was her lover?" Allan asked.

"Yes. We all joked and said if one of them was the werewolf, the other would be in real trouble. Well, unless both were the werewolves. But I knew better. You understand that none of them knew who the real werewolves were, except for me. I was the moderator for the game, so I made all the rules and made sure everyone stuck to them."

"So you knew Lloyd was a werewolf hunter and Sarah was a werewolf?" Debbie asked.

"Yeah. Really, they made a big deal of it to begin with when I first assigned everyone their roles. Sarah came and secretly told me she didn't want to be the hunter. And Lloyd did the same with his role as a werewolf. He wanted to be a hunter. No big deal to me. I swapped them out, though normally we play the roles we're given. So even though they made a big issue out of wanting to play different roles, they ended up being lovers. *Go figure.* But secretly? I think Sarah was really interested in Lloyd. There was some intense stuff going on between them.

"Lloyd?" Zeta shrugged. "I think he was interested in the sex, and I think he believed she was playing the part of a hunter. So it was okay to be with her. But I think she knew he was a hunter. Maybe he told her, and she let on that she was one too. Players are supposed to lie about what role they're playing while they try to convince everyone they're one of the good guys so they don't get killed off early in the game. It's all a matter of acting the part."

Zeta offered them sodas. Both thanked her but declined.

"If you had a part to play, which would you prefer?" Zeta asked. She sounded curious, maybe wanting to know if they thought her games were silly.

"A hunter," Allan said, not even hesitating.

"Hmm, whatever part I was offered, I'd play it the best I could," Debbie said.

Zeta smiled and Debbie felt she'd won her over a bit.

"Was there a man by the name of Guy Lamb in your group?" Allan asked, and Debbie snapped her mouth shut as she wondered what that was all about.

"Yeah, yeah, he was here. But he was here before the others arrived—Otis, Lloyd, Sarah. So what's this all about?" Zeta asked.

"Lloyd and Sarah are dead." Debbie wished she had better news for her.

"Oh my…ohmigod." Tears sprang into Zeta's eyes, and for an instant, Debbie wondered if it was all an act—if she hadn't known the deceased that well. Zeta choked back a sob and said, "I'll…I'll be right back."

Debbie glanced at Allan to see his take on Zeta's behavior. He raised his brows a little at her, but he had a dark look, and she wondered if he knew something more about this…Devlyn. And what was the business with Guy Lamb? Or maybe Allan thought Zeta was somehow involved in the murders.

Zeta returned with a box of tissues, set it on the coffee table, then grabbed one and blew her nose. She took her seat. "Sorry. I'd been upset with Sarah…" She paused and her eyes widened. "They're dead because of an accident, right?"

"No, they were murdered," Debbie said. "Why were you upset with Sarah?"

Zeta wiped her eyes again. "She moved here about six months ago, and we met at auditions to play roles in a local theater production. We really hit it off. We went to movies together and had lunches out. Neither of us was seeing a guy at the time, so it was perfect. I had started Wolf Zone about two months earlier, and some of the folks that had participated in the group had moved—like Guy Lamb—or their lives had gotten too busy.

"So I started a new game with some of the same players and some new ones. I asked Sarah if she wanted to play. She was all for it, but I thought she'd want to be a hunter, not a werewolf. Most of the time, the women want to be the hunters and not the prey. You never know people very well until something like that happens, you know?" Tears spilled down Zeta's cheeks, and she hastily brushed them away.

"I'm so sorry. I've had friends like that before—you know, one minute they're your best girlfriend, doing everything with you, and the next thing you know, they're stuck to some guy like peanut butter. And that's the end of the all-girl activities. So I was annoyed with her because she dumped me like I was no one of importance after we'd been really close."

Before Debbie could ask Zeta any more questions, Allan queried, "So what was she like? What did she like?"

Zeta stared morosely at the table. "I thought she would have a falling-out with Lloyd and come back." Then she frowned at Debbie and Allan. "Not that I'd just

take right back up with her. How she'd acted was not the
way to treat friends."

"Why did you think she might have a falling-out with
Lloyd?" Debbie asked.

"He wasn't right for her. I don't know. Something
was off with both him and his friend. They said they
were actors, and they really acted their parts, but they
just seemed—intense. *Too* intense. Like they were getting into their roles a little too much. They had one of the
women in tears because they thought she was the wolf
and really bullied her. I had to put a stop to it and told
them if they didn't obey the rules, they had to leave the
group. They were fine after that. I really thought they
should have been the wolves."

Why? Because the wolves were always growly, aggressive, and needed to be put down? Allan hadn't heard
of any Vaughn Greystoke, but many *lupus garous* used
"Grey," "Gray," or "Silver" in their names to portray
their gray wolf heritage, so that immediately caught his
attention. Particularly if Sarah had been in this man's
pack and he was trying to track her down.

Allan had heard of a Devlyn Greystoke, a gray wolf
pack leader in Colorado who had mated a red wolf. He'd
been in Portland, Oregon, where she had been incarcerated at a zoo and the incident had made national news.
Naked woman in the Oregon Zoo penned up with a real
red wolf in freezing weather? Then she disappears from
a hospital?

Even Allan and his pack members had heard the news
and knew the two had to be wolves, though the media

thought that Devlyn and Bella were animal advocates, intent on releasing the red wolf into the wild.

Debbie asked, "So what was Sarah like?"

"She was really different from me. She loved to stay out really late, and she was raring to go early in the morning. Who can burn the candle at both ends and still function? Not me. Anyway, she loved the woods. We went camping one night, not really my thing, but she was so enthusiastic about it. So I thought maybe going with her would make a difference. But then she left the tent in the middle of the night. She had me worried sick because she took so long to return. I thought something had gotten her. A wolf or bear or cougar.

"Anyway, she finally returned and I gave her hell for leaving me all alone for so long, well, in a sleepy way. She looked worn out but really happy and climbed back into her sleeping bag. I asked her where the hell she'd gone. For a run, she told me. I knew she was just teasing me. I figured she had to go to the bathroom. But sheesh, I'm not a camper. It scared the tar out of me to be alone in the woods with all the wolves howling, bugs making their racket, and owls hooting."

"Wolves howling?" Allan asked.

"Well, maybe just one. All it takes is one to send shivers up your spine."

"Did she have a passion for anything in particular?" Allan asked.

"She ate barely cooked steaks. We'd go out and she'd say she wanted them rare. Not medium rare. But just seared for a couple of seconds on the outside. Yuck. I'm vegan, so it was really hard for me to watch her eat something that was bleeding all over the plate."

"Did she have family?" Allan asked.

"No. She said she was an only child and her parents had died. So she was footloose and fancy free. Me? I've got four sisters and tons of cousins, but I'm not close to any of them. Not like I was with Sarah. We just, I don't know, had fun together. Kind of an odd pairing, I know. But we still had fun. She used to play her wolf role to the hilt. With me. She couldn't with the others.

"She'd mention how she'd behave if she were a werewolf. Like she was trying to convince me they could be good, and if it wasn't for the villagers trying to kill her, she wouldn't have to kill them. She really wanted to change the villagers' minds, convince them werewolves were really good guys, not creatures to fear." Zeta sniffled. "I just laughed it off and told her that wasn't what everyone signed up to play. No one would believe it. It wouldn't be any fun. Someone had to be the villain. She said the hunters were."

Allan disagreed. Some *lupus garous* were just as evil as humans could be.

Then Zeta sobered. "I can't believe she's dead. And Lloyd too. What happened? A home invasion? His home? I checked at hers, but she was never there, so I figured she was at his place. But I didn't know where it was. The address he gave to play the game was false. It didn't exist at all. I checked when she just disappeared. That had me worried he was a criminal. And Sarah was no longer answering her phone.

"When I told the police, they said they needed more to go on than what I had. Which was nothing. She had gone off with her lover. They thought the game we were playing wasn't important enough to keep her here if the two of them wanted to go off somewhere else. I checked to see about Otis's house, but it was the same way. Bad address. So I told the police. Since it was just for a game, no evidence of any crime, they couldn't do anything about it. She wasn't working at the time, so she hadn't left a job behind." Zeta took a deep breath. "How did they die?"

"Lloyd was found dead in a stolen vehicle, and Sarah was shot in the forest, both up north," Debbie said.

Zeta frowned. "Did Otis do it?"

"Why would you think he had anything to do with it?" Allan asked, interested.

"Because he hated Sarah and he was furious that Lloyd had started seeing her. I overheard them in back of the park restrooms where we used to meet to begin our game. We would sit at one of the tables under a pavilion and discuss where we were in the game, trying to figure out who the wolves were. Then armed with whatever evidence we thought we had—or the players had, since I was just the observer—they would go off and hunt were-wolves. Anyway, the restrooms were a few hundred feet away, but I heard this argument between the two men.

"Lloyd and Otis were trying to talk softly, but it got really heated and their voices began to rise. Otis said that if Sarah was a wolf, she was dead meat. And if Lloyd got bitten, he was too. I thought they were playing the game a little too seriously again, but they sounded too angry to be playing. The police assumed they were just actors who really got into their roles. But I checked their applications and the places they said they'd acted in theater and couldn't find that they'd been in the plays either."

She motioned to the walls. "You can see my name on all the playbills. So false addresses and they lied about the plays they were in? And then they all vanish at one time? Something had to be wrong with the two men. Then here comes this private investigator out of the blue."

"Could we have a look at their applications?" Allan asked.

"Sure. The local police weren't interested." She pointed to the table. "I got them ready for you just in case."

"Thanks," Allan said and took a look at Otis's, while Debbie looked over Lloyd's and then Sarah's. "Can we have the photos? We'll turn them over to the homicide detective in charge of the case."

"So he's making you do all his legwork and he gets all the credit?" Zeta asked. "Sure, take them. They're duplicates."

"Were their phone numbers bad too?" Debbie asked.

"They were disconnected once the men left the area. Those are copies for you. I"—Zeta choked on the words—"I thought you might be able to find Sarah. I didn't think she'd be… Well, I worried about it, but I thought she might just be with Lloyd. Not that I really liked it; he wasn't good for her. But I wish she was with him rather than dead." Zeta wiped away fresh tears. "Otis's unaccounted for, right?"

"He's not dead, as far as we know," Allan said, although if Otis was responsible for Sarah's death and turned up in Cunningham pack territory again intending to kill, Allan sure wanted to end the man's career as a werewolf hunter.

"You said the car Lloyd was driving was stolen? The blue Impala?" Zeta asked.

"Yeah. Do you know what he was driving before that?"

"A blue Ford pickup. He apparently liked blue vehicles."

"So what happened to it?" Debbie asked.

Zeta shrugged. "The day before the three of them vanished, he was driving the Impala. I figured he traded in his truck for the car."

Another stolen vehicle?

"Do you know what Otis was driving?" Allan asked, hoping they'd get another good lead.

"A red Camaro."

Immediately, Allan thought of Franny. But the guy she knew had a different name. Still, Allan didn't like the coincidence.

"He had this hunter look about him. He wore camo gear a lot, except when it got snowy. Then he was wearing a white parka. So I'm thinking—to fit the look—pickup truck, antlers in the back or a rifle hanging in the window. But a red Camaro?" Zeta shook her head. "It didn't fit the picture."

She glanced at her watch and continued, "Listen, I'm so sorry about what happened to Sarah. I wish the police could have saved her. Or that I could have convinced her the two men were bad news. But I'm glad you're looking into this. If you ask me, Otis did it. I've got an audition in half an hour, so I need to get going. If you need to ask me any other questions, feel free. I'll help any way I can to bring him to justice."

"You've been a great help," Debbie said.

"Yes, we couldn't have asked for more," Allan

agreed, "although I have one last question. What did the PI drive?"

"A black sedan."

The investigator had to be a wolf working for Devlyn Greystoke, another wolf from Colorado, leader of the pack, and his cousin. Allan didn't have his number, but Tessa, his SEAL team leader's mate, was distantly related to Devlyn, so she should have the information. Allan would have to call her when Debbie wasn't around. At least he was glad to know that the driver of the black sedan was on their side.

"If you learn Otis did it, will you let me know?" Zeta asked.

"Sure." Debbie and Allan rose from the couch and said their good-byes, then headed out.

"What do you think?" Allan asked as they got into the hatchback.

"I wonder if Otis ditched that car. It would be easy to spot if he was following anyone. If the one Lloyd was driving was stolen, maybe the red Camaro is too. We're in the area where these guys lived. Can we check out Sarah's place? Even though the men gave false addresses, we know she didn't."

"It's worth a shot."

"Okay. Here's Sarah's address. What did you think about this Vaughn Greystoke, PI? Think he is for real?"

"Sounds like it. I'll see if Paul can run him down."

"You looked like you might know of him."

"I might know of Devlyn, but I'll have to let Paul check into it. We both would know of him if he's the man I'm thinking of."

"But you don't know Vaughn?"

"No."

"Okay, what about the red Camaro? I'm sure it had no bearing on Franny's accident, but still, if Otis was driving it, and he killed Sarah and then ran Franny off the road, that seems like a coincidence we can't ignore."

"Agreed. Lori can get with Franny on it. I'll ask if she can check with her since they're good friends." Allan couldn't help but be annoyed with Franny if she knew more than she had been letting on.

When they arrived at the apartment complex, the manager showed them in, complaining the whole while. "I have to steam clean the carpets. It was paid up for two months, so I didn't know Sarah wasn't coming back. Not until the private investigator came and wanted to look her stuff over. Don't you guys talk to each other?"

"With PIs? No. Besides, even if he was with a police force, we each look at the investigations differently and ask different questions," Debbie said.

"Well, this is a complex that doesn't allow pets. No kids either. It's a no-pet, no-kid place for adult living. Swinging singles, except no loud partying. Mainly young professional couples. Once they have kids, they're out of here. And no pets," she reminded them, as if pets were the bane of her existence. "But you know what I found? Tons of fur. Shed all over the place. On the furniture, tile floors, and carpet. Probably fleas all over the place. I'm going to have to have the carpet cleaned and a pest exterminator in here. She wasn't going to get her deposit back." Then the manager swallowed hard. "Well, I mean if she had been alive. So when are the police going to release the place so I can rent it again?"

Debbie and Allan put on gloves and began searching

through things, but they didn't find anything that would help them in the investigation. No laptop, cell phone, photos, or notes of any kind. When they left the place, Debbie asked Allan, "Fleas?"

"Luckily, if she had them, they don't bother me. What about you?"

"No, thankfully."

"Do you want to call Rowdy and let him know we learned who the two murder victims were?" Allan asked as they climbed into his vehicle.

"Sure, I'll do that. But he's not going to be happy."

"Hell, we practically solved the case for him. He'd better be happy."

She smiled at Allan, but he knew she dreaded calling Rowdy. He was sure to be mad about it, but Allan had to find out if this case involved pack business. The only way to do that was to learn what he could before the homicide detective arrived. Otis sounded like a werewolf hunter out for blood. Had he killed both Sarah and Lloyd? It was beginning to sound like he had. But they still didn't know if the man who murdered Sarah had been turned.

"Hi, Rowdy. I'm putting this call on speakerphone. It's me, Debbie. We've got some information pertaining to a Sarah Engle and Lloyd Bates. Sarah was the leg-trap murder victim, and Lloyd was the man found in the submerged car in the Van Lake murder."

"And you know this how?" Rowdy sounded annoyed as hell.

After asking them a million questions, Rowdy told some of his team what to do to look for new evidence in the case. Then he dismissed them and chewed Allan out for investigating this on his own when he should have run it all over to Rowdy and let him handle it. He ended the call. Abruptly.

"Sorry," Debbie said. "Rowdy seems to think it's entirely your fault we went down there."

"It is. I had the clue and I was going whether you wanted to join me or not. Besides, he still likes you, so he's not going to hurt his chances with you."

Debbie had thought the issue of who was dating whom was behind them. She wasn't dating Rowdy. And now it seemed she really wasn't dating Allan either. Somehow she thought that had changed between them last night.

Annoyed, she waffled between wanting Allan to stay the night and letting him know it was time for him to get on his way. Rowdy could help her get her car from the shop.

But halfway to Whitefish, she didn't have a chance to decide either way when Allan got a call. "Ah, yeah, okay. I'll be there as soon as I can. I'm an hour and a half out. See you, Mom. Thanks. Give her my love."

Debbie suspected what it was about right away, and she wished she hadn't been annoyed with him. "Rose?"

"Yeah, she's in labor."

"Tell her I wish her all the best."

"I was going to take you to dinner, but—"

Debbie smiled. "No problem. Being with your sister is way more important."

"Thanks. If you don't mind, we'll do it another night. On the way home, we can stop at a drive-through and grab something to eat."

She wanted to tell him she'd just fix herself something to eat when she got home, but he would probably have a long night at the hospital with his mom and sister. He needed to eat, so she agreed. "Sure." She wanted to congratulate him on being a new uncle soon, but multiple births sometimes didn't turn out well, so she reserved comment. "They'll be fine," she said instead.

But he didn't say anything in response. She understood how he felt. She was feeling anxious about Rose, and she wasn't even related.

Chapter 13

WHEN HE DROPPED DEBBIE OFF AT HER DUPLEX, Allan gave her a light kiss on the lips, but she pulled away so quickly that he didn't have a chance for more. After telling her good-bye, he headed to the clinic outside Bigfork. He knew Rose would have good care. If she got into too much trouble, she could shift into a wolf and have her babies as wolf pups, which was sometimes easier for one of their kind. He was still sick with worry though. He wondered how Everett was holding up if Allan felt this bad.

When he arrived at the clinic, at least half the wolf pack was there, which wasn't good if the werewolf hunter was around and knew who some of them were.

Everett was in with Rose, and so was Allan's mom. Allan met up with Lori, who looked anxious, rubbing her own belly.

Emma Greypaw, Lori's grandma, was shaking her head at Lori. "I told you girls you'd both be fine. Quit your fretting."

Paul took Allan aside. "What did you learn?"

Allan told Paul everything—that the driver of the black sedan was Vaughn Greystoke, a PI supposedly hired by a man named Devlyn to search for Sarah Engle.

"Devlyn? The gray wolf pack leader in Colorado? The one with the mate who was incarcerated in the Oregon Zoo?"

"That's what I suspect."

"Okay. In other news, the Van Lake murder victim? He was a wolf." Paul immediately got on his cell, then put it on speakerphone. "Tessa, Paul Cunningham here."

"How is your mate? Twins coming soon?"

"Yeah. And Allan's sister is having her triplets right now. We're at the clinic, but we're investigating a possible werewolf-hunter murder and Vaughn Greystoke came up in our search."

"Good luck with hunting him down. I don't know the wolf though."

"He's a cousin of Devlyn's."

"Then he's got to be my distant relation. Here's Devlyn and Bella's number. Tell them I said hello."

"Thanks, will do."

"Good. Take care of your wife. We'll be talking again, I'm sure."

"Thanks, Tessa."

Then they ended the call and Paul contacted Devlyn. "I'm Paul Cunningham and I'm checking into a Vaughn Greystoke, who claims to be a PI investigating the disappearance of a Sarah Engle for you. If you're the right Devlyn."

"I am, and I've learned she was murdered."

"Right."

"Vaughn is my second cousin, and, yes, he was investigating Sarah's disappearance. The woman the hunter killed wasn't part of our pack, but she was looking to join us. Anyway, we just thought she'd changed her mind about joining us. But then she called me and said a werewolf hunter was after her. I contacted Vaughn and asked him to give her protection. Before he could locate her, she called me back and said to never mind. She had taken care of it. So I figured she had killed the hunter. I still sent Vaughn to investigate what was going on anyway. He's been on a merry chase ever since then."

"He drives a black sedan and has been following some of our investigators and pack members," Paul said.

"You know how it is when entering a pack's territory. No one knows who's running things. Some packs get really antsy about usurper wolves trying to take over a pack. So he's been trying to learn if there truly is a pack up there and who's running it. I take it you are the pack leader?"

"Yes."

"A woman named Emma Greypaw was in touch with Sarah before she vanished. Then Vaughn learned Sarah had been murdered. But he didn't learn it right away. He's been following Lloyd and Otis's trails."

"Did Vaughn kill Lloyd?"

"And leave evidence behind? No. We suspect Lloyd's partner Otis did. Here's Vaughn's number. I'll give him a call and let him know you'll be calling him. He'll work with you to help in any way that he can."

"Thanks. We appreciate the assistance," Paul said.

"If we had werewolf hunters in our neck of the woods, we'd feel the same way. Good luck."

When they finished the call, they heard a baby cry. Allan's heart nearly stopped. Lori was on her feet in an instant, wringing her hands. Paul walked over and wrapped his arm around her shoulders. Five minutes passed, and another baby began to cry. But they were all on pins and needles until they heard the third baby. When it cried, they all smiled and everyone there took turns hugging Allan and congratulating him for being a brand-new uncle. And now he had his work cut out for him.

He was surrounded by love and family. Yet all he could think of was Debbie sitting home on this wintry night—all alone. And wishing he could be there.

———

After having another meeting with Franny, her husband, Lori, Paul, and Allan about her stalker trouble and putting the whole pack on alert, Allan went to see to his mother's needs while she was seeing to the babies' and Rose's. Three days later, Everett looked bushed as Lori and Emma prepared a meal for the whole family to show their support.

"How's Debbie?" Lori suddenly asked Allan in the living room, while everyone was busy putting food away in the kitchen, fussing over the babies, or taking care of Rose.

He thought he was alone and hadn't heard Lori come up behind him.

"She's fine." He didn't know why Lori was asking. Debbie hadn't had a major upheaval in her life. And as far as he knew, the department hadn't had any emergency calls requiring divers. They'd get a team that was ready to go anyway, and since he was going to be here for another day or so to help out, they'd call on another team.

"You've talked with her?"

Allan frowned down at Lori. "Yes. I called her and told her that Rose was doing fine and all three babies were healthy boys."

"What is she investigating while you're here and not doing any dive work?"

"Lori…" He tried not to sound exasperated. He suspected her intuition was picking up something about the way he felt about Debbie, no matter how much he tried not to show it. But he wasn't about to discuss it with her, even though she was a good friend and a pack leader.

She frowned up at him. "Didn't she tell you she's been doing some investigating on her own?"

"What? Not on this werewolf case." All of a sudden, his heart was racing, and he had no control over it.

"She called Rose to congratulate her on the babies and sent a present for each of them. She said she'd come by later, when they were a little older and Rose was more rested. She knew Rose would be too worn out for company. Debbie said she was busy working a case, but as soon as she could, she'd drop by."

Allan was already pulling out his phone and calling Debbie.

"Oh, Allan. I was just going to call you," Debbie said, "but I didn't want to bother you if you were needed there. Someone's been shooting down near the lake. It's probably nothing, but I'm in the vicinity and investigating it."

"Where are you? Wait for backup."

"A quarter mile south of Polly Meyer's cottage. I can't wait. If he's shooting something illegally or he's our murderer, I can't let him get away."

Allan told Lori he had to go and where he was going, then sprinted outside Rose's house to the car. "I'm twenty minutes from there. Wait for me. I'm on my way," he told Debbie. It could just be a hunter, but after Sarah and the two wolves were shot in the same vicinity, he didn't want to risk not investigating. But he wondered why Debbie would jump to that conclusion. "What else, Debbie?"

"I saw a red Camaro up on the logging trail. I'm having Rowdy run the plates now."

Hell, if the shooter was a werewolf now, they couldn't get Rowdy involved. They had to take care of the shooter on their own, though Debbie would be clueless as to why.

He'd kept his phone open on the drive to the lake road to reach the area. "Talk to me, Debbie. Tell me you're waiting for me."

"He's shooting something. I'm in the trees and getting closer to where I can see the beach. What if it's... Ohmigod, he's shot a wolf."

Allan's heart nearly stopped. It was probably a genuine wolf, not one of their kind. But what if it wasn't? What if it was one of their own people?

Debbie shouted, "Police officer! Drop the weapon!"

"It's not what you think it is!" the man shouted back.

Hell, Debbie. Allan couldn't drive any faster on the narrow, winding, snow-covered gravel road. If the shooter was Otis, he most likely wouldn't obey her. But Allan couldn't talk to her now. He couldn't distract her. He wanted to call for backup, but he couldn't disconnect the line. Not when he was listening to her heavy breathing, her life pounding through her veins, and his own heartbeat thundering in his ears.

"Drop the weapon!" she hollered again.

"Hell, I know you're not one of 'em, but if you're going to protect 'em, you're just as bad as them."

Shots rang out.

Stricken and numb, Allan barreled the vehicle in her direction and then saw her car. He slammed on the brakes, bringing his hatchback to a sharp stop on the packed, crusty snow. Then he threw open the door, having enough presence of mind to grab the medical pack, and ran toward the sound of gunshots fired in the distance. "Damn it to hell," Allan said, running full-out.

As soon as he reached the location, he found Debbie alone on the shore of the lake, getting ready to shoot a wolf lying nearby on its side.

"No!" he shouted, racing to save the *lupus garou*. From here, he knew the tan-colored wolf was Tara Baxter, Everett's sister. Allan had to save her. Besides it being a devastating loss, if Tara died before he could rescue her, she'd turn into her human form in front of Debbie.

"It's wounded, wild, and a predator. We need to put it out of its misery," Debbie warned him, weapon still readied.

"No, don't shoot the wolf!" His heart drumming, he raced to the location, but he didn't see any sign of the hunter. "Where's the shooter?" Making sure the place was secure was a priority, but Tara looked to be in bad shape, so he didn't have any choice but to take care of her and hope no one would shoot them out in the open like this.

"I wounded him. He fired back at me, then ran off," Debbie said, sounding a little winded.

"Hell." Allan got on his knees in front of Tara. "Hope you hit him somewhere that's going to slow him down and force him to seek medical attention." Better yet, that would kill him. Tara's heart was beating way too slowly, and she was bleeding from three bullet wounds. All the wounds had evidence of burning. Silver rounds. He yanked out his cell phone and said to Debbie, "Get a blanket for her, will you?"

He called Paul and told him the emergency. "One of our wolves is wounded. Shooter's gone but could still be in the area. Debbie says she thinks she shot him." Allan gave him the location.

"Lori told us you might be in trouble. We're already on our way. Where's Debbie?" Paul asked, his voice dark with concern.

Allan knew what he was worried about—the wolf dying and turning human in front of her.

When Allan didn't hear Debbie leaving to get the blanket out of his vehicle, he glanced back at her. She was sitting on the snowy beach now, blood soaking her pant leg and dripping onto the pristine snow.

"Hell, Debbie." Allan realized then she was in shock. "Debbie's been shot. Leg wound, it appears. She saw the red Camaro up on the logging road and called it in to Rowdy's office." Allan pulled out his knife. "No telling who's going to be up here and when."

"Okay, we're on our way. We'll have to salvage the situation the best we can. Out here." Paul ended the call and Allan knew he'd get hold of their EMTs and doctor, and the alert roster would be notified. They had to get Tara out of here ASAP.

He was afraid he was losing her. He had to remove the rounds quickly and ensure she wouldn't die. She was so sweet and innocent. He'd never heard her say anything bad about anyone. She was meek and mild mannered, a real beta wolf. He couldn't imagine anyone shooting her. He quickly cut out the rounds digging into Tara side, then bandaged her. But then she quit breathing.

Damn it to hell.

"Where exactly are you injured?" he asked Debbie again, not liking that she had taken a bullet, but hoping she hadn't been hit more than once and it wasn't critical enough that he had to take care of it immediately. He had to revive Tara before he could see to his partner.

"Leg," she said, sounding so weak, not being able to take care of her too was killing him. Her breathing was rapid and shallow, and she was leaning over like she was about to collapse. She knew first aid, but she appeared to be too injured to do anything for herself.

Even so, Tara was worse off at the moment.

He started CPR. Tara still wasn't breathing. He prepared to give the wolf mouth-to-nose resuscitation, cleared her airway, placed his mouth over her nostrils, and blew four quick breaths.

He did this again after two to three seconds, allowing the air to exhale, then continued breathing into her nostrils until normal breathing finally returned.

As soon as she was breathing and seemed to be stable, he turned to see to Debbie and heard vehicles parking back at the road. Thanking God that he'd have help and the shooter hadn't returned to finish them off, he began working on Debbie. She was on her side now. From the way she was lying, her gaze was turned in Tara's direction.

He found where Debbie's wound was bleeding and tore open her pants so he could bandage the wound.

He should have turned her away from seeing Tara. But
Tara was still a wolf, and he was too busy trying to stem
the bleeding from Debbie's wound to move her. Her
skin was cold and clammy, her pulse weak. Her gaze
seemed unfocused.

But then her heart went into cardiac arrest and Allan
had to begin CPR. This would go down as one of the
worst days of his life.

He was sweating up a storm despite the frigid
air. Suddenly, the EMTs were taking over, stabilizing Debbie and placing her in the ambulance.
They also had to take Tara—but not as a wolf. She'd
already turned.

"Did Debbie see Tara shift?" Paul asked Allan after he
had gone home, showered, changed, and washed the
blood out of his clothing, then met up with Paul at his
lakeside cabin.

Allan was staring out at the lake, some of its surface
frozen near the shoreline. "What?"

Paul said, "Allan, listen to me. I've asked you three
times. Did Debbie see Tara shift?"

"Debbie was unfocused, in shock. She was looking
in Tara's direction, but I don't think she really was
seeing anything."

Paul ran his hands through his hair. "What about
the shooter?"

Allan shook his head. "I don't know. I was concentrating on Tara. I didn't even realize Debbie had been
hit. What about Tara? Debbie? How are they doing?"
Allan couldn't believe Paul had made him come here

when he wanted to see the women at the clinic. Yet deep down, Allan knew why. He just didn't want to deal with the truth.

"Both are in stable condition at the clinic. But we have a real problem."

"I don't think Debbie saw anything. And if she did, she was in shock. I doubt anyone would believe what she had to say if she did see anything."

"We can't risk it. You know it, Allan."

Allan swung around and scowled at Paul. "What do you mean? She was out of it. If she saw anything, which I doubt, it was that I was giving CPR to Tara as a wolf. After that, Debbie was in such bad shape, she went into cardiac arrest, and she wasn't able to witness anything at that point."

"We can't assume that she didn't see Tara shift."

"You're not serious. Give her a chance to talk about what she witnessed, about the shooter and whatever else she saw. And then we can go from there."

"You're not thinking rationally about this," Paul said. "You care way too much for her, for one thing. Pack takes priority. We have to protect our kind, no matter what."

Allan's heart raced. He thought his best friend meant to eliminate her. It would be easy enough to do. She had gone into cardiac arrest once. She could do it again, and this time she wouldn't make it.

He whipped around and headed for the door.

"Allan, it's for the best."

He wasn't listening. As pack leaders, Paul and Lori had the final say in matters regarding the pack. When he took over the pack, Paul had said he'd be as democratic as could be. He was normally really reasonable. Allan couldn't understand what had gotten into him to take this stand against Debbie. Even if she had seen Tara shift, no one would believe Debbie.

Maybe something else had gone wrong. But Allan couldn't let them kill her.

When he finally reached the clinic, he found Everett and Rose there, waiting for Tara to get out of surgery. "Where are your babies?" He didn't know why he even asked. He knew someone would be watching them. He just felt thoroughly rattled and angry.

"Emma and some of her quilting friends are enjoying them for a moment," Rose said, dark circles under her eyes.

He thought when Paul had said Tara was in stable condition that she was already out of surgery.

Allan's mother and Lori intercepted Allan. "Debbie's in the ICU. You can't go in," Lori said. "She'll be out in a little while."

Allan was confused. He thought Paul meant they had to eliminate Debbie. Maybe Paul was just trying to prepare him for what might happen. Allan couldn't relax. The adrenaline was still pumping through his blood after saving both the women's lives, and now with the concern that the pack would want to eliminate his partner, he couldn't settle his anxiety.

"Christine took her into surgery first because she's human and was more at risk of dying at this point," Lori said. She let out her breath. "Allan, Paul called and said you were ready to do something rash. Why don't you come with me and your mom and we can discuss this in the doctor's office?"

"Is Debbie going to be given the chance to share her side of the story?"

Lori took his arm. She led him from the patient waiting area to the doctor's office in the back of the clinic. The well-appointed office was filled with a sitting area of leather chairs and a redwood coffee table, a desk, and an office chair. Once inside, Lori said, "Okay, I know how Paul is sometimes. He's rather to the point and yet he means well for all concerned."

"For us, but not for Debbie."

"Can I be perfectly honest with you?"

"You know that's the only way I want both you and Paul to be." As long as it meant Debbie was safe from harm.

"You were getting yourself way in over your head with Debbie."

"I'm not dating her or thinking of any such thing. We just enjoy working with each other." And so much more, but he couldn't mention it to any of them.

Lori took another deep breath. His mother had taken a seat in front of the doctor's desk and was looking concerned, her brows knit together in a tight frown.

"She died," Lori said.

Allan felt dizzy, like the world had slipped out from under his feet. "You—"

Lori held her hand up to stop him from speaking further. "We didn't have anything to do with it."

"You said she was in the ICU. In stable condition. What the hell—"

"She died in the ambulance. They brought her back a second time."

Allan stared at Lori, shocked to the core. Should

he have gone to her rescue faster? But if he hadn't removed the rounds from Tara and done CPR, *she* wouldn't have survived.

"Because of what she witnessed—" Lori said.

"She was in shock. She couldn't have seen anything."

"Allan, she saw Tara shift."

He sat in the chair, his legs no longer able to hold him up. "She's in the ICU. How—"

"She came to, but they're keeping her in there a little longer. She was terrified, her words slurred because of the heavy-duty pain medication she's on, but she wanted us to know she saw a wolf turn into a woman. And she said her partner knew all about it."

Allan felt the air leave his lungs. "What now?" His voice sounded oddly hollow to his ears. He realized how much he cared for her. She wasn't just another human or his dive partner, but someone real and caring and devoted to helping others.

"It's done."

Allan's mouth gaped. "What?" He felt light-headed. He couldn't remember a time he'd felt like his mind was in such a fog except when he'd been shot on a mission and lost too much blood.

Lori bit on her lower lip, then said, "She's…one of us."

"What?"

Catherine patted his arm. "Now you can date her."

Allan stared at his mother's concerned expression. He wasn't grasping what had happened. "Someone bit her?" He was ready to tear into whoever would have done so when she was in such grave shape.

"She received some of my blood intravenously," Lori

said. "No one bit her. But she was going to die if she didn't have our healing genetics."

He gaped at Lori. He still hadn't grasped the situation. "Wait, you didn't do it because she'd seen Tara shift?"

"Partly, yes, but, Allan, she was in critical condition. She still is. But our faster wolf healing abilities will help her to pull through. We could have let her die. She would have without our help. She wouldn't have made it in a human-run hospital."

He couldn't believe Lori and... "Does Paul know what you've done?"

Lori smiled. "Of course. We were in total agreement as soon as we learned she would have died without our intervention. And that she'd seen Tara shift. Not only that, but you were headed down a path of no return with her."

"I wasn't dating her." He couldn't even think in those terms right now. This was going to be a complete nightmare for her.

"Our original pack members—your mother, sister, me, Paul, and my grandma—will take turns watching her."

Allan noticed she had left him out of the loop on that one. "And me?"

"Only if the two of you are agreeable. She's going to have to be taught our ways. She'll have to be watched because to begin with she'll have trouble having control over her shifting. And of course she needs to realize how important it is to keep our secret. We could send her to another pack, like Hunter's, where they know better how to deal with newly turned wolves, like his mate and her brother are."

Hunter Greymere was their SEAL wolf team leader, and Allan was certain he'd *love* to have another newly turned wolf under his command. *Not*.

"But Paul and I believe that if we all work together, the rest of the pack included, we'll get through this just fine."

Allan bet Paul hadn't expected anything like this to happen when he and Lori took over the pack. He was always saying how glad he was that he didn't have a newly turned wolf in the pack. Allan guessed it was inevitable that it would happen someday.

"When can I see her?" Allan asked, feeling overwhelmed with negative emotions. No way in hell had he wanted her to have to experience all that she would without being given a choice. And now she would be just as much a werewolf hunter's target as the rest of his pack.

"Maybe not right away," Lori said pragmatically. "She knew that you saved Tara's life before she turned into her human form. Debbie may be afraid of you. It might help if she sees someone she won't automatically connect with Tara."

"Everyone's connected. Her brother, her mother, my sister who's married to her brother. Me. Paul, because we were raised together. My mom. You, because you're mated to Paul. I just don't see how any of us are going to be able to see her and not make her think we're all in cahoots."

"For now, the doctor and the nurses will see her. She will get used to them and not know we're part of this whole situation."

"She's my partner. I have to see her."

Lori shook her head.

His mother said, "I think Lori's right."

"She's going to have to learn about us sooner or later," Allan said. "Hell, the full moon appears in a few days."

"Which is why we need to make sure she stays with one of us at all times," Lori said.

"I'm seeing her," Allan said, and no one was dissuading him. Both his mother and Lori looked worried, but he asked, "Is that all?"

"We need to know what the shooter looked like," Lori said.

Allan's jaw dropped a bit. "This isn't all about that, is it? She was turned so she could live and tell us what she saw?"

"Allan," his mother said.

Lori held up her hand. "No. As important as the information is and as much as we need to know it as soon as we can, that's not why we did it. We knew how much she meant to you."

Allan swallowed hard, and tears sprang into his eyes. *Hell.* He quickly rose from the chair and headed for the door. "I'll be in the waiting area for when she comes out of the ICU and then I'm seeing her."

Pack meant everything to them, and he realized then that not only had they given Debbie a chance at life, as different as it would be for her now, but they'd done this for him. And yet it could be a real problem for all of them. For them, if she was totally out of control. For him, if she hated what she was now. For herself, if she was so horrified about what she had become that she didn't want to live.

Debbie felt like hell. She didn't think she'd ever felt this out of it.

For a while, she just lay there, trying to recall what had happened to her that she needed to be in a hospital bed.

Then she remembered flashes of scenes—the gunman shooting the wolf three times, even after she told him to drop his weapon, then him turning the gun on her and firing. Her firing a shot back and hitting him in the shoulder, she thought.

And the wolf near death. She meant to shoot it and put it out of its misery. But then Allan was there, saving the wild wolf. Was he crazy? An injured dog could be dangerous, but an injured wolf? She wanted to stop him, but she couldn't muster the strength. She remembered him telling her to get a blanket for the wolf, but she didn't have the energy. The next thing she knew, she was sitting on her butt on the snow-covered beach.

She had seen the concerned look on Allan's face when he was trying to save the wolf and again when he glanced at her and saw her sitting there. The pain hadn't hit yet, since the bullet had severed nerve endings, but she could see the blood pooling in the white snow. She had watched it for a moment, thinking it looked like cherry coloring spreading over ice in a snow cone.

She thought Allan would come to her aid, but instead, he was giving the wolf mouth-to-nose resuscitation. She'd never seen anyone do that before. She had been fascinated in an abstract kind of way, as if she wasn't quite there, just watching from far away.

And then the wolf turned into a woman—Tara, if Debbie recalled her name correctly. She was the sister to Everett, the man married to Rose, and really quiet. She was lying in the snow, bandaged after Allan had removed the rounds from her body. She was naked, and Debbie hadn't gotten the blanket for her like Allan had asked her to. She remembered feeling bad she hadn't done so.

She had been so cold herself, she felt as though *she* was naked as Allan rushed to take care of her wound. She must have passed out because the next thing she knew, she was in an ambulance, and that's all she remembered.

"Debbie," Allan said, and she opened her eyes to see he was holding her hand, a worry frown etched across his brow.

Dozens of roses filled a nearby table, and she wondered who would have sent all the flowers. Everyone in the sheriff's department? Did anyone even know she was here?

She swallowed hard and with a dry throat said, "Allan."

"God, I'm so glad to hear your voice." He hurried to get her a cup of water. "How are you feeling?"

"You don't want to know."

"Okay." He pulled up a chair and took her hand again. "How much work have I missed?"

"None."

She frowned at him. "You're an awful liar. How many days have I been out?"

"Three."

She sighed. "Any news about the case we're working on?" Then she grew concerned because Allan seemed so worried about her. "I'm not...dying, am I? Unfit for duty?"

The worry frown remained. "You're not dying," he said.

"But I can't work."

"Not for a while."

"How long?"

"We're not sure. We'll have to see how quickly you can get back on your feet."

"But I'm going to live. Not physically incapacitated from diving?"

"No. But you're going to have to take it easy. And you're going to need around-the-clock care for a while."

She smiled just a little bit. "You wouldn't be volunteering for the position, would you?"

His jaw hardened. "Hell, yeah, if you're all right with it."

She relaxed a bit. "I know you won't be able to be there around the clock, but—"

"I'll make arrangements to have someone come in and stay with you whenever I need to be out."

She smiled and felt better. She knew Allan cared for her. She wouldn't have wished anything like this to happen to her on purpose, but looking on the bright side, maybe this would turn out to be the best thing that ever happened.

"How will your family feel about that?"

"They'll be glad to hear it." He motioned to the flowers. "From family and more."

"They're beautiful." She eyed them, trying to determine which might be from Allan, if he'd gotten her any.

"The one with the dozen roses," he said, as if reading her thoughts.

"They're beautiful."

The nurse knocked on the door, then came in. "We need to do some more blood work on you, Debbie, if you don't mind."

"As long as I'm going to live, no, not at all."

Chapter 14

ALLAN LEFT THE ROOM, HATING THE DECEPTION OF THE whole matter. All the pack members had been both welcoming and wary about the situation.

For the last ten days, he'd practically been staying at Debbie's room at the clinic, though often when she woke, he'd been taking care of business and the nurse had been attending her. So he was glad to finally see Debbie awake and conscious enough to talk and recognize him and everything around her.

But he hated that she didn't know what she'd become. After what Lori had told him about Debbie being suspicious of him as far as Tara was concerned, he'd worried about Debbie's reaction to seeing him.

So far, she seemed fine. He assumed she hadn't seen it happen, or if she had, she didn't believe her own eyes. After all, who in their right mind would believe it? And she'd been in really bad shape at the time.

He knew he had to tell her sooner than later, because the sun was nearly lighting the moon to the fullest extent, and she would most likely shift. That would be a terrifying experience, he imagined. Having been born a *lupus garou*, he'd never given it much thought. They were proud to be who they were.

Everyone was affected differently too. Some newly turned wolves were more accepting of the enhanced abilities they had. Others were not, particularly about the shifting when they didn't have much control over it during the pull of the full moon. Or that they had to be watched at all times by other pack members. It could be frustrating if the man or woman was used to being alone or doing things their own way in their own good time and without being accompanied.

He talked to Dr. Christine Holt, wondering if Debbie was really well enough to go home with him.

"She's healing just fine, Allan. You know how our faster healing abilities are. She'll need to take it easy for another week or so, but after that, she'll be able to do anything she wants to. As long as she's being watched because of her wolf condition, she'll be fine. Do you think you can handle it?"

He wanted to say it would be no problem, but what did he know? She was a wild card until he told her the truth and she shifted, and then how would she react? He had no idea.

"Paul said you wanted to do this alone if she was agreeable to stay with you," Dr. Holt said. "But I still wonder if it wouldn't be better if we had more pack members involved. Maybe some of the original members and someone on the medical staff in case she needs a sedative."

Allan shook his head. "We'll try my idea first. If it doesn't work, we can have a wolf pack intervention."

"All right. Paul was wondering if maybe one of the newer turned wolves of Hunter's pack could come and talk with her. To share how he or she felt in the beginning. One of them might be able to show her that there's life after being turned and that new wolves are perfectly comfortable in their new skins."

"Maybe. If this doesn't work out, we could call Hunter and see if his mate wants to talk with Debbie." No way did Allan want a male wolf to speak with her. He could see one of them sympathizing with her, and the next thing he knew, she'd be angry with Allan and the rest of the wolves who were born that way and join Hunter's pack.

That notion didn't set well with Allan in the least.

"Are you really okay with taking care of her?" Christine asked. "It's a big responsibility. I know you're a highly trained SEAL and have dealt with all kinds of crises, but this is different. It doesn't take guns and bullets or teeth. It takes a lot of patience, loving, caring, and understanding."

"I understand. I can handle it." But he wasn't sure how it would all work out. How could anyone be? He had no idea how she'd react to what she was now. But he had every intention of giving it his best shot and hoping to alleviate her fears as soon as possible. She'd trusted him before this, cared for him, knew him the best, so he figured it was better if he worked with her than someone else. "When can she go home?"

"She needs to stay for three more days at the clinic. That will give you time to get your place ready for her to move in. Make sure that you can secure the house so that she can't get out in case she tries to run. And don't hesitate to call any of us if you need some help with this."

"We'll be fine."

Afterward, Paul and Lori talked to him about what he needed to do, and even Hunter's mate, Tessa, called to give her two cents.

The day Allan went to pick Debbie up, she was as

cheerful as she always was when he visited her. Which meant? She couldn't possibly know what had happened at the shoot-out. He thought she looked positively thrilled to see him because he was taking her home from the clinic. Only not to her home. He'd already talked to her about it, and she seemed eager to do it. But first, she wanted to go to her place to get some clothes for her stay at his cabin.

As he helped her into his hatchback, he thought she still looked pale and tired. He pulled a blanket and pillow out of the backseat, tucking the pillow behind her and wrapping the blanket around her.

"How do you feel?" Allan tried not to look as worried as he felt, but tonight the full moon would be out in all its glory and he had to tell her what to expect.

He pulled out of the parking lot and started driving toward Whitefish.

"So much better. I can't believe I could have been so bad off and feel so great."

The faster healing genetics. Allan would talk to her about those later too. He glanced over at her, but she appeared to be drifting off to sleep.

When they were nearly to her place, she yawned.

"Feel any better?"

"Some. Still feeling a bit wiped out. I guess that's why I need to stay with someone for a while. I guess we'll be missing the Penguin Plunge in Whitefish."

"There will always be next year. And I'll definitely take you to it." He would take her to anything her heart desired, if she was still speaking to him by then. "Paul said you told him the man who shot you was so bundled up, you couldn't tell what he looked like."

"Yeah, unfortunately. I was hoping I could positively identify that friend of Lloyd's, Otis. The man was wearing a ski mask and a bulky winter parka so I couldn't tell. He wore snow boots and he was dressed all in white—to blend in with the snow, I imagine. Zeta did say that Otis wore a white parka when it was snowy out."

"True. It's a wonder he didn't get shot by a hunter. Did you see the color of his eyes?"

"His eyes were wintry blue. I didn't remember until now, but we stared at each other for a moment before he shot me and I shot back. But they were icy blue."

"Okay, I'll let Paul know. And he can contact the police. In the photo, Otis was too far away and turned to the side a bit, so I couldn't really see his eyes."

"Me, either." She stretched out in the passenger's seat, pulled the blanket under her chin, and yawned. "Are you sure this isn't going to be too much of an imposition?"

He'd already learned what she'd like to eat, so he had stocked the pantry and fridge at his cabin with her favorites. He'd asked her if he could pack her things and haul them to his place, but she had wanted to return home and pack for herself.

"No, not at all." As much as he'd like to see this as a way to get to know her better, he knew things would change between them in a heartbeat as soon as she knew what she had become. It was his fault for not moving her so she wouldn't see Tara change. Not getting there sooner so she wouldn't have been shot in the first place. Not treating her wound fast enough. If Allan had confronted the shooter first, he wouldn't have hesitated to kill the bastard and not waited for him to fire a round first.

"When do we start back on the case?" Debbie asked,

as if she hadn't just dealt with a life-threatening trauma of her own.

"When the doctor okays you going back to work." He wasn't sure how that was going to work out now. She'd have to take a leave of absence. He could just see her in a skintight wet suit trying to shift into a wolf. That would be a sight.

"She said you've been hanging around the hospital the whole time I've been there. Thank you."

"I had to know you were going to be okay. Early on, you were sleeping nearly every time I came in."

"Allan, you know none of this was your fault. I know you, and I know you blame yourself. I should have waited for backup. I'm so sorry. They said Tara went home today. She was going to be all right too. What... happened to the wolf? Did you save it? Everything was such a blur. I...I thought they were one and the same." She laughed a little.

"Rowdy's rubbing off on me with all his paranormal musings. And I watch too many paranormal shows. Anyway, I don't know how I didn't see Tara and how injured she was. Only the wolf. I wish I could have helped you more by assisting her and providing a better description of the shooter, but I guess I was fading fast. They say you saved both of us. When I asked about the wolf, they said they hadn't seen it. So it must have been okay and run off."

Nobody had told a lie. They'd seen Tara, but not in her wolf form. He really didn't want to discuss this with Debbie right now. He could talk to her about everything at his place—with the cabin locked tight in case she tried to bolt.

"I was busy with Tara and you at that point," he said again, not really lying.

"What about the red Camaro?"

"It was impounded at the scene. The serial number had been removed. License plates had been stolen from another vehicle."

"Wow, okay. I called Rowdy's office. What happened on that?"

Thankfully, Rowdy had been in the middle of another homicide case and wasn't called until after Tara and Debbie arrived at the clinic. He'd dropped in a few times to see Debbie, but she'd been so out of it, he hadn't learned anything from her. One of the nurses had always been present. At least Rowdy hadn't let on that he figured anything was amiss. He had talked to the doctor and learned the seriousness of Debbie's injuries.

"He came to visit you several times, whenever he could. I'm sure he's still looking to date you. He sent roses."

She smiled. "That was sweet of him."

Debbie continued to chat away in a lighthearted and cheerful way, while Allan was feeling the onerous duty of speaking about all of this to her later and was in gloomy spirits.

When they reached her duplex, she waited for him to get the car door for her.

"Are you still tired?" he asked, concerned that she might have needed to stay longer at the clinic.

"I felt so good for a bit." She sighed. "Maybe because I could leave the clinic. But yeah, I'm exhausted. I feel I need to sleep for a week to get over feeling this way."

"Do you want me to pack for you?" He offered his

hand to help her up. She relied on his strength, which worried him all the more.

"No, as long as you don't mind me taking a while. I want to shower too. If you don't mind, could you fix us something to eat? I've got an ice chest that we can fill with some of the food."

He didn't want to tell her they would be moving her completely out of her duplex. For right now, they'd left everything as it was. But once she was settled in with him or someone else who she trusted in the pack, they'd move everything that was hers. She might not want to stay with him once she learned about what she'd become, but she was going to have to stay with someone in the pack. No way could she live on her own until she had her shifting under control.

"Sure, I can do that," Allan said.

"The ice chest is in the garage. Plenty of ice in the freezer. Oh, what happened to my car?"

He hadn't expected that question. Catherine had taken it to an outer barn for safekeeping until Debbie was ready to drive it again. But he didn't want to tell her that and make her suspicious. "It's parked in your garage."

"Oh. Good."

He unlocked the door for her, and she headed inside. "Is there anything in particular that you want me to fix for lunch?"

"Maybe chicken à la king? I've got noodles to go with it. Anything you don't mind making."

"Okay, I'll let you know when it's ready." Paul and Lori had already told the duplex manager about Debbie's injuries and that she was going to be staying with family for several months and would need to move out. Thankfully, the duplex came furnished, so they didn't need to move any of the furniture.

He just hoped Debbie didn't learn about it until after they were settled at his place and he told her the truth.

He was glad she was feeling so good, but he could tell she was still tired. He was afraid she wouldn't take the news well when he told her the truth tonight, and he would have to deal with the mess. For now, he had to play along—feed her, help her pack. When they reached his mountain cabin, that was another story. He'd had security alarms put in so that if she managed to some-how get through a lock on a window or door, an alarm would go off. He didn't think she would be able to, but he wanted to be prepared.

He had to even put a lock on his wolf door.

He opened the cabinet and pulled out a can of chicken à la king and a bag of egg noodles, dreading taking her home and what would happen as soon as the full moon reached its zenith. It was one thing to deal with an angry human. Another to deal with a wild and angry wolf. Especially one that would have no idea what her strengths and capabilities were.

Debbie had never taken acting classes, but she sure hoped she had snowed Allan over. And the rest of those associated with him. Sure, she was half out of it when the wolf had turned into a woman. Yes, she had seen Allan giving the wolf CPR. And she hadn't seen any sign of Tara. Then suddenly, Tara was there and the wolf was gone. Even so, Debbie still hadn't believed they were one and the same. Not until she overheard the doctor and nurse talking in another room. What had scared her the most was that she now knew the real reason the doctor said she had to be with someone for some time—not because of health issues, but that they were afraid she'd tell someone what she had seen.

Not that anyone would believe her. But the werewolf pack must have been worried enough that they didn't trust her on her own. If she'd had family or a friend, she could have suggested staying with them, but she was afraid the werewolves wouldn't have allowed that either.

She wasn't without resources. She locked the bedroom door, then looked for her cell phone. No purse, no phone. Figured. She hurried to change out of her clothes, packed a small bag, turned on the shower, and went straight to the bedroom window. She didn't know what to think about all of them, but she felt like she was in a horror flick where everyone was an alien and she was the only human. Now that she had discovered they were aliens, she had to flee. She planned to get in touch with Rowdy, but what if all his talk about werewolves wasn't just in good humor, but because he was one too? She had no idea how big the pack was or who all was in it.

She didn't know where she would go or what she was going to do. If she fled the state, would they come after her? Kill her? For now, they were just keeping an eye on her, being extra polite and really nice to her. But if she told on them, then what?

They thought she hadn't heard them, but one time she overheard the nurse say that Tara didn't want to shift into her wolf ever again after she'd nearly died. If Debbie hadn't heard their conversation when they thought she was still under, she would have believed she had imagined the whole nightmare.

Then the business with the guy who shot the woman with silver rounds? A naked woman, just like Tara? Debbie heard them say these rounds were silver too. But since Allan and his pack mates hadn't known who Sarah was initially—Debbie just couldn't wrap her mind around it—she must not have been with their werewolf pack.

Debbie was afraid someone would bite her and change her into one of them. So she was really trying to keep her wits about her, act cheerful like she didn't think she had anything to worry about, and then run—before they knew what she intended to do.

She grabbed some spare cash she had in a sock in a drawer, then climbed out the window and headed to the garage. This was going to be tricky. She was afraid that as soon as she opened the garage, Allan would hear it and stop her. Or *try* to stop her.

Here she had thought he was one of the nicest, sexiest, and most caring men she'd ever met. Until he gave mouth-to-nose resuscitation to a wolf who happened to be a werewolf and a friend of his. She suspected all of his extended family were werewolves too. No wonder they were such a close-knit family. She tried to think back to what she'd said about werewolves before this. When Allan had said if he'd played the LARP game he would have been a hunter, she'd really thought he meant he was against werewolves or the concept. Now she suspected he meant he wanted to hunt werewolf hunters. The PI? Vaughn Greystoke?

She put a hand to her temple, feeling light-headed all

at once. Another wolf? Another wolf pack? She had to get out of here...now.

She opened the side door to the garage as carefully as she could and stopped dead. Her car wasn't in the garage, but Allan was. He looked up from grabbing the ice chest. *Crap.*

His brows raised in one big question mark. What was she doing in the garage when she was supposed to be taking a shower? This was so not good.

Plan B. She would have to come up with a story really fast about why she was in the garage and go along with him to his mountainside cabin—despite wishing she had any other choice. Then when he was sleeping, as long as he didn't handcuff her to a bed, she'd escape using *his* vehicle.

She thought of just screaming, but what could she say to the police? A werewolf pack had abducted her? Allan was one of their divers and so was Paul. They were SEALs, for heaven's sake. Paul's wife had even trained a couple of men at her dojo who became police officers. So no, Debbie wouldn't be able to get anywhere with that.

"Hey," she said, frowning a little. "I thought you said my car was here." Can't come up with a story? Get on the offensive.

"I guess they parked it at someone else's place for safekeeping since you were going to be staying with me for a while. I thought you were taking a shower." He looked like a really wary wolf.

And she felt like Little Red Riding Hood. So where was the werewolf hunter when *she* needed one? "I had a bag in my car with all my emergency supplies.

I was going to add that to the stuff I wanted to take to your place."

"Oh. I've got mine so if you need anything from it, you're welcome to it." He escorted her back to the house. She was certain he didn't believe her one iota. And the feeling was mutual.

When she returned to her bedroom, she took a shower, glad that she had only been running the cold water or she wouldn't have any hot water now.

It would have felt good—it was her first shower in days—if she hadn't had to worry about what came next. But the problem with washing up was she felt even more tired, like she could lie down in the tub and go to sleep. She guessed the doctor was right. She still needed time to recuperate.

Debbie decided to take a bath instead so she could soak and relax before her next attempt at escape. She began filling up the tub, hoping she wouldn't drown in it if she fell asleep.

———

Allan picked the lock of Debbie's bedroom door so he could make sure she was in the shower and hadn't tried to take off again. This was really not good. Somehow, she must have figured something was wrong, despite acting as though everything was fine.

He heard her stop the shower, then start running water in the tub.

While he waited for her to actually get into the tub, he texted Paul: She's acting like she knows nothing about us, but I think it's a ruse. She left the house to get something out of her car when she was supposed to be taking a shower. She didn't need to get anything out of her car. And of course, the car wasn't there.

Allan glanced at the bedroom window and texted: She had to have slipped out the bedroom window. She's taking a bath now. But I suspect I'll have trouble with her.

Paul texted back: Let me know if you need backup. You've got the sedative that Doc gave you, don't you?

Allan: Yeah, but I only want to use it as a last resort.

Paul: Gotcha.

Allan heard her turn off the water and step into the tub. He left the bedroom and closed the door. He couldn't lock it. He wasn't going to give her an explanation for that if she asked. He figured she knew to some extent what was going on.

He didn't want to start making lunch if she was going to be a while soaking in the tub either. But when she didn't leave the tub after a good twenty minutes, he knocked on the bedroom door. "Debbie? Are you all right in there?"

He was afraid she had slipped out the window and...

His heart pounding, he headed back through the duplex, and when he reached the front door, he opened it. Covered in an inch of snow, his hatchback was still there. He closed the front door and returned to the bedroom.

Worried about Debbie even more now, he knocked on the bathroom door. "Debbie? I'm coming in."

He was afraid she'd accidentally drowned in the bathtub. He twisted the doorknob. It was locked. He used his lockpick on it and yanked open the door, afraid of what he might find.

He hadn't expected to see a wolf shaking water from her fur coat and had no time to react before she lunged.

Chapter 15

DEBBIE HAD FALLEN ASLEEP IN THE BUBBLE BATH ONLY to wake to find she was a damned wolf! She couldn't believe it. She hadn't discovered any bite marks on her anywhere when she stripped out of her clothes. The oddest thing was that her scars had vanished. Yet it hadn't really registered in her tired brain until she turned into a wolf.

How had they turned her? Maybe it was like with vampires, even if they weren't real. But in some stories, the vampire could seal the wounds and then the bite marks were gone.

Now she was soaking wet and staring Allan down as he stood in her bathroom doorway. He had to have picked her lock!

She shook off the excess water, getting him all wet.

She was so angry, she wanted to rip Allan to shreds. He just stared at her in disbelief, as if he had never seen a wolf before. As if he wasn't a part-time wolf himself. Maybe he wasn't. Maybe he was a minion to a wolf pack, like Dracula had minions working for him.

Ohmigod, this was so unreal. She growled, and she couldn't believe she'd made such an angry growly sound, right before she lunged at him.

She slammed her paws into Allan's chest, but he quickly grabbed her head to keep her from biting him. He was strong and she thought she could yank free of him, but after her injury and surgery, she was way too weak. Her growls sounded menacing though, and she snapped her wickedly sharp teeth.

He held her head securely, despite the fact that she was shaking it, snarling fiercely, and trying to break free from his titan grip.

"Debbie, you were going to die if we didn't save your life the only way we could. Your heart quit beating twice. We have faster healing properties. No one else would have been able to keep you alive like we could."

She called him a liar, only the word was just a menacing growl. It didn't matter that she looked like, felt like, and sounded like a wolf. The notion just didn't register in her brain, and she'd expected to hear human words, not an animal growl.

She likened it to a scenario in which she suddenly had elf ears or purple skin. When she looked in the full-length dressing mirror hanging on her bathroom door, she had expected to see her usual self—brunette, brown eyes—not a wolf with gray, tan, and black markings. Not a wolf with a long tail and big ears and teeth.

When she'd first seen her huge wolf feet and wolf legs in the bathtub, she thought she'd somehow turned into a German shepherd. Which was beyond bizarre. She had watched lots of horror stories and thought maybe she'd received a body organ from a canine and now could turn into a dog. But instead of a dog, she had been a long-legged wolf with a shocked expression—*her* shocked expression. No matter how much she tried to rationalize what she was seeing in the mirror, she couldn't.

"You're going to be all right. You've got a pack to

take care of you, and you have me. We'll teach you
everything you need to know."

She felt the tension leaving her body. Not because
she was done being angry, but because she couldn't
keep the fight going. She felt like sinking into the floor
and sleeping for an eternity.

As soon as he felt her relax, he released his grip on
her, yet he was ready to tighten his hold again. She could
feel the tension in his hands and arms.

Then he let her go and she dropped to her paws, sat,
then lay down. She kept her head up, watching him, but
she was too tired to battle him any longer.

Allan warily kept his eye on her and pulled out his
phone. "Hey, Paul, the wolf is out of the bag. I'm going
to need some help here."

She growled softly. The whole pack would come and
get her. She felt she was the blood sacrifice for some
pagan satanic wolf pack.

Still lying down, Debbie didn't look like a threat now,
but Allan didn't mind admitting she had scared the shit
out of him when she lunged at him. A wolf's teeth could
rip him to shreds. He was lucky she was either holding
back and her lovely, true nature still had some control
over the anger she harbored against him for what she
had become, or she was still so exhausted from her
ordeal that she just didn't have the strength.

Whatever the reason, he was thanking God she hadn't
killed him. "I'm taking you to my place and we'll talk
this all out."

After about half an hour, though it seemed like

forever, he heard trucks pull up and was surprised when Everett arrived with the owner of the Italian restaurant, Fred Garafalo, and his chef, Gary White—all three new to the pack.

They hurried inside to help Allan with Debbie.

"What can we do?" Everett asked, eyeing Debbie.

Despite the arrival of Allan's new help, she hadn't moved from where she was lying down. She'd rested her head on her legs, kept her eyes on Allan, and lifted her head when she heard the men arrive, but she didn't move to attack anyone.

Thankfully. Maybe she was coming to realize they only wanted what was best for her. And they didn't mean to hurt her in any way.

"She's got some food in the freezer if someone wants to pack it in the ice chest. Someone can get her toiletries. Someone can pack some clothes for her. I'll stay with her." Allan would have packed her things for her so that someone she knew better was doing it, but it couldn't be helped. If she got vicious again, he wanted to be the one dealing with her. He still had the sedative in case he needed to use it, but he hoped he wouldn't have to.

She didn't seem to care. He half expected her to growl again. Maybe she was too tired.

"Paul told me to bring a crate for her in case you need it. I put it in the back of your hatchback."

Allan didn't want to have to crate her, but he couldn't risk her getting all snarly with him on the drive back to his place. It took about a half hour, longer in this weather, and he really had to concentrate on his driving.

"We'll follow you home and help unpack everything so you can stay with her," Everett said.

Everett was really good for the pack and Allan was glad he had mated his sister. He always seemed so diplomatic. Saying that Allan could keep an eye on Debbie would have sounded much more antagonistic than saying he could stay with her, as if to comfort her, which he wished he could. He didn't think that was going to happen right away.

When they were all packed up, Everett and the other men waited to see what Allan wanted to do about the crate or if he was willing to risk letting her ride with him without being locked up.

Everett left for a moment, then came back with a heavy-duty leash and collar.

Allan really didn't want to put her on a leash. But if they tried to get her out to the hatchback and she wasn't on a leash, she was sure to run. Chasing her down could be a real nightmare for them and a danger for her. But he really didn't want to have to leash her.

"Debbie, come on. Let's go and get settled at my place and then we'll talk."

She was watching him, but she didn't lift her head.

Everyone waited.

"I'll carry her out, if someone can grab some towels for her." Allan hoped that carrying her wasn't a mistake. He wasn't sure if she was playacting, or she really was being submissive and going along with the program. Or she was still exhausted.

She was so relaxed, he had a hard time lifting her. Everett helped get her off the floor, then Allan carried her to his vehicle.

Everett got the back door for her and the other men laid out the towels in the backseat since she was still so wet. Allan supposed she'd have an easier time stretching out in the backseat if she didn't want to sit up front and watch out the window.

She stretched out like one sleepy wolf, yawned, sighed, closed her eyes, and went to sleep. At least she appeared to be sleeping. But that could be just a ploy. She could wake at any time, ready to renew the fight between them.

Allan closed the car door.

"That was easy, but it might not be when we arrive at your place." Everett gave him the collar and leash.

"True. And it's wilderness out there. She might think it's safer there than running through this more heavily populated area. But she won't know how to manage on her own in the woods. Not with all the cougars, wolves in real wolf packs, and bears out there. Thanks for all your help," he said to the men, then got in his car and led the caravan to his mountainside cabin. He had mentioned the dangers for Debbie's benefit as much as the men's, hoping he could dissuade her from attempting to run.

They reached the cabin after about forty minutes and Debbie continued to sleep. At least he didn't have any neighbors that could see his place. He carried her to the bedroom Rose always used when she came and stayed up there. His mother had even dropped by to leave off all the flowers from the pack members and fellow law-enforcement officials. The pack truly hoped Debbie would adjust without too much trouble. No one was a newly turned wolf, which was good, but it also meant she had no one to talk to about what she was experiencing.

Allan figured that when he could, he'd ask Tessa to talk with Debbie.

Then Allan helped the men carry in Debbie's things, leaving the bags with her clothes and toiletries on the living room floor. While Everett was putting away her groceries, Allan thanked the other men and they left.

"Good luck," they said.

"Thanks." Allan suspected he would need more than that. Then he called Paul with an update.

"Do you want me to send Lori over? Would it help for Debbie to have a woman to talk to?"

"Debbie is sound asleep. I think for now, she's fine. I'll call you in the morning or if things get out of hand."

Allan waved good-bye as Everett quietly left.

"Everett's headed back to his house. I think we'll be good for the night."

"All right," Paul said. "Don't hesitate to call if you have any trouble at all."

"Thanks. Talk to you in the morning." At least Allan hoped he wouldn't have to call anyone else tonight. He carried her bags into her bedroom and set them on the floor. Then he watched her sleep for a few minutes. Satisfied she was fine for the time being, he stalked down the hall to the master bedroom. He stripped out of his clothes, tired from all the late nights of worrying about Debbie and ready for a good night's sleep. Though with her here now, he didn't think he'd get one for long. He walked into the bathroom to take a shower.

He was lathering up when he sensed he was being watched. Then he saw her sitting on the tile floor, observing him through the lightly fogged-up glass shower doors.

Hell. He sure hoped she didn't try to take a bite out of him when he left the shower stall. He realized too late he couldn't even reach his phone to call for assistance. He should have locked his bedroom or bathroom door, but he wasn't used to doing so, and he'd never even given it a thought.

"We don't bite people," he said calmly as he finished washing himself, as if he did this all the time — washed up while a hostile, newly turned wolf watched him through the glass doors. "We don't kill people or hurt them." Unless the people were trying to hurt his wolf pack. Even so, if they were human, his kind tried to ensure that law enforcement officials dealt with the crime through legal channels. He didn't figure he needed to get into that right now with Debbie though.

He finished washing, hoping that delaying the inevitable would give her time to cool down. But now that he was done, he had to leave the shower. Sure, he was plenty alpha, but from her posture, so was she. And a human didn't stand a chance against an angry wolf, unless he could discuss this rationally with her human side.

He wanted to reason with her, tell her the steps he was going to take, as if he were a police officer trying to talk someone down from doing something criminal. But wouldn't she know what he was going to say and do anyway? Not a lot of choices here.

He figured he'd try and talk her down anyway, just in case it helped. Using his calmest voice, he said, "I'm coming out now. Don't bite me. Your wolf teeth can crush bones and there's no recovering from that."

He turned off the water and then opened the glass

doors. In that instant, looking into her beautiful brown eyes framed by the tan mask and reddish fur, the black hairs covering the tips of her ears, he thought how lovely she was. Her ears were perked, expectant, waiting for his next move as he stood still in the shower, dripping wet, naked, and vulnerable. He didn't think he'd ever felt this imperiled in his life. Maybe because normally if he felt threatened, he'd take care of the threat in any way that he could. But in this instance, he wanted to make her feel safe and protected, and reassure her everything would be okay. That *she* would be okay.

So he was attempting to act calmly with no hint of aggression, which could escalate the already tense situation.

Her posture was stiff, indicating she was ready to spring into action, but her face was an unreadable mask. Wolves could be unpredictable when they were newly turned, or even if they were from another pack. Like old friends playing card games, wolves in a pack gave away their intentions in minute ways—the twitching of ears, shifting of the body, facial expressions—all kinds of visual cues. But she was an unknown quantity, totally indecipherable.

At first, her eyes were on his, a pure alpha challenge. But then her gaze moved and settled on his package. In a purely sexual way, he would have become aroused, but not in this instant. He didn't even want to think what she could do to him if she was *that* angry. He hoped his nervousness didn't show.

"You're family now," Allan said, trying to coax her down. "You're one of us, a *lupus garou*. Before, I couldn't date you, given what we both were. But now I want to, if you're of a like mind." Even if she wasn't, he wanted to give them a shot. It might take years, he figured, but she wasn't leaving them and he wasn't giving up on her. He wasn't certain this was the time to approach that subject, but she had seemed interested before. He wanted her to know how much he cared about her. That he would be there to help her through this every step of the way and, at the same time, give her his love unconditionally.

He slowly moved out of the shower to grab a towel, not wanting to move quickly and appear hostile.

Standing her ground, she refused to back up, which meant his legs were practically touching her nose. He tried not to think of it when she lifted her nose and smelled his package, those wicked teeth too close for comfort. Not that she was showing them, but it would only take a second to change from curious to vicious.

He had to remind himself that she was a new wolf and everything would be fascinating to her: the smells she could smell now, even the ability to identify distress and sexual interest, though he wasn't certain if she could tell the difference at this point. To him, it was instinctive, but then again, he was born knowing this. Maybe with her new wolf genes, it would be just as natural for her.

If so, she could smell his stress.

He slowly pulled a towel off the rack behind her, which meant he had to lean forward a little, something he really didn't want to do because he was getting even more into her space. When he grabbed hold of the towel, she licked one of his balls, and he swore he nearly had a heart attack. It could have been sensuous and arousing under totally different circumstances.

He began to dry himself off, and she licked some of the water off his thigh. So far, so good. But as soon as he wrapped the towel around his waist to feel as though he had a little armor to protect his masculinity, she backed up. The way she crouched, as if she were on a hunt and held her tail straight out, he knew she was getting ready to attack.

He could have shifted and pinned her down, could have done so easily as a much bigger male wolf. But he didn't want to scare her. Still, he had to get out of the damn bathroom in one piece. It might be his only choice.

She jumped, and he veered left, anticipating her move to the right. Just a slight turn in her body gave her away. He leaped out of her path, her teeth snapping, and she snarled. Wolves could be dangerous, and she sounded like a vicious predator, not a wolf in play. She grabbed his towel as if it was the only thing she could vent her frustration on. Teeth sinking into the blue plush towel, she yanked. Instinctively, he wouldn't relinquish it. For a second, he had ahold of one end, and she had the other.

She tugged with all her might, body close to the floor, teeth and lips closed over the towel, butt elevated a little as she pulled backward, shaking her head while she tried to jerk it away from him and growling ferociously.

He saw the opportunity present itself at once. He dropped the towel and dove out the door, slamming it closed on his exodus. His heart racing, he hurried to throw some boxers on. She was snarling and banging against the door, sounding like she would rip him to shreds if he let her out.

He had no intention of doing so. Until she turned into her human form, and he could talk to her more reasonably, she was confined to his bathroom.

—∿—

Debbie couldn't have been any more incensed than she was right this very instant. She'd woken to hear what she thought was Allan in the shower. She was surprised he'd left his bedroom and bathroom door ajar, maybe to listen for her if something happened. She couldn't believe how much she could smell things now, like the water from the shower in the next room—or the fluoride in it, she should say. And his scent everywhere in the place as he had walked through it. She thought she also smelled Paul's scent, because he'd come to see her in the clinic, and she recognized it.

God, why did Allan have to be so damned hot and a wolf? Seeing him washing himself, running the soap all over his glorious body, she had stared at him in awe. She had sensed he was nervous. Some devious part of her had wanted to push the envelope and show him she wasn't going to be pushed around, forced to do things that she didn't want to do. To show him he wasn't her boss.

On the other hand, as stressed out as he was, he had been so good with her—firm, letting her know how serious her biting him could be, but at the same time, gentle, reassuring—not all SEAL wolf tough. Which she imagined he could turn into in a second. She couldn't tamp down the anger she felt, but she did concede that he was trying hard to be good to her, even when she must have looked seriously dangerous. She sure sounded that way to herself.

So now she knew why he had been so reluctant to date her. And why the family had disapproved. Probably the whole pack. But now for her to date him? He had to be nuts! She wanted to take a bite out of him.

"Debbie," he said, and the bedsprings sank, so she suspected he was sitting on the edge of the bed while he was talking to her, "I didn't turn you. None of us bit you. They gave you our blood in an IV. But believe me when I say it was the only way to save your life."

She paced back and forth in the beige bathroom. It was nice and big, but not big enough for a pacing wolf.

"We have a wolf pack, as I'm sure you're well aware. The flowers in your guest bedroom are from all the members of the pack and a few from law enforcement friends. Everyone in the pack wants to welcome you and help you adjust to your new way of life. Our SEAL team leader's wife was recently turned, so she could speak to you about what you're experiencing. But everyone in our pack was born as a *lupus garou*. We don't turn into vicious wolves. We keep a low profile and run through the woods as wolves, which can be tricky with genuine wolves, cougars, grizzlies, black bears, or hunters around. Which is why we stick together to keep everyone safe as much as possible."

And they had multiple births. That's why Lori and Rose were having twins and triplets! They were a bunch of wild animals. Or half of them was.

Debbie groaned, but it came out a low, menacing growl.

"The worst part is the shifting when you least expect it as a newly turned wolf. The worst time for that to happen is during the full moon."

Great. How long did that last? Ohmigod, she

couldn't dive any longer? Or only when the full moon wasn't out?

This was so much of a nightmare. If she was supposed to have died...

Then again, no, if she'd been given the choice, she probably would have opted for something to help save her. Like a bionic heart or something. Being a part-time wolf? She shook her head. She wasn't sure she would have gone that far. Maybe. She'd have to see how badly this all turned out before she could make a final judgment.

"When you're up to it, we can run as wolves together."

Was Allan the one who had recommended she be turned so he could date her?

She growled again. Dating wasn't going to happen. Not with him or any other wolf in the pack. How many were there?

Ohmigod, the wolf killer. He really *was* a werewolf hunter. There really *were* werewolves. The woman who had been murdered? Most likely she *truly* had been one. And what about the other case? With the bank robbers? The shoot-out? A wild wolf biting into tires and killing one of the men, the other naked in the lake after he fell off the cliffs?

All the bizarre happenings all made sense now, if they all had been werewolves. *Rowdy*. He'd been right all along.

No wonder Rose and Lori had been upset to find the murdered woman! And for Allan to be upset about Tara nearly dying.

Then Debbie thought of Rose and Lori carrying all those babies, and she realized just how much of a danger they were in.

Every time she thought of one thing, she thought of a ton of other problems with this whole scenario. Like driving a car and all of a sudden getting the urge to shift. She could see herself sitting in the car while it was parked alongside the road. Then a police officer she knew would check her abandoned car out and discover a wild wolf. But of course he wouldn't know her. Not as a wolf. Then what? Tranquilize her and put her in the zoo? Kill her?

Oh, no, that's just what she had been about to do to Tara. Put her out of her misery when she was a wolf. Debbie whimpered at the thought. Now she understood a little of what their kind faced.

But weren't there evil werewolves? All the people she'd met—Allan, Paul, Lori, Catherine, Tara, and Rose, and the others—they'd all been really nice to her. And they'd been nice to everyone they met. No pretenses. They weren't vicious people. Well, of late, Rose and her mother were reluctant for Allan to date her, but *no* wonder!

She thought back to the way he had kissed her, so lovingly, passionately, wolfishly. Here she'd thought it was the SEAL in him. Now to learn it was the wolf!

She groaned, sat down in front of the door, and stared at it, listening. He hadn't moved from the bed. She frowned. He *better* not have gone to sleep while she was stuck in the bathroom.

No way was she going to allow that. She'd fix him! She'd had a puppy when she was young, and she remembered it missing its littermates when her mother brought it home. So for the first three nights, it barked bloody murder. She could do that. Bark until he couldn't stand it anymore and let her out!

But as soon as she lifted her chin to bark, she let out the most hauntingly beautiful howl instead. One wasn't enough. She had to try it out several times to see if every time the howl sounded just the same. But it didn't. It was just a little different each time. Long, low, beautiful.

The bedsprings moved.

She sat still in anticipation. Was he going to shoot her with a sedative? Shoot her with silver bullets? Wish he'd never taken her home with him?

Should she get ready to pounce?

Chapter 16

ALLAN WAS WOLF TIRED. LISTENING TO DEBBIE HOWL all night was *not* going to happen. Hell, everyone with wolf hearing within a two-mile radius could hear her. And with her in a tiled bathroom connected to his bedroom? Even worse.

She reminded him of a puppy that was being isolated from the pack. But she *wasn't* a puppy, and he knew she was frustrated with him and with what she had become. As much as he didn't want her attacking him any further tonight, he couldn't make her stay in the bathroom any longer while she was in her wolf form. Not when she was howling like she needed a rescue—*from him*.

Hoping this wouldn't be an awful mistake, he sighed, pulled his covers aside, and left the bed. She immediately grew quiet, which meant she heard him coming and was listening to his footfalls on the carpeted floor as he approached the door and making decisions about what she would do next if he opened the bathroom door. At least she hadn't been clawing at it.

Wearing only a pair of boxers, he felt vulnerable again, but he wasn't going to get dressed just to let her out of the bathroom.

He hoped she wouldn't lunge at him again when he let her out. If someone had shut him up in there, he would have been furious, but then again, he could shift at will. Then he wondered if she had to pee. Since she was still in her wolf form, she would have to relieve herself outside. He was sure she wouldn't be happy about that at all, but worse, she couldn't have any privacy. He'd have to put a collar and leash on her, and he could imagine just how unmanageable she would be.

All the things they did naturally as wolves would be first-time experiences for Debbie. All of this was just part of their nature, but dealing with a newly turned wolf, he realized just how much he took for granted.

"Debbie, I'm opening the door to let you out. You can either return to your guest bedroom, or you can join me in bed. If you have to go out to relieve yourself, I'll take you outside." Which meant he'd have to bundle up for the snowy cold first. "It's hard to say how long you'll remain in your wolf form, a couple of hours or longer. It all depends on the individual. But it won't last forever." He didn't want to mention that she would have no control over it for some time.

He really didn't think she'd join him in bed, the way she was so antagonistic, and he wasn't sure that was a good idea anyway. But he wanted to offer, just in case she felt more comfortable staying with him.

Slowly, he started to open the door, but he met resistance as the door bumped into her. She was sitting in front of it, and he had to wait for her to back up a bit so he could open it further and let her out. She was so unpredictable, he wasn't certain what she would do, and he tensed for the lunge. Instead, she brushed by him, tearing out of the bathroom, running in a couple of tight circles in his bedroom, then grabbing the hem of his boxers and giving them a tug, nearly pulling them off. Wolves had a hell of a grip. Then she released his boxers that now had teeth marks in them and dashed down the hallway to the living room.

Like a wild wolf, she raced around the couches. Before he could follow her, she tore back down the hallway into his bedroom.

Like a mad animal, she turned on the proverbial dime and raced back down the hallway. She needed to burn up some of that excess energy, and he was glad she wanted to just run and not attack him again. At least for now.

"When you're done playing," he said, tired and hoping that if he acted like this was no big deal, she'd settle down eventually, "you can join me or go back to your own bed." He climbed back into bed and hoped she would feel better and wear herself out. Wolves didn't like confinement. If running around the cabin got rid of some of her pent-up anger and frustration, so much the better.

He loved her howl, loved her beautiful, agile wolf form, and loved her high-spirited race through the house. If she broke something, it didn't matter. Just as long as she didn't injure herself in the process. He could envision taking her to the clinic and having to explain to the doctor how she had broken a leg.

Debbie raced up and down the hall, making hairpin turns in his bedroom as he folded his arms behind his head and watched her. The full moon shone through the uncovered windows. He hadn't thought he'd ever witness a newly turned wolf running into his bedroom and out again. She looked as wild as any genuine wolf. He thought of running with her in the forest as wolves, enjoying the crisp cold night in their fur coats, but he didn't believe she was ready for that. Not if they encountered a wild wolf pack or the hunter they still hadn't caught.

She began to slow down, tiring, her running spirit spent. She was trotting at first, then walking, cooling down, her tongue hanging out of her mouth. She stopped to peer at him as he observed her. He didn't smile because he knew how serious the situation was. How vulnerable her feelings had to be.

"If you want to join me, you're welcome." He wasn't certain it was a good idea, but he would do anything to make her feel welcome in his life.

She still hesitated. Then, before she made the leap, he saw the sparkle in her brown eyes, the way she crouched and then sprang into action.

She jumped over him, startling him, landed on top of the bed with one huge lunge, but her jump was too strong. She ended up hitting the bed with way too much force and slid off the side, taking half the comforter with her.

He tried not to laugh, not wanting to embarrass her. But he could see learning her new wolf skills was going to take some time for her, and for him, to get used to. Those born as *lupus garous* learned their own strength as wolf pups, and their parents taught them limits on biting and roughhousing. With a full-grown wolf, it was going to take some work. She wouldn't realize her own strength, and he was afraid she might hurt someone accidentally.

Which meant he'd have to turn into his wolf and teach her how to play. But not tonight. She needed to sleep. Hell, *he* needed to sleep.

She sat on the other side of the bed on the floor, waiting to see his response.

Still wearing a serious expression, afraid smiling would put her off because she'd think her action had amused him—which it had, but he was trying hard not to let on—he patted the bed. "Come on, Debbie. There's plenty of room up here."

She jumped up and landed in his lap. He groaned as her weight pressed against his groin. He hadn't expected that or prepared for it. He didn't think she'd planned it either.

She moved off him, then came around and licked his face—as kind of an apology, he suspected. This was much better. He ran his hand over her head and smiled a little. "If you need anything, just let me know." He was still thinking of her needing to relieve herself outside, but he was praying that wouldn't happen.

She moved around the bed, then around and around. *Find a spot already*, he wanted to say. *Patience*, he warned himself. He'd said he could do this, and he had every intention of doing it for her and for the pack.

She got settled, and he was about to drift off when she sat up, stood, circled, and settled again. This was going to be a really long night. He thought his king-size bed was big enough for the two of them, but when she finally went to sleep, she still kept moving around, restless, kicking him with her big wolf paws, whimpering and woofing while she had wolf dreams. So much for getting a good night's sleep.

She was so restless that at some point during the night, he finally pulled her against his body. She looked up at him with sad eyes, and his heart went out to her. Then she rested her head against his chest, and sometime in between sleeping and fully waking, he found her sleeping on top of the covers between his legs, her head resting on his crotch. He smiled down at her. At that point, he wanted to get up and start the day, but he didn't want to disturb her. After a few minutes he finally drifted off to sleep again, and when he woke, she was gone.

～～～

When Debbie had awoken after one of her many night-mares of being a wolf, she found herself asleep against Allan, her head resting on his warm crotch! She was all curled up in a ball, and she had quickly moved off him, realizing that not only had she slept with him as a wolf, but she was now sleeping with him as a human, and *naked*!

Not that she hadn't been that way with him before, but now he was a wolf, so that made a hell of a lot of a difference.

Well, she was too, but that wasn't *her* fault!

She was confused, angry still—who wouldn't be?—and having a horrible time dealing with this. She'd had to go to the bathroom as a wolf, but there was no way in hell she was going to go outside and squat in the snow. Besides, she knew he'd have to put a collar and leash on her, and she really wasn't going there. She had no plans to run off. Not now that she'd become this…this half animal, half human. She knew she couldn't handle it on her own. That she wouldn't be safe. And ultimately none of his people would be either.

As much as she didn't like what she'd become, she wouldn't jeopardize all of their safety. Not in that way. Maybe by accident. If she had to go outside as a wolf

and if he even could manage getting a collar and leash
on her, she would yank the leash right out of his hands
and do her thing in privacy, then return to let him know
she had no intention of running off.

So she was much relieved when she woke to find
herself back to her normal self…if sleeping naked with
Allan with her head on his crotch could be called normal.

Trying to take her mind off what she'd become
and needing to get on with her life—that was in total
shambles now—she made coffee and was going to fix
breakfast when she heard Allan stirring in the bedroom.
Normally, she wouldn't have been able to hear movement on the mattress or the sheets rustling slightly that
far from where she was in the kitchen. She guessed
with a wolf's enhanced hearing she heard sounds she
couldn't as a human. It was both wonderful and irritat-
ing. Hearing stuff she'd never heard before—the gentle
wind brushing against leaves, snow falling off overladen
branches, Allan's waking—was something she had to
get used to because right now it was unnerving. She kept
stopping to listen, to distinguish what she was hearing.

If someone tried to sneak up behind her, she could see
how hearing them as an early warning would come in
handy. As it was now, she kept thinking the sounds were
closer, on top of her, not in the distance. She couldn't
even imagine going to a movie now. They were loud
enough already. What would it sound like to a wolf's
sensitive hearing? Most likely deafening.

And smell. Ohmigod. She couldn't believe she could
smell the sausages before she even started to cook them.
The eggs and cheese, the same way. And Allan, spicy,
warm, and sexy, wolf and human. Those were good

smells. The bad odors would take some getting used to. Dead stuff? Even humans could smell dead things, if they were big enough and decomposing. But she imagined being able to smell dead plants and animals that were farther off, smaller, less pungent.

Still, she could see where that could help her in her police work too. She was a glass half-full kind of person, so she always tried to see the good in things. *Tried* was the key word.

She growled under her breath as she thought of Allan confining her to the bathroom with no way to open the door and bite him for it. The howling did wonders though. She just had to learn how to use her newfound curse to her advantage.

She stared out the kitchen window, the dark not so dark, just to see if she could see anything any better. And she could. Birds moving about, looking for berries. Leaves fluttering in the breeze, catching her eye, when they wouldn't have before. Anything that moved caught her attention.

Despite the restless sleep she'd had last night, she didn't feel as tired as she thought she would. Maybe she could get in a nap later on. She felt more alert than she normally did at this time in the morning. Even so, she poured a cup of coffee, filled it with cream, and sipped from it, her obligatory jump start for the morning.

She heard Allan stirring again. He'd probably worry when he found she was gone, thinking she'd escaped. Or maybe not. If she could smell the coffee and everything else so well, he probably would too. Yes, she was irritated to the max with him about confining her to the bathroom, but she had to admit he'd been really good about not turning into a wolf himself and taking her to task for threatening him so viciously last night.

And he had offered her his bed, which she should have avoided, but she'd been feeling so out of sorts, she hoped sleeping with him would help her to settle down. And it had. But she wasn't doing that again and waking up the way she had this morning.

The springs in the bed moved, the comforter and sheets were tossed aside, feet hit the floor, and then there was a pause.

Was he smelling the coffee? She put the sausages in the saucepan to start breakfast.

―――∽―――

Allan's heart did a leap when he discovered Debbie was not in bed with him any longer. He yanked his covers aside and jumped out of bed before he attempted to still his racing heart and listened. He didn't want her to think he was going to run her down every time she was out of his sight. He heard movement in the kitchen: footsteps, a mug clunking slightly as she set it on the counter, a spoon stirring. He smelled coffee and sausages. Everything appeared to be fine. She was just making breakfast.

Even so, he left the bedroom and then strode down the hall. When he reached the kitchen, he found Debbie dressed in pajamas and that fluffy robe and slippers that made her look so cuddly and lovable as she made coffee, sausages, and eggs for breakfast.

He was glad she was back to looking her usual self if it made her feel like she had more control over her life, and he hoped she was feeling better today. "Good morning."

She whipped around and glowered at him. So she

wasn't done being angry. She could be mad all she wanted, and really, they had altered her life to such a degree that he understood her animosity. But she'd have to deal with it. He'd help her cope the best he could by showing compassion and understanding.

Instead of backing off and allowing her the space she needed to get over this, he pulled her into his arms and gave her a sound hug. "I never wanted to turn you. Paul and Lori are the pack leaders. I'm a sub-leader and part of the original pack. They left me out of the loop on this one."

She stared up at him, her expression turning from surprise to realization. "They were afraid I'd be angry with you."

He smiled a little. "If that was the reason, they were right. But I was also angry with them. I didn't believe you'd seen Tara as a wolf. I tried to convince them to listen to your side of the story first. We've been family forever. I thought…" He hesitated. How would it sound if he told her they had only a couple of choices when a human saw a wolf shape-shift?

"They were going to decide to terminate me," she said, sounding sympathetic to his concern.

"We can't let anyone know what we are," he said, defending his *lupus garou* kind for what they felt they were forced to do when necessary.

"I understand. I had already died. They didn't need to revive me," she finally said, the tension in her body draining. She felt soft and lovable in his arms.

"Yes."

She frowned up at him. "You wouldn't have agreed to them changing me?"

He snorted. "What do you think? I've been head over heels over you since we first started diving together. And all I knew was the trouble that would get me into. I tried my damnedest to see you as just another dive partner. But it wasn't working."

"And the kiss?"

"I told you—it wasn't working. We mate for life, Debbie. One partner for life. Some of us have marriage licenses to prove to the human world we're together with regard to property ownership and for the children's sakes. If something untoward happened to the parents, the pack would raise the pups. You understand we're all in this together? We take care of each other's kids. Love them like our own. It's just part of our wolf nature. Our wolf half dictates we stay with one partner until death. Some take a new mate after that. Some never do. We do take mating seriously."

"Mating."

"It means courtship between our kind and then consummating the relationship. Once that's done, there's no annulment. No divorce. Normally, our instincts drive us to find the perfect mate. So once we find the mate we want to be with for life, we're good after that."

"So you're saying we're already *mated*?" Debbie asked, sounding and looking mortified.

"No. You weren't one of us before—a *lupus garou*, a wolf shifter. That part of us compels us to find a mate and to stay with him or her for life."

"Okay, so let me get this straight. Since you can't mate with humans, it's perfectly fine to fool around with them whenever you want? But you could never make a commitment?"

"Right. Although we don't 'fool around' as much as we want. We're not dogs."

"Dogs originated from wolves," she said.

"There's a big difference between dogs and wolves. Dogs don't mate for life. They…cat around. Wolves stick with their mate and they help to raise the pups. All of the pack does."

"Except when it comes to one of you taking up with a human," she reminded him.

He let out his breath. "All right. I see I'm not going to win this debate. Suffice it to say we aren't mated. Yet. And it's your choice. No one would ever force you to mate someone against your will."

"That's a cheerful thought. Okay, so when can I be on my own again?"

This was the part he really didn't want to have to explain. "Maybe a year, maybe more. It depends on how long it takes you to get your shifting under control and other things."

"Holy cow. No way." She paced around the room. "And what other things?"

"For some, it's not easy becoming one of us, personality-wise. Specifically, if the newly turned wolf is wolfishly aggressive and gets himself into trouble over it."

"Because newly turned wolves in jail during the full moon could cause real problems, I gather."

"Exactly."

"So you haven't found the wolf of your dreams and that's why you're not mated already?" She lifted a brow.

He nodded.

Then she frowned at him. "But I wouldn't have been the right one for you, since I was human."

"I agree. But at least for me, the mating instinct cut through the division between our species. Anyway, for the most part, you won't see a lot of differences in the way you are as opposed to the way you were before."

"Right." She stiffened in his arms and pulled away, turning the burner to medium heat to cook the sausages. "Being a wolf all night is no big deal."

"Well, sure, that is a big deal. And that's the part that will be the greatest issue to handle. You won't have a lot of control over when you shift, particularly around the phase of the full moon. It will get better over the years, but I won't pretend it won't be troublesome in the beginning."

With fork in hand, she turned to stare at Allan. "What do you mean by *particularly* around the full moon? Don't tell me we can turn anytime during the month. The werewolf stories all say when the full moon is out, they have no control over it. Nothing about any other time of the month. I figured they had been based on all of you."

"That's fiction. There's only one wolf I know of who writes werewolf stories, though she changes them up a bit. For the most part, she shows them for what they truly are."

"Who?"

"Julia Wildthorn. She's now mated to a Highland wolf. I only know about her because my sister and Lori are avid fans of hers. I think any wolf is, because they know she's one of them."

"They have them in the Highlands too?" Debbie took a deep breath. "I'll have to look her up. Maybe I can learn something about all of this."

"Her stories are fiction too. They're all about hot and sexy wolves in romance novels, so you can't put a whole lot of stock in them."

She considered his abs and her mouth curved up a little bit. He probably should have worn a robe.

"I guess I should have dressed for breakfast."

"You were worried about me. And for your information, if God forbid I turn into a wolf and have to pee, you better not put a collar on me. I don't plan to run anywhere." She glanced down at Allan's boxers. "I don't usually serve breakfast to half-naked men, but since I was sleeping naked with you this morning, it's a little too late to worry about such things."

"You were wearing a wolf coat. That doesn't count as being naked." He wondered what she would have done if she had woken up as a human, nestled against him and wearing nary a strip of clothes.

"Says you."

He stared at her for a moment, then slugged down his coffee and offered to refill their mugs. "Where the hell was I when all this happened?" How the hell had he slept through that?

"Don't worry. It won't happen again."

Well, *that* was a crying shame. He swore if she ever joined him in bed like that again as a wolf, he was staying awake the whole night. Not that he could do anything more than tuck her under the covers and fold her in his arms. But naked when she was now one of them? Hot damn, yeah.

Getting his mind back on the business of teaching her about their kind, he said, "Wolves that have genes going back several generations can shift at will, even during the new moon. That means several generations were pure *lupus garous*, no human mix. If a wolf has a parent that had been turned and one that was born a *lupus garou*, the wolf offspring won't change during the new moon, whether he or she wants to or not. Well, any new wolf, like yourself, won't either."

"Great. So only during the phase of the new moon do I get to pretend I'm human and won't have to worry about shifting at the wrong time, like in front of the world."

"Right. That means a week of no difficulty at all. As we get closer to the full moon, the pull to be a wolf is stronger, and it's strongest the night of the full moon."

"Great." She scrambled the eggs in the frying pan. "And there's no cure for it."

He sighed. "We don't have a virus or an infection. And we're not cursed. You're one of us until the end. The good news is you'll be able to smell, hear, and see better anytime, not just when you're in your wolf form."

"That could help with investigations if I was able to conduct them any longer," she said dryly.

"We can do night dives. During the week of the new moon, no trouble at all. We can check areas out at night otherwise. As a wolf, you'll be able to see better at night." He glanced at the kitchen light and realized it wasn't on. And it was still dark at this hour.

Her gaze followed his. "I guess that saves on electricity."

"Some. We still turn on the lights when it's pitch-black out."

"I'm not done being angry about this. I should have had some say." She served up the sausages and eggs.

He hurried to set the table. "And what would you have said? It was too late to ask. You were in bad shape."

"Dead or near death, you mean? What if I hadn't seen Tara shift? Or thought it was just my imagination?"

"Like you said, you were doing poorly. No way would you have been making eggs and sausage this morning. You could have had serious and permanent heart damage after what you went through. Health-wise, you might never have been the same."

"Like no longer being as physically active?"

"Right. As a wolf last night, you were raring to go. If you had been strictly human, you would have had months of recuperation and rehabilitation."

They sat down to eat and she let out her breath. "Okay, I get it. But I still don't have to like this wolf part of me." She picked up her fork and pointed it at him. "I'm not dating you or any other wolf."

"You can't go out with humans."

"Just for sex? No commitment?" She snorted.

"All right, you've got me there. But only once you've been a wolf for several months and only during the new moon."

"Like that would ever happen now. What a disaster. Not that sex with a human is high on my list of priorities." Then she looked up from her dish and asked, "Is Rowdy one of you?"

"No."

"I thought maybe because of all his talk about werewolves, he might be one."

"If you notice, we don't talk about werewolves in general unless drawn into a discussion about them."

"True. So how can you tell if he's one or not?"

"We would smell the wolf on him."

Her mouth gaped a little, and then she nodded. "Okay. Getting used to all of this." Then she poked at her eggs. "What if I was injured and ended up in a real hospital?"

"The clinic is like a real hospital, scaled down in size."

"Right. But you know what I mean. If a real—if a human doctor had to take my blood, wouldn't that show that I was a…well, mix of wolf and human?"

"No. Our entire system is either wolf or human, not a mix of the two. So if someone draws your blood as a wolf, they'll be looking at pure wolf DNA."

"So when Rowdy said he asked to check Sarah for wolf DNA, they wouldn't have found any." She relaxed a little, and he was glad some of his answers seemed to put her at ease.

"Correct."

Then she stiffened again and frowned at him. "Did Rose have her babies as…babies or wolf pups?"

Allan smiled a little. "Frankly, I wasn't in the birthing room at the time. You'd have to ask her."

Debbie's eyes widened. "She might have had them as pups?"

"Only if she'd shifted into a wolf first," he hurried to say. This was going to be so much harder to explain than he ever thought possible.

"Oh."

Again, the tension slipped from her expression, and he thought she might be okay with that.

"We need to learn who the shooter was who nearly killed me. And who nearly murdered Tara," Debbie finally said.

Allan didn't say anything, just watched her,

wondering if she knew what she was saying. Someone who got rid of the werewolf kind had to be good in her world, because he and his kind were all mad wolves—according to Debbie.

She finally made an annoyed face at him, wrinkling her nose, and said, "All right. Yes, I can see what you're thinking. I would now praise the man for what he did because I'd realize he wasn't a nutcase after all. But I can see your point. Tara's done nothing wrong, has she? She hasn't killed any people and that's why he's after her, right?"

"As a wolf, have you killed any people lately?"

Debbie frowned at him. "Of course not."

"Do you have any urge to kill humans? Or anyone else, other than me?"

She closed her gaping mouth, her eyes tearing up, and her cheeks coloring a little with embarrassment. "No."

He felt bad, but he had to break through all this crap she'd learned over the years about evil werewolves in fiction. "Well, there you go. You're as wild as they get because you haven't learned how to control your more primal wolf instincts, and you didn't want to kill anyone. For the most part."

"You have me all locked up in the cabin. What if I felt differently once you set me free?" She glanced out the window at the vista. Before he could respond, she added, "By the way, it's beautiful up here, like being on top of the world with a view of the lake and mountains. I really do love it here. Just not the confinement."

"I really appreciate the cabin and its location when I return home from missions. Lots of solitude and wildlife. Nature at its finest. Plus, I can run when I want without having trouble with neighbors or others catching sight of me. As to the confinement, it wouldn't be safe running off on your own. Not when you don't have control over the shifting. If you were on your own, what do you think would happen? You couldn't even go out to get groceries without worrying you were going to shift. You'd have no one to run errands for you until you can get this under control."

"I don't plan on running. I'm not stupid."

"No, you're not. But you did try to at your place."

"That was different. I thought you were going to bite me."

He smiled.

"You know what I mean. That you were going to turn me into one of your own kind. But then I took a bath and shifted. At that point, I knew I really had no choice."

"As to your point about killing someone, your human personality dictates what your wolf half does. Some of our wolf half is instinctual: protective of pack mates or others, being wary and curious, but our human half still dictates much of what we do."

She sighed. "Okay, no, I didn't feel like going out on a hunt and eating rabbits, deer, or any men last night. Not even you. I was just…angry when I jumped at you, all snarly and growly, and I'm really sorry. What did you expect? I'm normally not like that."

"I know you aren't. You were just upset about everything that had happened to you and acting on instinct. If you'd really wanted to bite me, you would have. Even though you might think I was keeping you from hurting me, you were a lot stronger than that. You were holding back."

"I was exhausted."

"Even an exhausted wolf could have injured me in a major way. Granted, some wolves are nasty. It's the human half that makes them so. Just like humans are good and bad. So sometimes we have to eliminate them. We can't go to jail so we take care of our own kind."

Her mouth was gaping again. Allan supposed it was a lot to take in at once. He needed to shut up and let her eat, and they could talk about nicer things for a change.

"So…you don't want to date me," he said.

She started to eat her breakfast and drank some of her coffee. "You know how I said I wasn't exactly a morning person?"

"Okay, so you don't want to discuss this first thing in the morning."

"Allan, no, there's no way I'm dating you."

"But you would have until this happened, right?"

She finished up her food and took her plate to the kitchen.

He scarfed the rest of his breakfast down. "Okay, no dating." But she was living with him, and that was even better. Dating was overrated.

"You don't mean it," she said, cleaning up, but he took the pan she was going to wash away from her. She smiled at him, just a little. "Don't think washing the pots and pans is going to change my mind."

"Hadn't even considered it." She would learn that he was always like that with the dishes. When his mother or sister cooked, he always did the dishes, his thanks for someone else cooking. But if Debbie thought he was trying to win her favor, then he was all for it.

Chapter 17

DEBBIE WAS CERTAIN THE WOLF STANDING NEXT TO her, scrubbing away at the scrambled eggs left on the frying pan, had every intention of dating her. He just thought he was going to give her time to get used to the idea. She had news for him. She was *never* mating any wolf. *Ever*. Mating for life? No way.

Her neat, orderly little life had been shot to hell when she turned into a werewolf. What did he call them? *Lupus garous*? Fancy name for a horror-flick creature.

No, she hadn't come to grips with being a werewolf. And no, she didn't think she ever could. The whole notion was so unreal. She kept thinking she'd wake up and the nightmare would end. But this was it. Her real life now.

She didn't see herself as the beautiful wolf he probably saw, but as a scary, snarling, growling, furry, biting predator.

She glanced at him. They didn't do it wolf style, did they? Ewww.

"What?" he said, not even looking up at her as he finished washing the frying pan. "Don't hesitate to ask whatever's on your mind. You need to know everything, but there will be things you'll think of that I won't. You can ask any of us anything you'd like."

"Do you...have sex as wolves?" She figured he'd either laugh at her or say yes, and she didn't know which would be worse.

"No. At least no one I know does. Humans get a lot more enjoyment out of the act. For wolves, there's a courtship phase and they are protective of each other, but it's just not the same with them when it comes to mating. It has more to do with the procreation of the species. They're innately wired that way, and only the alpha pair will have pups. That's to ensure the whole wolf pack has enough to eat and the rest of the wolves help to take care of the pups. Too many pups and yearlings would spell disaster for the whole pack. As humans, we have the human perspective. We have a mix of alphas and betas in a pack. Most of us end up pairing up with a mate and mating for life. We have our own kids, but all the pack members are eager to look after them."

"How will I know who is in the pack?"

"We'll provide you with a list. Also, when you meet them, you'll now be able to smell their wolf scent and know they're one of us. Of course, if you worked with wolves at a wolf center, you could smell like one, but it wouldn't mean that you were one. Out here, yeah."

Then she thought of the earlier rescue they'd made and how she had thought Allan's request so odd, and now she wondered...

She frowned at him. "When we rescued Franny and her baby, you told me to cancel the one ambulance and call for another. I couldn't understand because it could have meant precious minutes were wasted. Then they took her to the clinic where Tara and I were seen. Don't tell me that she and her baby are werewolves?"

"Yeah. She was so disoriented, I was afraid she was going to strip out of her clothes right then and there and turn into her wolf. Instinctively, she would have known her wolf coat would give her more protection from the cold. But she wasn't really thinking clearly because you would have seen her do it. Well, and you were cradling her baby, and babies shift when their mother does—"

"She would have suddenly turned into a wolf pup? I would have had a heart attack."

"Yeah, that was another reason to keep Franny from turning."

"So what about Franny and the red Camaro she said caused her accident? Was it Otis? Or just a really bizarre coincidence? Then again, if he killed Sarah, did he know that Franny was also a wolf?"

"I'm thinking there's got to be a common denominator," Allan said. "We need to have Franny come up here to speak with us." He couldn't have been more pleased that Debbie was focusing on the case and not completely on her werewolf issues now. She had made a valid point—something they needed to learn more about.

Debbie frowned. "Oh. My. God. The report I read about Sarah's autopsy—she had bitten her attacker. I was thinking with her human teeth, naturally, because his blood was on her teeth and mouth, and we never saw his bite marks. If she had bitten him as a wolf…has he been turned?"

"Possibly. Which may be why he disappeared for so long—he's been unable to control the shifting."

"And they said wolf fur had been caught on the trap. They believed that he had caught a wolf first and the fur was just stuck to it. But it had to have been Sarah's fur." Her mouth gaped. "I called Rowdy's office about the red Camaro when I found it in conjunction with Otis shooting Tara. What if he or any of his men had seen Tara shift?"

"That's a concern we always have to face. It's a real danger for us. Luckily, she arrived at the clinic well before Rowdy checked on the two of you and she had shifted back to her human self."

Debbie's thoughts were jumping from one scenario she'd witnessed to the next, realizing now how so much made sense. "And when the ambulance picked up Franny, I did hear a bark when she and her baby were inside."

"You asked if I heard a dog bark. I said no. Technically, she'd shifted into a wolf."

Debbie took a deep breath, thinking about what had happened to her, Tara, and Sarah. "I...I want to help bring the shooter down, Allan. I know it's going to be harder for me with the problem of shifting, but I want to help. I don't want to be left out of the loop. It's not a case of revenge either. I think of Lori and Rose and them being pregnant, well, now with Rose having her triplets, and their mates losing them and...well, maybe if I can still do this, I won't feel so...discombobulated. If Otis did try to kill Franny and her baby, we need to stop him before he hurts anyone else."

"I understand. You're staying on the case. We'll just be more careful about when we go out to search for clues."

"Was I too rough on you last night?" She felt a mix of emotions about that. Satisfaction that she had scared him a little, but she did worry he'd believe she was untamable and a danger to everyone. She couldn't imagine anything worse than being confined to his cabin for months on end without visitation rights.

"You were having a rough time of it. Nothing I

couldn't handle. And you might not think so yourself, but you're a beautiful wolf."

She gave him an annoyed look. She couldn't help it. She appreciated that he thought she was a beautiful woman. But a wolf?

His phone rang and she suspected it was Paul, as close as they were and as much as she assumed Paul was dying to learn how it went with her last night. Now she realized it didn't all have to do with having been raised as brothers either. He was Allan's pack leader. And hers now too? She groaned.

It was one thing to not like a boss and quit a job, but what if she didn't like the pack leaders' rules and wanted to just…leave?

She doubted they'd let her.

———

Allan answered the phone and said, "Yeah, Paul, we're both still alive."

Then he smiled and Debbie smiled back, though he thought her expression was a bit devious.

Allan had to be careful about what he said to Paul so he didn't antagonize Debbie, even though she left him in the kitchen and said she was getting dressed. She might still be able to hear him talking if she made the effort to eavesdrop on his half of the conversation.

"Any trouble?"

"Nah." Allan didn't want Paul to think he had to call on anyone else to help with Debbie. He thought if he and she kept an open dialogue, they'd be fine. *Eventually.* "Everything's fine. We just finished having a delightful breakfast that she prepared for us this morning."

"Really? She's back to being her normal self?" Paul sounded surprised and Allan didn't blame him.

"Yeah. She wants to keep searching into this business with the lake murder and find the shooter who nearly killed her and Tara. We can work it out."

"Are you sure? What with the phase of the full moon being out for several days?"

"We'll figure it out. She needs to do this. It'll help her to adjust if she feels some part of her life is still the same. With her enhanced wolf abilities, she'll see the usefulness in that aspect of her life."

"Okay, I trust you know what you're doing. Is she comfortable staying with you, or do we need to make some other arrangements?"

"I'd say after we managed to get through the night in one piece and she made a lovely breakfast, we're doing fine. But I'll ask her anyway."

"Can you do it now? That way I can line up someone else if she wants to move."

"Yeah, sure. She's in her bedroom getting dressed." Allan padded down the hall and knocked on her door. "Are you fine with the arrangements here, Debbie? Or do you want to stay with someone else?"

"You're going to work with me to find the shooter and you're my partner, so I'm fine with staying here," she said, not sounding pleased, but it was a start.

"Good." Allan told Paul, "She's staying with me so we can work out the details about the shooter."

"Just remember she can shift at any time, and she could get growly about it. It's got to be a frustrating time for a newly turned wolf."

Tell me about it. "I understand." Allan swore he

heard a low growl from the bedroom. "Got to go, Paul. I'll give you an update later." Before he hung up, Debbie howled and slammed into the bedroom door, sounding pissed off...*again*.

So much for keeping her progress a secret from Paul.

And so much for helping her get through this so she wouldn't feel so frustrated with her lack of control.

Allan stripped out of his boxers and opened the guest bedroom door. Instead of lunging at him this time, she sat still, like a statue, looking at his naked form, then lifted her gaze to his, puzzled, as if she wondered just what he was up to.

"We're doing this together," he said, thinking maybe if he was a wolf too, she wouldn't feel so alien. He hoped that he wouldn't scare her. He shifted and she watched, staring at him as if she were in awe, shocked, or surprised. Maybe a little of all three.

The shift was painless, just a quick warming of the muscles, a blurring of forms, and he was a wolf. A bigger wolf than she was. He hoped that didn't intimidate her.

She sniffed at the air, smelling his scent and gathering what he was feeling, which was a *lupus garou's* interest in another. Because that's just what she was now. He didn't know if it would ever work out between them. She had to want him too, forever, and she may never be prepared to mate with one of his kind.

He stood still, not getting any closer, letting her come to him. She remained where she was.

He wanted to smile, but he was certain she wouldn't understand that showing his wicked wolf canines in this instance meant he was smiling. He sighed, then moved forward. Her ears went back. She wasn't trembling, but she was unsure of his intentions. Or maybe just what it was to feel like a wolf getting to know another wolf. Again, he realized what a huge undertaking that was for her also.

―∼∞∼―

Allan was a huge wolf. Huge! Before he had shifted, he had dropped his boxers, and she'd wondered what in the world he'd planned to do. She hadn't expected him to shift into a wolf. The sight was extraordinary—so fast, the blurring of one form into the other—until he dropped to his feet as a very real wolf.

He was beautiful in a very handsome wolf way. His coat was shiny and thick. Striking silver and tan markings on his face, his chest white and his back a silvery, golden saddle. But he was so big!

He towered next to her and she tried not to cower before him. She didn't think she'd be some beta wolf, but this was a totally new experience for her. So maybe as a human she was alpha, and as a wolf, sort of beta?

She had to snap out of this and stand right up to him. Only she was afraid her legs would shake.

He licked her cheek. She bowed her head a little, and she was afraid that was cowering. She lifted her head and looked him in the eye, forced her ears to perk up, but she didn't lick him back. Wasn't that a sign she was interested in more? Like courting? Or mating? Dating?

No way did she want to go there.

She didn't know what to do in response to show there were no hard feelings right now. And that she appreciated he was trying to make her feel better by turning into a wolf. But she didn't want him to get the notion she wanted to do any mating nonsense.

So how was she supposed to react?

He moved away from her then. She was afraid she'd hurt his feelings, but then he bowed in front of her, his butt in the air, his tail wagging. She recognized it as a play bow, like the German shepherd they had raised when she was growing up did. He would do that in front of the neighbor's husky. She thought if she could relate what her dog had done to how a wolf would react, she could figure out some of this canine psychology.

The problem still was that she didn't know how to react. She wasn't ready to bow down to Allan and play with him. This was just too bizarre.

Good-naturedly and with lots of patience, he waited for her to respond.

Oh, all right. What could it hurt? Well, lots, if she bit him too hard or he bit her too hard. Then again, he would know not to. She wouldn't.

She twisted around and tackled him, growling fiercely because it just came out that way, even if she didn't mean to growl so wildly. He rolled onto his back in a purely submissive way and opened his mouth to play bite, but he was so gentle that it taught her to be gentle. Maybe they were supposed to do this in a rougher way, but for now, it was like taking baby steps.

She realized then that she couldn't have had a better teacher.

She was on top of him, going for his neck, mouthing him, when she couldn't have imagined anything yuckier than grabbing a furry beast by the neck before, but it felt right. All of it. Tackling him. Biting him. All in fun. Nothing sexual about it. She didn't think.

She noticed his tail wasn't tucked submissively between his legs, but straight out, showing he was allowing her to be on top, to feel empowered. She moved off him, giving the play bow a try to see what he would do in reaction. He watched her, then rolled off his back and rested on his belly for a moment, his ears up, his gaze on hers. Then he jumped up and she whipped around and ran. She hadn't meant to. She knew you never ran before a wild animal. And she knew he was so much bigger than her that he wouldn't have any trouble catching her.

He nipped her butt and she yipped in startled surprise. He did it again, but this time she rounded on him, and they were in his bedroom, standing on their hind legs, teeth biting at each other's mouths.

They played like that for half an hour, her tackling him, him tackling her, and then they sat panting in his living room, studying each other. He stood, then motioned to the hallway with his head.

He looked as tired as she felt after the restless night they'd had. He loped off toward his bedroom, and she followed him, only this time she nipped him in the butt. He barked at her, a happy kind of bark.

She'd like to think this was all there was to it. But she knew better. If she shifted outside his cabin, it could spell disaster.

Allan couldn't think of a better way to end their play than to take a nap with each other. Thankfully, Debbie seemed to like the idea, and he was proud of her for playing so well. He thought at first she wouldn't play with him. Or that it was too difficult to understand what he was trying to tell her while he was in his wolf coat. But she picked up really quickly on cues, so he thought this might not be so hard after all. The shifting without warning? That was another story.

They curled up together in bed, her head over his body, his head tucked close to hers. He thought they might even go for a run together tonight in the woods. But what if she turned into her human form in the frozen cold? He'd have to shift and carry her home, and they'd both be naked. If it were summer, it wouldn't be quite such a bad an idea.

He *could* take her for a walk in the woods as a human and carry a backpack of winter clothes for her so that she could dress if she shifted. It wouldn't be the best plan, but it would be nice for her to get out and smell the woods and animal scents. To get used to them as a wolf. He'd be with her so if any hunter showed up, he'd set him straight about his pet wolf. And he'd be armed.

He'd talk about it later with her to see what she'd like to do. He thought being confined to the house would drive her batty after a while. It would him.

His phone rang, but Debbie didn't stir, and he wasn't getting up and shifting to get it. It was probably Paul to see if he was all right. Allan didn't want to disturb what he and Debbie had for the moment. Peace. Quiet. Naptime. Until she woke, and then who knew what would happen next.

"Do you think Allan's okay?" Lori asked Paul again. She couldn't help it. She wasn't a worrywart, but she had been concerned when Paul said that Debbie had shifted and was growling in the background, and Allan had ended the call right away.

"I think they're fine. Maybe they didn't sleep well, and they're taking a nap now. I don't want to disturb them if he's making any progress with Debbie. They need the alone time."

"Like we had?"

"Well," he said, pulling Lori into his arms so her back was against his chest and he could gently caress her swollen breasts and her swelling tummy. "Our alone time was a lot different."

She sighed. "I thought maybe if I went over there and talked with her, she would be less growly, you know, because I'm so pregnant, and she'd behave better."

"I think she's in good hands with Allan. You know how much he cares for her. He'll handle this right."

"I hope she's not too angry with all of us. I wonder if he told her that she has my wolf genes."

"As long as it didn't make her pregnant and it saved her life, I'm certain she'll be all right with it. Speaking of napping and having a rough night of it..."

She sagged against him. "If you'll give me a back rub."

He smiled and kissed the top of her head. "I'll give you much more than that." Then he led her to their bedroom.

Chapter 18

ALLAN WOKE TO FIND A NAKED WOMAN CURLED UP against him, only he was still all wolf. He shifted and pulled the covers over them, wondering what the next phase in training would be. He realized that's what this was going to be for a while. An in-house boot camp for a *lupus garou* until Debbie could get her shifting under control. He'd never really thought anything about the full moon, except that he loved how it lighted the whole sky at night.

Because of the situation with Debbie, he was counting down the days when the new moon was here, and she wouldn't be able to shift for a week. He planned to pack in a month's worth of outdoor activities in that week—searching crime scenes, diving, shopping trips, eating out, and movies, anything that she wanted to do that she couldn't during the rest of the month until she could control her shifting better.

Maybe if she had a week of scheduled activities crammed in, she'd be ready for three weeks of not going places as much. At least he hoped that's what they could do. He'd propose it to her when she woke.

Her naked body resting against his had stirred longings again for something more. He felt driven to make her see the benefit of having him for her mate. Someone who could protect her, show her the ropes, and love her unconditionally. They would be perfect for each other, he thought, as much as they had been compatible before she was turned. He really believed if she hadn't been turned, and he hadn't been a wolf, they would have been perfect as human companions.

So he wasn't giving up on the notion.

He thought about what she'd said earlier. That she'd woken as a woman, naked against him. She must have fled the bed right away or he would have noticed.

Would she flee the bed when she woke this time? He hoped not. If not, he figured she had to agree they were dating, of a sort. Wouldn't she?

Debbie couldn't believe she had woken and found herself naked against Allan again, except this time she was sleeping against his naked body. And he had to have known it or she wouldn't be wrapped up in his arms underneath the covers in a totally human way.

She had to admit she loved being held in his arms like this. Loved the way he was so tender. She wished they could have done this as humans and she didn't have to deal with this wolf business. But she was glad she was alive and better than fit. She had to remind herself of it every time she shifted and was furious over it.

Right now, like this, she wasn't sure what to do. Unless she quit coming to bed with him as a wolf, she was bound to keep waking up against him as a naked woman so she might as well just get used to it.

He must have felt her tense, because he opened his eyes and sighed. "I've been thinking—"

"I'm not dating you." She closed her eyes and snuggled against him, giving up the pretense that she wasn't happy with this—here, with him.

"Okay. But I was thinking about the week of the new moon."

"Which is three weeks from now." She couldn't help but be irritated about it.

"Right. We'll do everything during that week. Investigations into the murders, diving, rescuing. Wherever we're needed. We'll do our investigative work at home until then. Internet searches, whatever we can run down. During the week you're free from shifting, we can go to the movies, eat out, shop, whatever you'd love to do."

"I can't really go anywhere for three weeks, can I?" she asked, hating that she would be confined like that. She loved the outdoors and she loved her job because she could go diving and help rescue others or help solve crimes. She hated that she'd be cooped up in the cabin for weeks on end, which she suspected would be the ultimate case of cabin fever.

"After a time, you only will have trouble during the full moon. We'll have get-togethers with other pack members. If you have to shift, you can do so in a bedroom, and then you can rejoin the party."

"As a wolf," she said skeptically.

"Yeah. But we're all *lupus garous*, so everyone will understand and have no problem with it."

"But me."

"It would be a safe way to learn to get used to it. After a while, it will seem like no big deal to you."

"I don't see how I'll ever get used to it."

"You will. Do you remember Michael, the artist?"

"Who paints pictures of wolves? Is everyone a wolf but me?"

Allan smiled. "He's fairly newly turned. He's just as happy as can be."

"No wonder he paints such beautiful portraits of wolves. I thought they were drugged so that they could sit and be photographed with people or out in nature."

"Nope. He's one of us, and the portraits he does? Only of the *lupus garous* who are willing to sit still long enough to have their portrait taken."

"You haven't had one made of you?"

"No. Nor has Paul. We couldn't believe he had Lori sitting long enough to do hers."

"Maybe he takes photographs."

"He says he can't capture the essence of the wolf unless he paints the actual wolf."

"How come he was turned?" Debbie asked, afraid he'd seen someone shift and was forced to be one of them.

"You know Hunter, the leader of Paul's and my SEAL team?"

"He lives on the Oregon coast."

"Right. He fell in love with a woman who had wolf genes from a parent. She wanted to be mated to Hunter, and she was really close to her brother."

"So they turned him?"

"Tessa did. He was glad because they are really close, and he would have been left out of the family otherwise."

"If he had these wolf roots too, it's not exactly the same as with me."

"Well, it is, in that they didn't have any of the wolf senses, the shifting, none of that. So since Hunter is Tessa's mate, he oversees her shifting, and others watch Michael because he has no mate."

"He came here to the art festival. I saw him. No one

was with him." Then she thought back to how either
Allan's mother, sister, or Lori's grandmother had been
nearby. They had a booth where they were selling jams
and salsas and hand-beaded moccasins. "Oh, scratch
that. I remember he was with your family. He must have
had the shifting down fairly well then if he was out in
public." She hoped it hadn't been long so she could have
some of her old life back. Although it would never be
quite the same again.

"He does. But it's been two years now. Even at that,
he has trouble during the night that the moon is at its
fullest and some days after."

"Two years? Ohmigod. I will never last two years
at this."

Allan rubbed her arm. "Yeah, you will. You'll learn
to cope with it and be just fine."

She couldn't believe being with him like this felt so
natural, but she figured it would have gotten to this if
they'd continued to make love like they had at her place.
Something about her playing with him as a wolf and
then napping…she didn't know. But she was already
feeling like she was closer to him than she'd ever been
to a man she had been interested in being with.

Had turning her into a wolf made that happen? She
didn't think so. She'd been fascinated with him from
the beginning. Maybe he was right in saying that somehow they saw in each other what they needed to feel
complete. Even before he should have thought that way,
because he was a wolf shifter.

If they continued to get naked like this and ended
up in bed together every time? She figured he wouldn't
need to date her. She'd be all marshmallows and agree

to a mating before she was ready. Until she turned into a wolf again.

———~~~———

Later that afternoon, Franny agreed to come and talk with them to see if she could aid them in discovering Otis's whereabouts and how he came to be here and caused her accident. She hadn't known him by that name, but when Lori had showed her the picture of Otis, Franny said he was the same man who had dated her and then stalked her.

It was sunny and a bit warmer when she arrived. Lori's grandmother was taking care of her baby while Franny's husband was busy with his chef duties at the Italian restaurant.

Franny sat across from Allan and Debbie, who was sitting on the couch in her wolf form, annoyed that she couldn't hold her human form for an hour or so while Franny talked to them.

"Debbie was concerned you would feel uncomfortable with her listening in on the conversation as a wolf," Allan said, not wanting to mention it because he knew Franny wouldn't mind at all. Like everyone else in the pack, Franny wanted Debbie to feel at ease around them in any form she was in. But Debbie had insisted he mention it, right before she had to shift.

Franny shook her head, looking tense.

"Okay, what we're trying to put together is when you were seeing Otis and then stopped seeing him. He killed Sarah around the day of your accident, maybe the night before, according to the autopsy reports. From what we understand, he was in a LARP group and Sarah became his best friend's lover."

"Lloyd."

"Right. So then she turned Lloyd. Had she then convinced him to come up here with her to join our pack instead of joining Devlyn's in Colorado? I assume she knew Devlyn wouldn't have approved of her turning Lloyd when he wanted to be a werewolf hunter. And he was best friends with Otis, also a werewolf hunter, who was ready to kill any werewolf he could locate and genuine wolves too. Because of her desire to come out as a werewolf, Devlyn wouldn't accept her in the pack.

"What if she and Lloyd were together still and she told him to come here? Then he told Otis? We never found any evidence she had a car anywhere in the area. Then Otis murdered Lloyd because he was also a werewolf. Lloyd had no defensive wounds on him, making it appear as though he didn't believe his friend Otis was going to kill him."

"Otis must not have had any of your names, or he would have tried hunting you down, don't you think?" Franny asked.

"I believe that's why he just shot wolves that were checking out the blood left at the site. But it seems like too much of a coincidence that he ran you off the road, that he knew you were here, when he was most likely trying to learn who else was a werewolf in the pack Sarah planned to join."

"He must not have seen Rose and Lori arrive," Franny agreed.

"Yeah, we got damn lucky on that."

Allan sensed Franny knew more than she was letting on. Suddenly, Debbie bolted from the couch, sending decorator pillows flying as she raced to the bedroom.

He suspected she was shifting again, but it was the first time she was able to do so that soon after the last shift.

He and Franny waited for Debbie to rejoin them, not wanting her to miss out on the talk.

When she stalked back in the room, she was wearing a pale blue sweater, jeans, and fluffy blue slippers. She curled up with him on the couch and he wrapped his arm around her, glad she was happy to be back to her human form.

"Did you know Sarah?" Debbie asked.

Allan had never considered such a thing. As far as he knew, Sarah was a stranger to the pack and somehow had heard they were looking for wolves—courtesy of Lori's grandma and his mother.

Franny hesitated, looking a little panicked.

"How did you meet Otis?" Debbie asked.

Franny let out her breath. "Through Sarah. We knew each other in drama classes at the community college in Boise. She was really wild; I wasn't. She'd met these two guys—Lloyd and Otis. Only Otis went by the name of Cleveland when I knew him. She started dating Lloyd, and I went out with Otis. Then I met Gary, my wolf mate, and I called it quits with Otis. He was really angry about it. Kept stalking me and Gary. Then Sarah left for southern Montana and said that Otis and Lloyd had headed out that way too.

"I didn't hear from her again until right before... before Lori and Rose found her. Sarah and I had been close friends. She had some notion we should come out as *lupus garous*—tell people what we were. That people would see we weren't vicious or anything. I'd hoped someone would convince her how foolish the notion was. I figured she might get in trouble with a wolf pack over her wild ideas. Not that she'd die at the hand of some professed werewolf hunter."

"Did you know Otis had notions of killing were-wolves?" Debbie asked.

Franny looked at her lap. "Yes. His talk about finding werewolves amused me. He hadn't found any, but he said he was looking. I said they could be just anyone, didn't he think? No way did I believe he'd ever really run across any, other than Sarah and me, and he was clueless about us. We figured he always would be. I feel I am to blame for indulging in his illusion too."

"Why didn't you tell us before that you knew Sarah?" Allan asked.

"She wanted to be a member of the wolf pack in Boise that Gary belonged to. He was one of the sub-leaders who voted her down. He said she should be put out of her misery before some of our kind were killed because of her wild ideas. When I met him and heard how he felt about her, I didn't want him to know I had been running with her. I hadn't wanted him to know about Otis either because I'd stayed with him much longer than is safe for our kind. I just wanted that part of my life to be over and to start anew with Gary."

"But you knew her name and the men who had been involved with her when we didn't. We might have caught up with him sooner," Allan said, annoyed.

"I was really shaken up with the car accident and nearly losing my baby. No one showed me the picture of the woman Lori and Rose had found."

"Okay," Allan said, backing off a bit. That had prob-ably been Lori's call.

"I didn't learn of it until recently… I heard you went to southern Montana to investigate some lead, but not anything about it. As far as I knew, Otis had learned where Gary and I were and was stalking me, and now he wanted to kill me for leaving him. I had no idea he was in the area because Sarah was."

"Sarah told Rose she was coming in a few weeks," Allan said.

"I didn't know she was coming. She had gotten in touch with me about my pack, sent me a letter and her new phone number. I had talked to her about it. I thought between you and Paul, because you were SEALs, you could set her on the right path. She never got in touch with me to say she was coming or had arrived. I just thought the dead woman was someone else who had come to check out the pack. Or a random wolf in the area." Franny swallowed hard. "I jeopardized the whole pack. She said she was leaving Lloyd. She never told me she had turned him. If she had told him about our pack, I believe Otis would have tortured her until he knew her contact."

"What if she told him you were the contact? And that's why he tried to kill you?" Debbie asked.

Franny chewed on her bottom lip. "Why didn't he try to coerce the truth out of me then?"

"Maybe he planned to but we came upon the accident scene too quickly," Debbie said.

"Did you see him stop, then leave?" Allan asked.

"No. I was trying to get myself unbuckled and get out of the SUV because it was filling up fast with water. I was upside down, I think I was unconscious for a few seconds. I don't remember the SUV flipping, just the rough ride down the slope. After I managed to get out, I was attempting to open the back door to reach Stacy. I don't believe I was thinking straight at the time. Now, I realize I should have crawled between the seats and released her. It didn't even come to mind."

Allan could relate. "That's understandable. You were hypothermic and in shock."

Franny nodded. "He might have figured we had drowned when I didn't leave the car right away, and then he left when he heard or saw you coming."

"Do you have any idea where he might be staying?" Debbie asked.

"We all went camping together. Lloyd and Otis might not be wolves, but they know survival training from their time in the military and growing up. Otis is a survivalist. He might be staying at some rundown motel, or he could be living off the land."

"It's damn cold out there," Allan said.

"He's originally from Alaska. I'm sorry I didn't tell you all this before, but I didn't even know Sarah was the one Otis had killed. When I learned about it, you seemed to already know everything I did. I...didn't want to talk about it."

"We're a pack," Allan said. "That means sharing any information that could lead to protecting our pack."

She nodded.

"Why would you want her to join the pack when your mate didn't like her?" Allan asked.

"She seemed so lost. I worried about her. I really thought you and Paul could help her."

"Do you want to have lunch with us?" Debbie asked cheerfully.

Allan and Franny looked at her. He was as surprised as Franny looked.

"I'm hungry, and I'm fixing lunch." Debbie got off the couch and headed for the kitchen.

"I should get back to Stacy. I didn't mean for Emma to have to look after her for that long."

"Nonsense," Debbie said. "From what I've heard, Emma and her quilting friends can't get enough of taking care of babies. They are all adopting the little ones in the pack."

Allan smiled. He hadn't thought Debbie liked babies all that much. Maybe just not the idea of having her own.

Chapter 19

WHEN FRANNY LEFT AFTER LUNCH, DEBBIE TOOK ALLAN to the guest room where he'd set up both their computers. "I want to check all the rundown motels in the area."

"I'll call Paul and ask if he can put someone on the detail. You can't go anywhere."

"I know, but that's what I would have done if I could have. What if they assign you another dive partner while I'm 'recuperating' from my injuries?"

"The sheriff knows I'm here taking care of you and I'm not going anywhere."

She was glad to hear it. She figured if the sheriff found another female diver for Allan to work with, she wouldn't be able to control her wolf half one bit.

"Why did you end the interview with Franny and serve lunch?" Allan asked.

"She had told us everything she knew. She felt bad her friend had died, and she felt she was responsible."

Allan pulled Debbie into his arms and hugged her. "Women are so much better at some things."

She smiled up at him and hugged him back. "I was afraid you'd be mad at me."

"No. I was surprised, but women and men think differently. I could tell you made a real friend in Franny this afternoon. And that's a good thing."

"She felt guilty that her actions could have resulted in Sarah's death."

"I think now she understands she has to keep the leaders informed if something might affect the pack. You got a lot further than I would have with her. We make a good team."

―⁓―

That evening, Tara came over with her brother and mother, Lori and Paul to Allan's cabin to discuss why she had been running as a wolf and what had happened to her.

Tara wrung her hands as she sat on the couch next to her mother and Everett. She reminded him of the way Franny had acted earlier—guilty, beta-like, anxious.

"I...know I shouldn't have done what I did," she said so demurely, Allan felt bad for her. Everyone had wanted him to date Tara, but she was so mousy, she just wasn't his type. He did care for her like a sister, and at that moment, he wanted to give her a hug and tell her what she had to say was significant.

By doing what she did, she had jeopardized all of their lives, not just her own. They wanted to understand her reasoning and ensure no one else was tempted to do anything like it.

"Everyone is important to the pack," Tara continued. "But me. I wanted to do something to help. I thought if I could draw him out, I could stop him. Not that I thought I could stop him in what he was doing exactly, but maybe I could locate his vehicle and learn where he was staying locally."

"So how did you find him? Or did he find you?" Paul asked.

"I followed six different hunters that day. All were

armed with rifles, and I was careful to keep out of sight. They were hunting elk, and none of the men looked like the picture that you had passed around to the pack. I really didn't expect to find him that day. But I prayed I would. I'd been doing this for several days, really. Every day, I'd find hunters, follow them, listen to their conversations, then look for others, hear shots fired, and check them out.

"That last day, I slipped down to the water's edge to get some water to drink. I heard a person coming, only when I looked at first, I didn't think it was him. Until he said, 'One less werewolf to hunt down!' And began shooting. I meant to bolt, but he shot so many bullets at me, I didn't think I could run away. Instead, I collapsed and played dead."

Except that she'd stopped breathing and had nearly died. Allan remembered the horror of that day as if it had just happened. Debbie's eyes filled with tears. He took her hand and held it, but it wasn't enough. He tucked her under his arm and she relaxed against him. He could only imagine what she was feeling—that she had intended to put the wolf, Tara, out of her misery. That if he hadn't stopped Debbie, she would have killed her.

"All of you have worked so hard to keep the pack safe from other wolves, from rabid wolves in the past, and from humans who would kill us if they knew what we were. I...I just wanted to help. I'm so sorry. I know what I did was wrong, and it could have gotten us all in a lot of trouble." Tara looked at Debbie. "I'm so sorry, Debbie. I don't know how you could be managing with all this thrust on you so suddenly. It's all my fault and I feel terrible."

Debbie swallowed hard. "We're both alive and the man responsible is still out there. He's the one who's at fault. Not you."

Tara's eyes filled with tears and she looked down at her hands, but then she turned her attention to Debbie again. "I'm sorry I got you involved in this, but for Allan's sake, I'm glad you're one of us."

Allan rubbed Debbie's arm. "I agree with you on that."

Lori then talked about protocols and how everyone was supposed to talk with her or Paul first before they ventured into something risky that might cause trouble for the pack.

Debbie was quiet and Allan wondered what she was thinking about all this. That she was living a real nightmare? He rubbed her arm and gave her body a reassuring squeeze.

With the pack leader business finished, Tara and her mother and brother left.

Lori said, "I hope we didn't upset you by having you join us in the meeting, Debbie."

Allan knew Lori and Paul wanted to include her because she'd been so involved in what had happened, and Tara had wanted to say she was sorry. They had also wanted to impress upon her, as well as Tara and her family, the importance of the pack and how everything that might involve them had to be cleared through the leaders.

"No. I was glad to be able to tell Tara it wasn't her fault I was injured so badly," Debbie said. "I didn't even realize she had felt she was responsible. I...felt awful that I might have killed her if Allan hadn't stopped me."

"You wanted only the best for the welfare of the

wolf, had it been strictly a wolf." Lori took Paul's hand. "Are you ready to go home? I think I need to lie down."

"That means I've got massage duty," Paul said.

"Did anyone learn anything about any local medical facility taking care of a man suffering from a gunshot wound?" Allan asked.

"No. I wonder if he took care of it himself," Paul said.

"Maybe he won't be able to shoot anyone else." Debbie sounded hopeful.

"Infection, loss of blood, or both could really hamper his ability to do anyone any more harm." Allan walked Paul and Lori out to their car. "Unless…"

"He's a wolf like us and his healing abilities saved his life," Lori said. "Wouldn't that be ironic?"

"And not in a good way," Paul said.

"I'm going to change," Debbie said. "Night, all."

As soon as she headed for her bedroom, Lori whispered, "Change for bed or shift into her wolf?"

"Shift," Allan said.

"How are things between the two of you?" Lori asked.

"No courting or dating." Then he smiled. "All that matters is a mating, so however we get there, if we do, it works for me."

"Today, we're starting a new routine," Allan said after the second week of Debbie's shifting. She was having a little more control over it as they approached the week of the new moon. He had seen how often she kept checking the lunar calendar he had bought her. She couldn't wait as she marked off the days in black Magic Marker. "We're going to have daily guests for a while."

She grumbled. "I'm being treated like a new puppy that needs to be socialized with others."

He smiled. She had often mentioned how she felt like a new puppy, learning all she could about living as a part-time canine. It had been like that for her to some extent, but she wasn't puppy age and she had her adult human perspective on life in general. She'd been really good about all the lessons, and he hoped this would help to show their pack unity and make her feel welcome. To start out, mostly just the members of the original pack visited: Paul and Lori, Allan's mom and sister and her mate, and Lori's grandmother. Everyone came at different times of the day on separate days and usually alone so Debbie didn't feel overwhelmed. Later, newer members of the pack visited. All had worked out well.

Today was special. They were having a mother and her twin five-year-olds over. This was the first time that Debbie would be exposed to the youngest members of the pack, besides Rose's and Franny's babies.

"Cindy Summerset is coming over with her twin girls after we eat lunch," Allan said as they sat down to eat grilled cheese sandwiches he had made. That was one of his specialties and she loved them, so he loved fixing them for her.

He didn't know why he reminded her of the pack member visits every day. Maybe to help her mentally prepare herself.

"I'll be out chopping some much-needed firewood while you visit with them." He'd tried to do a mix of visits, some where he was there with them, sometimes slipping out to give her more alone time with the pack members.

"They're going to be afraid of me if I shift. The girls, I mean."

"Not at all. You'll be fine. And for the last two days, even though you had the urge to shift, you didn't. So you're making real progress." He had seen the way Debbie had visibly tensed, as if she was holding back the urge to give in. Lori was visiting that day and quickly talked about swimming and diving at the lake anytime Debbie wanted. Though Debbie thanked her and seemed to want to do it, Allan noted that most of her concentration had been on forcing back the urge to shift. He'd seen the way she'd tightened her hands into fists and the strain on her face while he was cleaning out the fireplace.

It helped when a pack member talked away like nothing was amiss, though everyone could read the wolf cues. For Debbie to continue with the conversation and not totally freeze up said much about her gaining some control of her abilities. And that was a really good sign. Some newly turned wolves took much longer to adapt.

When the twins and their mother arrived, Allan made introductions and set the girls up at the table with milk and the homemade chocolate-chip cookies Debbie often made for pack visits. Rose had asked if she could sell them in her gift store along with the salsas and other things their mother made, and Debbie had loved being asked. And then Allan excused himself to chop wood.

Debbie didn't mind. She'd rather he didn't see her make a fool of herself if she had to shift all of a sudden when guests were here.

The girls were dressed in blue jeans and sweaters featuring flocks of fluffy sheep. The twins had backpacks, which they set on the dining table, unpacking coloring books and crayons. Debbie smiled. The twins were adorable. They glanced at her every once in a while as she and their mother talked, looking a bit curious.

"I started working out in Lori's martial arts classes. I have so much more confidence now than when I first began," Cindy said.

Debbie wondered if Cindy thought that if Debbie took some classes, she'd feel better about herself. She already knew martial arts so that she could apprehend criminals if she needed to, or to protect herself. She hadn't had any confidence issues until she began turning into a wolf. Taking martial arts classes wasn't going to cure that.

"She has all *lupus garou* classes and some that are just for female students," Cindy continued.

One of the girls, Eliza, was vigorously coloring large areas of her page with blue crayon. The other, Meghan, was carefully working on something small with a purple crayon.

Debbie wondered where Cindy's mate was, since they mated for life. She guessed she had lost him. All she knew was that Cindy had joined the pack and was raising the girls on her own.

"Do you take classes too?" Debbie asked the girls.

They both looked over at her. "Uh-huh," they said in unison.

"Yes, ma'am," their mother corrected them.

"Yes, ma'am," they both quickly said.

Debbie smiled at them. They were sure sweet.

"Momma said you sometimes shift when you don't

want to," Eliza said. Her blond curls were a little darker than her sister's, and she was an inch taller and her cheeks fuller.

Her eyes widening, their mother looked horrified, and she opened her mouth to speak.

"Are you going to shift? Momma said not to act shocked if you did," Meghan said matter-of-factly.

"I'm so sorry," Cindy said, her cheeks flushed.

"No, that's quite all right. I don't feel like shifting right now. Sometimes it just happens when I least expect it."

"Did you ever get stuck in your clothes when you started to change?" Eliza asked.

Often, but she wasn't about to tell the girls about those times.

"Oh, I did once," Meghan interjected before Debbie could respond. "We shift when Momma does so we don't get into trouble." Meghan's eyes grew big and she leaned toward Debbie as if she was about to tell her a big secret. "I wasn't listening to Momma when I was supposed to. She said we were to get undressed 'cuz we were going to shift."

"You never listen," Eliza said, coloring more of her picture blue.

"I do too." Meghan stuck her tongue out at her.

"So what happened?" Debbie was getting a kick out of the twins and was so glad Cindy had brought them over.

Meghan sighed dramatically. "I had my purple socks on still."

"That was funny," Eliza said, nodding vigorously. "Whoever heard of a wolf wearing socks? I would have laughed, but I was a wolf too."

"Yeah, then you tried to pull it off with your teeth and put holes in it. Then Momma got mad at both of us." Meghan gave her sister a pointed look.

"I was just trying to help you take off your sock. I didn't know my wolf teeth would put holes in it. But then you grabbed it back. So they weren't all my teeth marks."

"They were my socks and you were trying to take one away."

"You were almost standing on your head, trying to pull off the one, and I was just helping you."

"So you played tug-of-war with it?" Debbie could just imagine the two young wolf pups playing tug-of-war with the purple sock, both shaking furiously, growling, and finally catching Mom's attention.

"Yes," their mother said. "Believe me, with two wolf pups tugging on a sock, that was the end of it."

Debbie laughed. "I can imagine." She figured Meghan had forgotten her question, and Debbie was glad for that.

But then Eliza asked, "Did you ever do that? Shift when you were still dressed?"

"It isn't polite to ask," their mother said, "unless she wants to share on her own."

The girls looked from their mother to Debbie to see if she would fess up.

No way was she going to say how embarrassing it had been to have to shift when she wasn't ready. She hadn't wanted Allan to see her like that, but he hadn't laughed, well, smiled a little when she was still wearing her panties and bra one time. She could see where there was a real benefit to living in year-round warmer climates—fewer clothes to remove in a crisis.

"Your mother is right. I will say the first time I ever shifted, I was taking a bath, so I was one wet wolf."

The girls giggled.

"Momma never washes us when we're wolves because she's a wolf at the same time. But we swim across a stream to practice swimming at night sometimes and then we're wet wolves when we get home. Momma makes us shake a lot before we go inside."

Debbie was having a lovely time with the girls and their mother. But while she and Cindy were having hot tea and chocolate chip cookies, she felt the urge to shift. She swore Cindy knew it, and so did the girls.

Debbie wasn't sure what gave her away every time, but usually whoever was visiting would hurry to take over the conversation. She thought they were trying to help get her mind off the impending shift. In truth, she had to concentrate on making the urge go away while still acting as though she wasn't zoned out.

"Do you want to shift now?" Meghan asked. "If you do, we can too, and you can remember what we look like as wolves if we see you later like that."

Meghan and her sister looked back at their mom to see if it was all right with her.

"Sure, but only if Debbie wants to. She might not want to be a wolf right now," Cindy said.

Seeing the girls really wanted her to, Debbie hesitated for only a moment. "All right. That works for me."

The girls' faces lit up. They dropped their crayons on the table and then jumped down from their chairs.

"Be back in a minute," Debbie said, not sure what to expect or how to act around the girls when they were wolf pups.

For the first time ever, her company actually wanted her to shift. And she was actually happy to. When she returned as a wolf, the girls were wearing their wolf coats. Both were tan wolves with a little black on their faces and ears and the tips of their tails. Their mom was a wolf too. Debbie knew the girls were excited about it, but she hoped their mom truly hadn't minded.

They were cute, just like most pups were. Instead of being five-year-old wolves, which would have made them full-grown adults, they looked more like five- or six-month-old pups or younger. She'd seen yearlings on a TV show and they had been bigger than the girls.

They came over and sniffed her, which was a way of getting to know her scent and greeting a fellow wolf in the pack. And then they wanted to play with her. She had a blast. It was so different from when she played with Allan. They growled viciously and she tackled them in fun, but gently. She loved it and was glad Allan and Cindy had suggested she visit with the twins. This did not change her mind about having a litter of pups herself. But she loved this added dimension to her new persona.

Maybe she could get used to this new business after all. Not that she really had much of a choice.

Chapter 20

AFTER THE GIRLS AND THEIR MOTHER LEFT, ALLAN said to Debbie, "Let's do some more investigating into Lloyd and Otis. Maybe we'll find something that might lead to a location for Otis now."

They had two velour high-back chairs at his desk, and though she had a computer of her own, they did this together, each searching for clues the other might miss. Instead of watching a movie, reading books, or playing video games, this was what he and Debbie loved doing most. Trying to catch the killer out there.

They'd been searching for clues all along, in between visits with the pack members. After they discovered some information about Lloyd's and Otis's stints in the army—they'd both been snipers, with nothing remarkable about the five years they'd each served—Debbie began searching for their Facebook pages. Both had listed themselves as werewolf hunters in a LARP group in Helena, Montana. Allan and Debbie knew they had hit pay dirt. They began reading all of the posts about werewolves—how to locate them and kill them. One of the men had said, "If you want to join us, we're hunting every last one of them down."

They had hundreds of comments from people who loved the idea of pretending to be werewolf hunters. They also had hundreds of comments from "wolf packs" condemning them for their stand against werewolves.

It all looked fairly harmless, except that Otis most likely had murdered both Lloyd and Sarah. The day that Allan and Debbie had searched Lloyd's submerged car, hoping to find the driver alive, was the last time Lloyd had posted on Facebook. Even then he was touting his werewolf-hunter status, although he had been a *lupus garou* for some time.

Just as they found his status comments on the page, Debbie swore, jumped out of her chair, and began stripping out of her clothes. Allan wished she was doing it because she wanted hot sex with him, not because she couldn't control the urge to shift.

Instead of growling and pacing like she often did until she got her annoyance under control, she jumped back on the chair as a wolf and began reading the comments again. Allan smiled at her. "Tell me when you want me to scroll down."

And that's how they did it. Her wolf half wasn't going to stop her now, and he loved that they could deal with this in a more positive way.

Lloyd wrote: *We've found a nest of werewolves near Bigfork and have caught one already. I've been pumping her for info on where the rest of the pack is. We'll keep you posted.*

And that was the last time he had been on Facebook.

Debbie nodded her wolf's head, and Allan scrolled down a bit more.

Otis wrote: *We're working on infiltrating one of their packs, and we've learned some things we didn't know. You can drown a werewolf. He's not invincible. Of course, we all know silver bullets will kill them.*

Debbie barked.

"Sarah must have told Lloyd our kind could drown, unless Otis had already killed someone that way," Allan said. "Although he killed Lloyd with a blunt instrument and then submerged the car. In any event, Otis wrote this before he murdered his friend. Lloyd must not have seen it coming. On the Facebook page, there's no indication that Lloyd had been turned. He acts as though he's a hunter and nothing more. There's no sign that he wanted Otis to kill him for what he had become either. But it appears he knew about our pack."

Debbie suddenly shifted and began pulling on her clothes. "Because of Sarah. Did she then tell Lloyd her good friend Franny was one? And he told Otis?"

"Good bet if Lloyd was trying to stay on Otis's good side. But we've had protection for Franny, so if Otis thought to locate her again to learn who was in the pack, he's not going to be successful."

In the three weeks before the phase of the new moon passed, Allan had taken Debbie on several runs as a wolf at dawn and dusk. She was learning the pack's scent trails and how to get back to the cabin on her own from anywhere they ended up. She was still sometimes aggravated by the sudden urges to shift. At first, he carried a backpack with her clothes in it and remained in his human form in case she needed her clothes. For the first week of the full moon, that had been important. Three nights in a row, she'd shifted at dusk when they were out on a run.

If he had been her, he would have felt just as exasperated. He couldn't blame her. Having little control over her life was frustrating. He tried to be patient and let her work it out on her own until she could deal with it. He had to because he wouldn't be with her always. They'd planned so many activities for the week of the new moon, he assumed they'd be dead tired every night. If they could even get to everything she'd planned.

Today was the first day of the phase of the new moon and of her weeklong freedom from shifting. She was up at the crack of dawn, having prepared breakfast, and had already packed her diving gear in the car. He worried about her frame of mind when the full moon returned and she couldn't do this for the other three weeks of the month. At least not for a while. As the days went on, she'd get better at it, except for the week of the full moon.

He smiled at her and wanted to say that she looked like she was ready for Christmas, but thought better of it. She'd be reminded that this wouldn't last forever. He was glad she was so excited. It made him feel just as glad to see her so happy.

He sat down to eat his waffles and maple syrup. She had already scarfed hers down, taken her dish to the kitchen, and begun going over her list and checking it twice. He couldn't stop thinking of the day as though it was Christmas.

This morning, they were going diving before it was even light out. Just a fun dive in the same spot where Lloyd's body had been discovered in the stolen blue Impala. Allan didn't think they'd find any other evidence, but since Debbie wanted to dive and do some out-of-doors investigative work, they decided to go to that location, just in case.

Sometime later today, they would pick up her car at his mother's place so Debbie could use it anytime she wanted to. That was part of the deal. She could run off and do her own thing for the week too. With the caveat to be careful in case the shooter was looking to target her. They hadn't had any breaks in the case and no further shootings or killings related to it, so they assumed the shooter had left the area.

Allan wanted Debbie to feel as normal as possible, like she had her old life back, except that she was living with him now and could only do police-contracted dive work this week.

"I don't want you to feel bad about the way I feel, but I'm so excited," she said, hurrying him out to the hatchback.

"I'm thrilled for you, Debbie. You always brighten my day."

"Ha, not when I'm all snarly and growly because I have to shift when I don't want to."

"Always. It's understandable. If I were you, I'd feel the same way, but it'll get better. And I want you to know I love you even when you're being a growly wolf. Hell, you should see me when I'm all growly."

"Oh?"

"Well, not around you. But if I'd seen that damned shooter, believe me I would have been growling with extreme killing precision in mind."

"I wish you could have. I wonder what Otis is driving now that the police impounded his Camaro."

"If it had been me, I would have put a tracking device on it and let him come back for the car."

"Which he might have expected anyway."

"True."

When they arrived at the scene, it was just as cold as the last time. Getting used to the chilly temperature of the lake always took a few minutes.

They dived as long as they could, and when they were through, they did their safety stops and left the water. They hadn't found anything new in the water or anywhere around the area. But Debbie looked so pleased to be back to work, he was glad they'd come here first.

The pizza place was on their list, and though Allan wasn't real fond of the idea, she had invited Rowdy to join them for her coming-out. They'd played it cool, telling the sheriff's department her recovery would take months, but when she felt well enough, she'd step in wherever needed. They figured if she did a lot this week with the department, they would say next week that she'd had a relapse. Maybe by the time another month had rolled around, she would be doing well enough to work a little at a time.

After they got out of the water, they removed their tanks and masks and headed for the road where they had parked their car.

"Didn't think you'd take that long on the dive," a man said.

Parked behind Allan's hatchback was the black sedan.

With his brows raised, Vaughn Greystoke was leaning against Allan's vehicle, arms folded across his chest and looking like a military man with a mission.

Chapter 21

DEBBIE'S HEART WAS BEATING TRIPLE TIME WHEN SHE saw Vaughn Greystoke leaning against Allan's car.

The lethal-looking man was wearing a white parka and black cargo pants, shit-kicker boots, and mirrored sunglasses, his dark-brown hair cut military short. He wasn't wearing gloves, his arms were folded across his chest, and no gun was visible, but she suspected he was wearing one. He'd talked to Paul about coming to help them out, but then he hadn't come all these weeks, so they figured he'd gotten busy with some other pressing issue.

"Is there somewhere that we can talk...privately?" Vaughn asked. Despite his dark look, the man was ruggedly handsome, his attention focused on Allan.

"You were at the crime scene. Witnesses saw your vehicle," Debbie said accusingly. "Your cousin said you had no hand in the murder, but he's your cousin."

Vaughn shifted his gaze to her, his hard look chiseled in place. "Yeah, I was there. That doesn't mean I had anything to do with the man's death. His hunting partner did that."

Debbie frowned at him. "Witnesses saw *you*. No one said they saw *him*."

"He was there. Watching. In the woods. But others had arrived on the scene. I went to see if the victim was dead. He didn't survive. No one tried to rescue him. I knew he'd never last that long underwater unless he was a SEAL. Then I left, looking for the other one, Otis."

"We expected you sooner," Allan said, his voice darkly gruff.

Debbie shivered. "I'm freezing, folks."

"Let's talk this over at your place." Vaughn sounded genuinely concerned about Debbie's physical health. "Call in your...friend Paul, if you'd like. Or as many of your friends as you want, if you feel the need. But I'm on your side."

Allan took a deep breath. So did Debbie, but she couldn't smell Vaughn's scent, even though the breeze should have carried it to them. She wasn't staying out here and freezing to death though. She headed for the car.

"Let me drop Debbie off at a friend's place and we..."

"No way. I want to know what's going on just as much as you do." She got into the hatchback and slammed the door. She was working the investigation every bit as much as Allan was. Even if she had to do some of it stuck at his cabin.

"My place then. Have you learned where Otis has disappeared to?" Allan asked.

"Let's just say I'd rather discuss this in private."

"All right. Let's go." Allan got in the car and headed out while Vaughn climbed into his sedan and followed them. Allan got on his phone and Debbie assumed he was calling Paul. "Update: no more evidence in the lake pertaining to the murder case, but Vaughn Greystoke just met up with us. He's joining us at my cabin."

Allan put the phone on speaker so Debbie could hear Paul's response, which she really appreciated.

"I'll meet you there. If you're at the lake where the body was found, I'm closer to your place than you are."

Within twenty minutes, Paul called Allan back. "Looks like no one's been here. Checked all around the cabin and inside. See you in...?"

"Twenty minutes. I've been watching for a tail, but the only one following us is this guy."

When they finally reached Allan's cabin, Paul was standing on the porch, looking dangerous. Debbie wondered if Vaughn knew that both Paul and Allan were highly trained Navy SEALs in addition to being wolves.

She was so cold. Neither she nor Allan had removed their wet suits before they took off because of the situation with this man, so when they got home, she excused herself to get out of hers. She grabbed a change of clothes, her gun and holster, and then went to the bathroom and locked the door. Before long, she was enjoying a hot shower. Using warm water made the wet suit much easier to peel off. Then she hurried to dry and get into warm clothes. Her hair was wet, though she towel dried it some, but she wasn't spending the time to dry it all the way when she wanted to learn what was going on.

She grabbed her gun and tucked it into her holster, then joined the men in the living room.

As soon as she did, Allan excused himself to change. She thought he would have already done so. She could see how well the men worked together as a pack and as Navy SEALs. No one discussed what they were going to do, just did what needed to be done.

"We were waiting for you both to get changed before we discuss this matter," Paul said, and she so appreciated that they would.

She fixed them all cups of coffee, and when Allan joined them, they took seats in the living room. Paul had started a fire and the place felt toasty warm, while the cold wind howled through the pine trees surrounding the cabin.

"First off, I'm Vaughn Greystoke, from a pack in Colorado."

"Devlyn's pack," Paul said. "We thought you'd be here sooner."

"I meant to be. I followed that bastard's paw prints through the wilderness for weeks as a wolf. No way to check in. Not only is he a danger to our kind, but he left a trail of dead wolves in his wake."

"Hell. So Sarah managed to turn him," Paul said.

"Before he murdered her? Yes. Last laugh on him really, because he wanted to get rid of us and now he's one of us. Well, as in he's a gray wolf. He'll never be one of us."

"Not after he murdered two people and attempted to kill a woman and her baby," Allan said.

"We have a bit of a problem," Vaughn said. "Not only is Otis a survivalist and damn good at escape and evasion, but the human police are involved. I'd hoped I could catch up to him in the wilderness and end it. We still have to eliminate him."

"Agreed," Paul said. "If you're here now—"

"He's returned to the area. He has to be holed up somewhere in the vicinity. Instead of being housebound like Debbie must have been all these weeks, he took off for the wilderness."

"But he couldn't have stayed in his wolf form all these weeks, could he?" Debbie asked.

Vaughn eyed her warily. "Could you have? If your life depended on it?"

"You mean if I was out in the snow? No. I went with Allan a few times on runs through the forest, and I didn't make it all the way back before I had to shift."

"He might have waited through the week of the full moon, but he's also been a *lupus garou* for longer than you have. So he may be able to force himself to remain longer as a wolf. At least until he could reach cabins where he broke in and stayed for a day or so. I found a pattern of break-ins. I was always a day behind him, as if he knew someone was following and would leave sooner the next time or stay longer if he could. When he headed back here, I had to see you and warn you that he has returned to the area."

"What were you doing at the lake if the other hunter killed Lloyd?" Allan asked.

"When Sarah talked to Devlyn and Bella about joining the pack, she stated right away that she was a pacifist. She didn't believe in killing humans who learned about us."

"Even if one was trying to kill werewolves?" Allan asked, surprised.

"Devlyn didn't think to ask about a werewolf hunter, per se, since that's mostly unheard of. He did ask what she'd do if a human saw her shift and tried to kill her. She said that turning the human would make him see we weren't evil and change his mind about us. Devlyn disagreed. Since she left, that was the end of any further discussion on the subject. He thought she didn't want to join us because we would kill men like those."

"Otis doesn't seem to have known who our pack members were. Thankfully. So why not come forth with this information earlier?" Paul asked.

"I've been playing chase with this bastard. I followed the two women who located Sarah's body to ensure that Otis hadn't followed them. If he had, I would have taken him down. Then I followed Debbie from one of the women's houses—for the same reason. He knows I'm after him. He gave me the slip, but before that, he was headed back here. I thought he intended to target the rest of your pack, but he never knew who the members were. He got sloppy, killing genuine wolves exploring the blood left behind at the scene of Sarah's murder. He thought they were werewolves."

"Where were you when Otis shot Tara and Debbie?" Allan asked.

"Across the border in Idaho. I was trying to figure out how Sarah was connected with Otis and Lloyd. I discovered they'd all lived in Idaho and thought maybe he'd returned there."

Paul told him about Franny and her involvement with Otis and Sarah. "She was from the same area."

"Okay, so Otis might be after Franny to eliminate her, or maybe to discover who her pack mates are. Or he could be just planning to get his stash and leave for good now that he's a wolf. I keep thinking his focus will change, now that he's one of us. But he might be so angry he was changed, he'll try to infiltrate werewolf packs and kill them. Just on principle. The problem is that he may believe Franny made a fool of him, not only by dumping him and finding someone else, but in knowing werewolves were real. He might think she was laughing behind his back all along. Both her and Sarah."

"Agreed," Paul said.

A thought suddenly occurred to Debbie and she turned to Allan. "So that was the reason we went down south to talk to Zeta? Because Sarah had wanted to join your pack?"

"Sorry, Debbie. I couldn't tell you at the time why Rose knew about her." Allan reached over, wrapped his hand around hers, and gave it a squeeze.

She couldn't help going over all the stuff that had happened and realizing how much of what she had believed had only been half-truths.

"Do you want to help us on this?" Paul asked Vaughn.

"Hell yeah," Vaughn said. "I'll continue to try and locate his lair."

"I'm game," Debbie said. She told herself it wasn't for vengeance, that they needed to take Otis down before he killed any more innocent people, but who was she trying to kid? She wanted him dead. It wasn't her growly wolf side that wanted it. She'd come to realize that the members of Paul and Lori's pack were hard-working, law-abiding citizens, just like any other decent folk raising families and earning livings.

Wolf pups like Meghan and Eliza were just like any other five-year-olds, only they had a wolf side too.

The werewolf killer was the monster, not the werewolves.

"If you'll follow me, I'll take you to Franny and Gary's place so when you're not tracking Otis, you can have some good home-cooked meals and watch out for him if he shows up there," Paul said.

"Sounds good to me. I could use some good meals."

"Gary's a world-class chef," Paul said, "but he's not trained in protection like we are."

"Then that works out well for all of us."

They said their good-byes. Debbie just sat on the couch, pondering the case.

Allan rubbed her arm. "Did you want to get your car?"

She had scheduled a million things to do. None of them had taken into account they might learn that the shooter was back in the area.

She shook her head. "Where would he have his stuff stashed? His rifle, silver bullets, hunting traps? Clothes, all that stuff while he was running as a wolf?"

"Storage facilities? Motels that rent by the week or month? Furnished apartments that rent biweekly? Once he learned he was a wolf, he had to have found a place where he could store his stuff without making anyone suspicious. We never figured on him doing that. We assumed he had packed up and gone."

"We could split up and start investigating storage units and the other places by sections of the city of Bigfork and surrounding areas."

"We don't split up," Allan said. "But if he has to deal with turning into a wolf, that might narrow it down some."

"To more wilderness settings."

"Right."

Allan wanted to find and catch the killer, but he knew how important it was for Debbie to have her time to do as she wished. He figured even if she hadn't allowed for it, she was going to fall asleep at some point. He really didn't want her to miss out on a chance to do some fun things without the worry of shifting.

She stood and took his hand and pulled him close. She might not agree to date him, but this was all they needed—the intimacy, the baby steps. He was certain she'd come around before long.

"I know what you're thinking. You wanted me to do everything on my list today and for the rest of the week. Think of it this way—if we can eliminate the werewolf killer, we'll be all set to—"

"Date?" He couldn't help it. Even if she said she didn't want to, he wanted to, and he wanted her to know it.

She smiled up at him. "We'll be all set to accomplish the rest of the schedule we'd worked out. We could catch up on what we missed today and finish some of it each day for the rest of the week."

He rubbed her shoulders and smiled down at her, loving her. "You know you only scheduled four hours of sleep a day."

She shrugged. "Sleeping is overrated."

He laughed. "Okay, we'll skip sleep then." But that had become one of his favorite parts of the day because he got to snuggle, cuddle, and spoon her every night.

"Let's check out the places online first and then go from there." She snagged his hand and headed for the guest room. Seated at the desk, they pulled up the rental cottages in the area, then began calling the owners to learn which were currently occupied and by whom.

"Okay, so five people are staying at your lakeside cottage. Can you verify that four adults and a baby are staying there? Who made the reservations and picked up the key? Thank you," Debbie said.

Allan was listening to the call while he waited for

an answer on his. "Hello, Mrs. Edmonds? I'm with the sheriff's department, and I'm checking on renters for your three cabins. I need to know if they're families or—"

"Rental unit one is being rented by two middle-aged women. Rental unit two, a family of six—two adults and four children from the age of three to twelve. And the last unit is rented to two fishermen," Mrs. Edmonds responded.

"Have you met all of them?"

"Yes. I actively speak to each of the renters. Not trying to be intrusive, but we only have one driveway into the rental units and our house. We keep an eye on things."

"So you'd know if one of the renters came and left and hasn't returned for some time?"

"Well, that would be the fishermen. They do a lot of ice fishing and cook their own meals, so no, I don't see them coming and going. The two women, yes, they ate at the restaurant across the road and went shopping and sightseeing. And the family? They've been in and out of here a number of times."

"And you've actually seen the parents and the four kids?"

"Yes."

"Can we take a look at the cabin where the fishermen are staying?"

"You can search the perimeter."

"That would be fine. Thanks."

Debbie thanked someone and ended her call. "A man rented a cabin in the woods, but it has a lockbox so the rental manager never really saw him and couldn't say whether he is there or not. He never personally met him."

"Okay, and the two fishermen could have been Otis and Lloyd staying at one of the cabins."

After calling for a couple of hours that afternoon, then breaking for lunch, they finished up. They'd checked storage units that were in more countrified settings and the cottages or hotels that were also out in the woods.

Allan said, "Are you ready to do this?"

"I sure am."

They grabbed their coats and headed out the door.

"I know you're not serious about us getting so few hours of sleep a night and you figure I'll just fall asleep anyway," she said, climbing into the car.

He just smiled. Even though she had gotten used to sleeping with him, she still hadn't moved her things into his bedroom. He'd hoped she'd continue to sleep with him this week when she couldn't shift. He had half a notion to join her in her room, if she opted for staying there. Of course, it would have to be up to her, but he would try, if she attempted to keep her distance from him. So far, she hadn't. A good sign.

"Are you certain Vaughn's who he said he is?"

Allan glanced at her. "Yeah. He's wearing hunter's spray, but he's one of us."

"How can you tell?"

"When you were taking a shower, we questioned him about things he wouldn't know unless he's one of us."

"Unless Sarah told him about some of the stuff."

"We called his cousin Devlyn. He confirmed information about his wolf pack and sent us a news clipping about his mate, Bella Wilder, being put in a zoo when she'd been a wolf. It all matched up. And he sent some other information—a photo, some key things that only his cousin would know—to help identify him."

Debbie gaped at Allan. "Devlyn's wife was put in a zoo?"

"Yeah. She couldn't hold her form during the full moon. It sure caused a stir."

"A zoo," Debbie said, shaking her head. "She must have been terrified. She couldn't hold her form. Was she newly turned?"

"No. Her *lupus garou* roots don't go far back enough to prevent her from shifting during the night of the full moon."

She gaped at him. "You mean I'll never be able to either then?"

"As long as you're fine for the rest of the month, you should have no problem."

"Easy for you to say."

"It all turned out well in the end for both Bella and Devlyn." Allan wasn't about to mention that a male wolf had been in the exhibit with her and was interested in a mating. Debbie had enough to worry about as it was. "Bella and Devlyn mated, run the pack, and have..." Allan hesitated to say. He didn't want Debbie to balk at being his mate because of the real possibility she'd have a whole litter of pups at one time. The *lupus garou* were born knowing that. They were used to having lots of siblings who were the same age. Although occasionally an only child was born. But that was rare. Like having multiple births instead of one baby was rarer for humans.

Debbie was waiting for him to finish his sentence.

"Lovely children," he said.

She raised a brow and folded her arms.

"Triplets," he finally admitted. He thought about seeing Debbie when she was playing with Cindy and her twin girls. He had worried when he heard Debbie growling in the cabin and then Cindy growling back, her little ones adding to the ruckus. When he'd peeked in through the living room window, he'd seen them all roughhousing, and he was glad they had been playing.

He'd worried Debbie had shifted and couldn't control it, until the girls told him before they went home that they had wanted Debbie to shift so they could play with her. She'd gotten along with them just fine, careful not to hurt them, nipping them a bit when they got too wild, and playing more vigorously with Cindy, but not as wildly as she played with him. He realized her playing with others was important: she-wolves, pups, males. Except that when it came to males, he wanted to be the only one she frolicked with.

Then he changed the subject. "Devlyn said his cousin wasn't around much because of his work—he's a SEAL like us, on his own SEAL wolf team, but he was visiting when this situation arose with Sarah. He said Vaughn has great instincts and that's why he sent him to check into the matter."

"A SEAL? I'm not surprised. I'm glad Vaughn is not another suspect," Debbie said.

"I'm glad he's here to help us," Allan agreed.

When they reached the first rental unit on their list of fifty-two possible places to investigate, including seven that weren't being leased at the time, Allan thought he would show the owners the photos of Otis, Lloyd, and Sarah, in case she had been alive and didn't know what they planned to do with her. He'd also try to catch their scents. Even if Otis and Lloyd had been wearing hunter's spray, Sarah probably wouldn't have been and he would recognize her scent from her apartment.

They hadn't hit the road until three and they'd only managed to get to four places, as scattered as everything was and on snow-covered dirt or gravel roads in the country.

"This is going to take longer than I thought," Debbie said. "I'd really like to eat out tonight at that Italian restaurant, Fame del Lupo. What does the name mean?"

Allan smiled as they traipsed around the fourth cottage that afternoon. "Wolfish appetite. And I'd sure love to take you there."

She appreciated that he wanted to make her feel better this whole week so she could deal with the shifting for the next three weeks. And she decided, well, mostly decided, that she really couldn't live without Allan's sense of humor, his passionate lovemaking, which she'd been dying to have, and the way they could disagree and still get along.

"It's going on half past four. How about we make dinner reservations for six, and go home first and get changed." She didn't want to tell him what she had in mind until they got home.

"We'll be there at a quarter of five. Did you want to check out another place?"

"No."

He glanced at her.

She let out her breath. She wanted to discuss some more things before she agreed to change her life even more than it had been already.

Chapter 22

"ROWDY WAS RIGHT ALL ALONG ABOUT THE PACK. What are you going to do about him?" Debbie said as Allan drove them back to his cabin.

"He could just be joking. If he's not, he has no real proof. If he tells anyone, he'll be the laughingstock of the force. So I doubt he'll want to share what he believes with anyone. As far as we know, he's just having a bit of fun because he loves the paranormal."

"And if he's trying to gather evidence against us?" Debbie didn't believe Rowdy was just having fun with this. Sure, he acted like he was making a joke of it, but she thought that was because he was afraid of how she would view his allegations.

"Maybe we can convince him to join the pack."

"Coerce him, you mean."

"Maybe he just wants to belong. Don't worry about it. What will be, will be."

"Like with me."

Allan reached over and took Debbie's hand and squeezed. She loved how he did that—connected with her and treated her as though she was precious to him. "As long as we don't turn him and then he wants to date you."

She smiled. "I'll keep saying no."

"About us?"

She sighed. "Multiple babies?"

"Is that all that's holding you back?"

"Is that *all*? You're not the one having them!"

"We have a whole pack to care for them, and we can wait on having them as long as you want to delay it. You might even have just one child. Some do—look at Franny. You might not have any. No matter what, I'd be there with you every step of the way. You want to dive, I'll take care of junior. Whatever you want."

"You say that now…"

"It's in our genes."

Before she knew he was a wolf, she'd wanted this— envisioned being his wife, teaming up on police business, taking diving vacations, enjoying sunsets and hiking, and fishing when it grew warmer.

But now? She was a wolf, and that meant? Well, truthfully, she loved the way Allan played with her and taught her their ways, was infinitely patient with her, and loved her unconditionally. She was one of them and that meant forever. She couldn't imagine being with anyone else.

"So…how does this work, exactly? I mean, do you get on bended knee and propose a mating?"

"This is why you wanted to have an extra hour at the cottage before dinner? You want to mate me? Hot damn, yes, woman!"

She laughed. "Well?"

Allan chuckled. "Truthfully, it begins with a lot of kissing, and you know all the rest."

"And a marriage license?"

"We can do that. First or afterward. A wedding. Whatever makes you happy."

Allan was holding her hand, his expression serious

now, as if he was anticipating her next move—hopeful and eager, and that made her feel appreciated and loved.

"And we can wait on kids? Especially while we're getting to know each other as a couple. And take some vacations? Well, I guess during the week of the new moon on occasion."

"Absolutely."

"You're so enthusiastic." And she truly did love him for it.

"You're perfect for me, Debbie. I didn't think I'd ever meet someone who was more suited to me…"

"Except that I was human."

"And I still loved you. Once you became a wolf and we were able to share that aspect of our lives, I knew you were the only one meant for me. So, is that a yes to a mating?"

"Do you have to get Paul and Lori's permission?"

"No. Only yours."

She swore he was speeding a bit before they arrived at the house.

This was it, Debbie thought, and she saw the relief in his expression. Because he would have his way—her as his mate every bit as much as she'd have him.

He parked the vehicle and hurried to get her door.

He was perfect for her. Now that she had changed so much—though in many ways she hadn't changed at all. She needed him as a mentor, a lover, and most of all, a companion for life.

She hadn't expected him to lift her in his arms and rush her into the cabin. He closed and locked the door, then carried her into the bedroom as if he was afraid she'd change her mind.

After setting her on the floor, he began kissing her slowly, softly, as if he wanted to draw this out—their first mating, the real commitment, a relationship that would last for a lifetime.

She loved how he slowly undressed her, his hands all over her skin, caressing and tender. She was trying to unbutton his shirt and not get caught up in the way he slid his hands inside her bra and cupped her breasts, his mouth fused to hers.

His tongue urged her lips apart and she inhaled him, loving the sweet and spicy wolf that he was, and smelled something else—a sexy scent that turned her on fast and hard.

He pulled his mouth away from hers, he eyes glazed with desire, his lips curving up slightly. "Our pheromones," he said, his voice husky with lust. "Hot damn, honey. Really hot."

Then he was kissing her again, pulling her bra off and dropping it to the floor, cupping her breasts with reverence.

She pulled away, kissing his throat and nipping at his chin. She couldn't believe how sexy it felt to do that, even when he had a little stubble just appearing. The feeling had to be something to do with her wolf half. She couldn't imagine doing such a thing when she was only human and enjoying it.

He rubbed his body against her, showing just how hard she'd made him already. She rubbed him right back, lifting her leg over his and rubbing her crotch against his thigh.

He moaned, sounding like his attempt at taking this slow and easy was getting the better of him. But instead of taking off her jeans, he caressed her leg and held her tight against his thigh, fondling her.

Damp heat filled her panties and she swore she would come right then and there. She smelled the pheromones between them, igniting them even more, and pulled away from him, wanting them naked—bare flesh to bare flesh.

He was still trying to take it slow, his hand seductively sliding between her legs, firmly enough to make her come.

She quickly began working on her belt, the jeans button, and zipper, and yanked her jeans off.

He cupped her mound through her panties, sliding one finger against her clit. She groaned, wanting him inside her now but loving the erotic feel of him like this too.

She skimmed her hands over his nipples and felt them harden into small pebbles. When she ran her hand over his rigid length in his jeans, he forgot slow and easy and hurried to get out of them.

After that, he lifted her and carried her to the bed. Then he was on top of her, kissing her, moving against her, and simulating what he would be doing inside her soon.

All the kissing and touching and scents brought out the wolf in her—the raw primal need to mate. She not only felt her wolf, but his wolf too—the scents, the pure driven need. He plunged a finger between her feminine folds and stroked, his tongue sliding into her mouth and stroking her with the same urgency. She felt the world tilting on end, the pinnacle so close she could taste it, but right before she reached the climax, he pushed his cock into her in the joining, the mating between human and wolf, humanity and the wild.

She came apart under his thrusts, his deep driving compulsion to have her, and she encouraged it, pushed for it, relished it. She cried out his name in a strangled, happy, fulfilled way as he followed her into that world of bliss and sank down on top of her.

She stared up at his beautiful face, his dark stubble making him sweet and sexy and roguish-looking. And then she realized their mistake. She groaned out loud and pushed him off her. "You didn't use a condom."

"Ah, hell..." Allan said, looking worried and annoyed with himself at the same time. "I had every intention of doing as you wished."

She shook her head. "What are the odds that I would get pregnant after having sex with you only once?" Except the odds were fairly good, she thought morosely. She considered when she'd had her period last and when she should be ovulating—yeah, pretty good. Which *wasn't* good. She wasn't ready for multiple babies. Certainly not when she didn't even have her shifting under control.

It was bad enough she had to deal with that herself. Think what a mess it would be if she had twins and the babies shifted too! She could see it now—her half dressed as a wolf and the two pups half dressed in diapers and bunting. That reminded her of Meghan, Eliza, and the purple sock. At least in their case, the mother had told the girls to get ready to shift. With Debbie? She might not have time.

"I'm so sorry, honey," Allan said, dragging her into his arms and covering them with the comforter. "It won't happen again until you're ready to have kids."

As long as it might take for her to get the shifting under control, that could be never.

———w———

All week long they'd slipped in some meals out and late-night movies, but every minute of the day had been spent searching for Otis's hideaway. Vaughn had stuck close to Franny and the baby while Gary worked, so they felt she was safe enough for the time being. Paul had a couple of men assigned to watch Gary at the restaurant, in case Otis tried to do anything to him.

What took the longest for Debbie and Allan to search were all the places that either had been abandoned or were privately owned and unoccupied during the winter. They had started with a ten-mile radius and now were up to a twenty-mile radius.

Early that morning, Debbie got a surprise call from Rowdy. He'd been working a triple homicide all week and she knew he'd been ultra-busy, so she really was surprised to hear from him.

"I've heard you've been checking out dozens of places—storage facilities, cottages. What's up?"

"We just had a hunch Otis might have left some of his stuff behind when he vanished from the area," she said, being perfectly honest with him.

"Is he back in the area?"

"We haven't been able to locate anything that might have belonged to him or any sign that he's been in the area." Again, she hadn't lied. She realized this business of being a wolf made it difficult to be perfectly honest with human friends, and she could see Allan's dilemma when he was so interested in her but had to cool it with her.

"Is Otis a wolf now?"

How could she answer that? She glanced at Allan. He was listening, but he wasn't offering advice. She realized he trusted her to be one of them, to say the right things.

She took a deep breath. "He might be."

"I imagine he is. I assume newly turned wolves can't hold their human shape. Am I right?"

"You could be right."

"Okay. So if I arrest the guy, then it's going to be real trouble for…their kind. Correct?"

"Correct."

"So what do you want me to do about this? It's my case. My murder investigation. I have one of the best success rates for solving murders, resulting in successful trials that land the criminals behind bars."

"Maybe he'll just die of a heart attack and save all the taxpayers lots of money?" she asked.

"That doesn't help me with solving the cases."

"If we learn where he is, we'll give you a call."

"After the fact."

She hesitated to say. "Well…"

"I understand. Allan's with you, isn't he?"

"Yes."

"There's no hope for me, is there?"

"I'm afraid not."

"Thought so." He let out his breath. "Okay, I'll give you forty-eight hours to locate him and let me know where he is."

"What if he's a…wolf?"

Rowdy didn't say anything for a moment. "Full moon? Gotcha. I just hope if he has difficulty living, he's not naked when I find him."

"I've got to go, Rowdy. Allan's wondering what in the world we're talking about."

"I just bet he is. Tell him I said hello and I'm ready for our next pizza outing. Take care and be safe, Debbie."

"You too." She ended the call and tucked away her phone. "Thanks for letting me deal with Rowdy the way I saw fit."

Allan smiled at her. "Only you could pull that off and not get us into a lot of hot water."

Allan and Debbie had been tromping through the snow for days now, thinking they were never going to locate the place where Otis had stashed his stuff. Maybe Vaughn was wrong and Otis hadn't kept his things here locally while he ran off as a wolf. Maybe he'd come during the phase of the new moon, packed up his things, and left. Or maybe they'd been searching in all the wrong places.

"We're approaching the full moon like the first time you shifted," Allan warned her. He was carrying a mostly empty backpack, with only a few medical supplies, because he wanted to be ready if she shifted and he needed to carry her clothes for her. "Are you feeling the shift coming on?"

He worried about her. She'd been awfully quiet while they'd been hiking to a hunting cabin, the trail impassable for vehicles in the winter. The owner lived in Florida and came up here to hunt on occasion in the winter, but he said he'd already been up there and wasn't planning to return for another month. It was twenty-two miles from Van Lake, so beyond their search area, but they were starting to expand their search another ten miles out.

"Debbie?"

"Yes, yes. Let's just get to the cabin."

But would he be hiking with her while she was running as a wolf? As aggravated as she sounded, he thought so.

"Damn it," she suddenly said and stopped.

As soon as she started to pull off her parka, he asked, "Do you want me to help?"

She loved when he helped remove her clothes for sex, and vice versa. When she was turning into her growly wolf, sometimes she did, sometimes she didn't. So he always asked.

"Yes!"

He knew she wasn't mad at him but panicked, fearing that she would soon be a wolf half dressed in clothes.

He began pulling off her hat and then crouched to unzip her boots. The sun was setting, washing the sky in pink and purple, and reflecting off the snow.

"We still have three more cottages on our list to check tonight after this one. We're not going home until we do," she said, her voice ferocious.

"All right."

They still had another mile hike to this cottage.

If they located Otis, they didn't know how this was going to end. Unless the guy had a heart condition, forcing him to have a heart attack wasn't going to happen. They wanted to turn his body over to Rowdy but make sure it looked like an accident. They didn't want to kill him as a wolf, which could provoke a wolf hunt.

Then Allan's phone buzzed. He finished helping

Debbie undress, and she shifted almost immediately. He yanked out his phone and saw that it was Vaughn calling. Figuring the PI must have some news, Allan answered, "Yeah."

"I've found Otis's stash in a storage unit in Bigfork."

"Everything?"

"Hard to tell. Clothes—mostly the camo kind, ammo, a rifle and a Glock, personal stuff. Possibly the gun used in Sarah's murder."

"Anything that might clue us in to where he is now?"

"No, but he's been here recently and he wasn't wearing hunter's camo scent. So I've got his scent. And I'm taking some of his T-shirts to share his scent with the pack."

"Good. What about security cameras?"

"Yeah. Sending the pictures now. He was driving a black Jeep. We got a partial tag. Problem is we don't want the police to run him down."

"Yeah, gotcha."

"So we're having one of Hunter's police officers do the trick. Any progress there?"

"Just checking out four more cottages situated around twenty-two to twenty-five miles out from Van Lake."

"How's Debbie doing?"

"She's a wolf." Allan gathered up her clothes and tucked them in his backpack.

"Okay. Now that I've found his scent and that he was staying in Bigfork, I'll drop these off with Lori and Paul, and then I'm going to start checking into the places where he might be staying."

"You don't think he's taken off?"

"Nope. Not when he's left so much of his weaponry here."

"What about Franny?"

"Paul and Lori are there, providing additional protection."

"All right. If you locate him, let me know."

"Will do."

As Allan and Debbie drew closer to the cabin, he noted no lights were on, but he smelled the faint odor of wood smoke. He didn't have to tell Debbie. She lifted her nose and took a whiff of the air and huffed a little, her body tense.

"Stay close," he warned, his voice hushed.

Without warning, shots rang out from the direction of the cabin. Allan dove behind a tree as the rounds pelted the snow inches away. He glanced in Debbie's direction, but she had run off in a wide arc—and then headed toward the shooter.

Damn it to hell and back. He didn't want her shot. What if the resident was just a hunter? Using the cabin illegally, true, but not their killer?

"Police!" Allan called out to let him know what kind of trouble he could be in if he shot and killed him or his dive partner.

More shots were fired in his direction.

Screw this. He made a wide arc through the trees and around to avoid being shot. Either the shooter had night-vision goggles, or he was a wolf and could see well at dusk. He just hoped Debbie wouldn't get herself shot.

He wanted to yank out his phone and tell Paul they were going in to grab what could be their suspect, but he figured they were on their own right now. Certainly with Debbie up to who knew what, he had to act quickly to protect her and himself.

A screen door slammed and he assumed the shooter had left the cabin, not wanting to be caught inside.

As soon as he did and Allan bore down on the door, a wild growling—Debbie's wild growling—made Allan's blood run cold. It turned to ice when he heard a much larger wolf growl back.

The full moon of January—appropriately, the wolf moon—illuminated the trees and snow, some snowflakes sprinkling from the trees as the branches stirred in the breeze.

Then he saw them—a large tan wolf snarling at Debbie a short distance from the dark cabin, only the tiny glow of a fire inside.

He wanted to kill the bastard quickly with a well-aimed shot, but he couldn't, not with the way Debbie was tearing into the guy and the way he was tearing into her. Allan had to stop and strip, then shift. It was the only way to protect Debbie, who was attacking and not backing off. The wolf saw Allan then and tried to run, but Debbie pursued him, biting his tail, and he turned around to tackle her again. By then, Allan had shifted and was running full-out, because right this instant, Allan was in a killing mood. Nothing would stop him now.

He bit at the wolf in a vicious way, distracting him. He smelled Debbie's blood on him, and that incensed Allan all the more. His phone was vibrating in the pocket of his pants nearby, while Debbie bit again at the wolf's tail. Was the wolf Otis? They had no way of knowing at the moment.

What he did know was the wolf wasn't calling a truce. He'd tried to run as a wolf. He had something to hide. Paul suspected the wolf was their man.

Debbie was still snarling and growling, and Allan prayed she hadn't been injured too badly.

The wolf he was tackling was growling just as ferociously as Debbie, but he wasn't able to overpower or outthink Allan. Not as a new wolf.

Instinctively, the wolf knew to go for the throat, but Allan kept indicating he was going one way and then sweeping back to tackle him another. That was why it was so important for wolves to learn to read body language. This wolf was still clueless. He hadn't played with another *lupus garou*, hadn't learned the techniques to use. But Debbie had. She knew what Allan was going to do and complemented his actions, move for move.

He couldn't have been more proud of her. Suddenly, as if the wolf figured he wasn't going to make it out of this alive and he would kill the easier prey, he swerved around to attack Debbie. She read the signs before he lunged. And so did Allan.

She yipped and bolted away from the wolf. Allan charged into him, his teeth sinking into the wolf's neck, breaking it with one killing bite.

The wolf sank into the snow, tree branch shadows cutting across him and weaving a web of darkness.

Allan and Debbie stood panting and watching him. They saw that he was no longer breathing and heard his heart stop beating. The wolf shifted to human, and though a beard covered his jaw, it was him—Otis, the man they'd tried to locate forever. Allan joined Debbie, smelling her blood and checking her over. She licked his muzzle, then motioned to the cabin with her head. He nodded and ran off to get to the field pack and his clothes resting on top of the snow. He shifted, dressed, and slung the bag over his shoulders, then headed for the cabin. She paced in front of the screen door. The man had cleared the step recently, or the door wouldn't have opened.

Allan opened the door for her, and she ran inside, smelling the scents like he was. She didn't seem to be injured badly, if the way she was moving about was any indication.

They found Otis's rifle, more silver rounds, camo, another Glock, hunter's spray, and enough canned food to last a couple of weeks. The cot had been slept on, the sheets and blankets not having been washed, from the smell of it, for eons.

Debbie paced, her wolf nails clicking on the wooden floor. Allan pulled out his phone, saw a missed call from Paul, and quickly called him back.

"We got him." Allan gave Paul the coordinates. "Cliffs are nearby. Should we take him there and drop him off them? He died, a wolf checked him out, bit into him, and left him?"

"Yeah. Sounds good. If we don't report finding him, animals will feast off him. Vultures, what have you. How's Debbie?"

She was curled up by the fire, licking her leg.

"She's still a wolf, a few bites, but nothing serious. She's one hell of a wolf partner."

She lifted her head and howled.

Paul laughed. "Good. You?"

"Same here. He's got more ammo, rifle, guns. Let's report the find in the storage facility, then we'll dump his body off the cliff. Maybe we can let someone find the rest of this stuff in another month when the owner comes for another hunting trip. Maybe at spring thaw someone will discover his remains down the mountainside. Or not."

"Sounds like a plan to me."

"Okay, well, I'm out of here with the body. I'll call back in when that's done and let you know when we're on our way home."

"Okay. I'll let everyone know the killer has been caught and his killing spree has ended."

"Thanks. Out here."

Allan looked down at Debbie. "Did you want to stay here, and when I'm done, I'll come back for you?"

She woofed and rose to her feet, then ran over to him. He took that as a no. They were in this together.

Chapter 23

NEVER IN A MILLION YEARS WOULD DEBBIE HAVE believed she'd be running alongside Allan as a wolf while he was carrying a dead, naked body. She hated that they couldn't tell Rowdy the case wasn't cold. That they'd solved it for him. She couldn't believe she had a mad-wolf self, but when the guy began shooting at her and Allan, and continued after Allan identified himself as with the police, she knew she had to help take him down in any way that she could. Since using a gun hadn't been an option, she had to use her wolf teeth.

He was too big, too powerful for her, but she'd hoped Allan could shoot him and that would be the end of it. He returned fire in self-defense. There were enough rounds fired at Allan and her to support their case. But killing him as a wolf screwed everything up. At one point, she had thought real wolves wouldn't matter to the *lupus garous*. But she could see they treasured them as much as they did their own wolf packs and would protect them at all costs by covering up a wolf killing.

She was glad she had turned into the wolf because she had managed to stop Otis in his flight from justice. She wouldn't have if she'd been running as a human.

Even though the bad guy was a bad guy, she still

hated knowing he would be left for the scavengers to feed off instead of being turned in to the police. She realized it was for the best though.

After leaving Otis in the wilderness, Allan and Debbie headed back to where they had left their vehicle. Allan was quiet, and she wished he'd talk to her—not that she could respond much as a wolf. She finally woofed at him.

He smiled down at her and ran his gloved hand over her head.

"Sorry, gathering wool again. I hope that what we did worked. That if anyone's up here, either the snow will have fallen again and covered up the fight and our walk toward the cliff, or everything will have melted off and left no trails behind."

She woofed in agreement.

"You did a hell of a job back there."

She growled a little. She'd do it again in a heartbeat to protect her...mate. She'd mated with him, sure, but this was the first time she'd actually thought of him as her mate and not her lover, her friend, confidant, dive partner, and the one she dearly loved.

Her phone vibrated in the field pack. He pulled it off his shoulders as they continued to trudge through the snow, keeping to the same path they had used to get there. He found her phone in her pants pocket and said, "Hell, it's Rowdy."

She nodded.

"I wonder if he's been told already about the find at the storage unit."

When they reached the car, Allan unlocked the door and opened it for her, but as soon as she jumped in, she bit at the field pack as he tried to drop it on the floor. She was ready to shift again. She sighed. She hoped she would have better control over this soon.

Allan closed her door and got in on the driver's side while he watched her shift and begin to get dressed. "Ready?"

"Yeah, I can dress while you drive."

"What are you going to say to Rowdy?"

"Depends on what he says first." She sighed again and pulled her sweater over her head.

He glanced at her again. "How are you feeling?"

"Like I could snuggle with you in bed, as a wolf if I have to, for a week. But only until I have more control over the shifting for the rest of the month."

"Next phase of the new moon, we're only going to have fun."

She smiled at him. "You know what? Being with you is all the fun I need."

He chuckled. "Even when I'm being my mad-wolf self?"

"I was so thankful you had one. Me too."

"So about the rest of the schedule...I guess we can fit it all in the next time."

She pulled out the list and examined it studiously.

"Well? Where did you want to go next?"

"I know it's not on the list," she said, reaching over and running her hand over his thigh. "But I thought we might return to the cabin for a week of hibernation during the full moon."

He raised his brows. "So you *did* want to sleep some."

"Ha! No way. I need me some wolf loving."

Fully dressed, she pulled out her cell phone. "Wait. If Rowdy figured out where I called him from, he could come to see why we were out here." She was about ready to tuck her phone away when she had another thought. "I'll wait to call him from the cabin. But you said you'd talk to Paul. I'll call for us."

"Good thinking."

"Paul? We're on our way home."

"Helluva job, Debbie. Welcome to the pack."

When they arrived home, Allan was concerned about how she was feeling, emotionally and physically. She loved him for being so sensitive.

"I have to admit, this whole situation is disturbing, but I can see how important it is to keep our kind secret. Wish me luck when I call Rowdy."

"Should we have a fire after showering or—"

"I'm all for going to bed after we take a shower together." With great reluctance, she called Rowdy, grateful that the case was solved to their satisfaction, even if it wasn't for Rowdy. "Hey," she said as Allan helped her out of her parka.

"Hey. I'm at the storage unit where the weapons and such were found. Is that Vaughn Greystoke another wolf?"

She just sighed. "I guess just about *everyone* is."

"Not me."

"Except for you."

"They've run ballistics on the rifle. It's not the one that was used to shoot you and Tara."

She hadn't thought he even knew about Tara. Just

that she had been shot. "No? I thought Vaughn believed it was Otis's."

"It is. It was registered to him. But it's not the one he used in the shootings."

"Ah, okay. Well, I thought you might have had it all tied up."

"I need Otis's body first."

She didn't say anything for a moment as Allan helped her out of her boots.

"You still there?"

"Yeah. Well, Vaughn said that the surveillance showed the kind of vehicle he was driving. Did you put an APB out on it?"

"Yeah. But I have a feeling in my bones that he's no longer among the living."

"You mean like a sixth sense?"

"Yeah, you know me and my paranormal musings. Anyway, yeah, like a sixth sense."

"You think maybe a hunter got him?"

"I 'spect we'll be finding him come spring, if not sooner, wearing a few predatory bite marks. Nothing ominous—just a hazard of running around in the wilderness in the dead of winter when on the...lam."

"So you're no longer worried about him?"

"Are you?"

"Not when you're on the case."

Rowdy sighed. "Are you really doing okay?"

"Yeah." She was naked now and so was Allan, wrapping his arms around her and kissing her forehead, cheeks, and chin. "I'm fine. Thanks, Rowdy, for everything."

She swore Rowdy knew the truth. But why let Allan

and his pack know it? Why not pretend they didn't exist? He didn't seem to fear that they might turn him or eliminate him.

"I've been hearing you're marrying one of them," Rowdy said.

"Ah, Allan. Yeah. I finally caught my man."

"Well, more power to you. You can't say I didn't try to save you, but I figured once he wanted you, it was like a dog with a—"

She cleared her throat.

He didn't finish what he was going to say.

"Allan says it takes one to know one. Are you sure you're not one of them?" Debbie asked.

"Not yet. But I imagine that it's coming."

"You don't mind?"

"It's either that or end up like that poor fool."

"He murdered innocent people. And you would never do what he did."

"You think? It's hard to say. If I saw one of them killing another, I don't know. Whole different world out there."

"Well, all I know is Allan's the right one for me."

"What about our Friday night pizza?"

"Maybe once a month now. We have some newlywed time to nurture."

"No pizza night during the full moon though, right?" Rowdy asked.

"Only if you like living dangerously," Debbie said and kissed Allan on his throat. She was certain Rowdy was taking notes. New moon—no wolf change.

"You're on. Usual time? I'll be there," Rowdy said.

Then they ended the call.

"What's up?" Allan asked, pulling her toward the shower.

"He knows. Or at least he suspects. I think he believes we're the good guys though."

"Well, we are."

"Is it wise to keep meeting with him?" she asked.

"Yeah, it is. If only to ensure he knows we're just average folks like everybody else when we're not wearing our wolf coats."

"And so we can keep up on what he's thinking or doing with regard to our kind?"

"Absolutely. Vaughn said to watch out for Rowdy. He believes he's sitting on the fence—he can either try to prove we exist or join us. So we've got to prove we're worth joining."

"Or just turn him against his will."

"If we have to, but it would be a whole lot better if we could make him one of us because he wants it."

"But you can't tell him we're werewolves for real."

"No. That's the problem. Once that's done, he doesn't have a choice."

She nodded. "Thank you for loving me, Allan, and for having a pack who cared enough about the two of us that we could be together as wolf mates, even if they didn't know how it would work out between us."

"I was angry to begin with, afraid of how you'd feel. On the other hand, I wanted you for a mate and I'm glad you've found a family with us. With me. I can't tell you enough how much I love you."

"In your every action, you've shown me. I was so stuck on you before I learned what you were, but you know what?" She pulled him into a warm embrace and kissed him. "That's what intrigued me the most about you. Here I thought it was just because you were a SEAL."

He smiled down and kissed her right back. "You have to know you've made me the happiest wolf in the world." Then he took her into the shower, the one where she had sat as a wild wolf watching him soap that hard body of his, only this time *she* was soaping that hard body of his.

Allan knew beyond a doubt that when he'd gone diving for trouble, he'd gotten lots more than that—one human turned wolf, his dive partner, the love of his life, his wolf mate. Nothing could be better than that. He couldn't have asked for a better teammate for making sure the good guys came out on top.

She was everything he needed in a mate, wolf or otherwise. And he couldn't have loved her any more than he did as she began to soap his body while he soaped hers.

Debbie had thought she loved Allan the most for his mutual appreciation of diving. But it was so much more than that. He'd opened up a whole new world for her, and she was actually looking forward to a whole lot of wolf play inside the cottage and out. She'd actually missed being a wolf during the phase of the new moon, and she was ready to take advantage of both worlds now.

"Do you ever wonder what would have happened between us if I hadn't been turned?"

"I believe what was meant to be would be. And we were meant to be together."

She rubbed her soapy body against his. "I think you're right. Rowdy would have convinced me of what you were eventually, and I would have made you bite me."

Allan smiled at her. "Would you have been as growly about the shifting then?"

"Absolutely. I probably still will be when it happens and I don't want it to. Just so you know, if we have babies before I've got the shifting under control—"

"I'll be there to take care of it. You've got me and a whole pack to help out." He was silent for a moment, and then he said, "You're already pregnant?"

She let out her breath. "You never know."

He smiled, looking perfectly pleased with the notion.

She sighed. "I should have known how much trouble you could be."

He pulled her into his arms and kissed her mouth soundly. "Ditto, partner. We make a helluva team."

Read on for a sneak peek at Terry Spear's

Alpha Wolf Need Not Apply

As a law enforcement park ranger, Eric Silver hadn't expected to be chasing down pot-growing wolves at San Isabel National Park. Humans, no problem. He would get hold of his boss, who would contact various law enforcement agencies to take the criminals down.

But Eric couldn't let anyone know about this—*not* when the lawbreakers were wolves.

The moon was full, the cool, dry wind whipping the pinyon branches around, and he caught the scent of a wolf—one of the wolves involved in growing the illegal cannabis—that was loping through the trees dead ahead. Eric and his pack had to catch the bastards running this operation before humans did. Keeping *lupus garous* secret from humans was paramount.

Eric had been doing one of his usual searches for more of the illegal plants when he'd come across the scent that evening. He'd already found ten areas where they'd been growing. But he needed to actually catch the culprits, and this was the first time that Eric had been this close. Yet Eric was in a real quandary. Darien, his cousin and the leader of their pack, would be furious if he learned Eric had gone after the wolf on his own without calling for backup, but what could he do? He couldn't let him get away.

All he could do was concentrate on the wolf's scent ahead of him. It was confident, not fearful—the wolf didn't yet suspect that Eric was trailing him. Eric glimpsed a tuft of black fur stuck to some of the under-brush, and it smelled of the wolf he was following.

They reached a goatlike path that led to a secluded patch of marijuana. So far so good—there was no sign of any other wolves in the area.

Eric moved in to take the wolf down, but saw movement to his right. Another wolf, this one more beige than gray, had been hiding in the brush. Hell, one gray wolf against two big gray males? Darien would kill him for getting himself into this bind, if Eric lived through it. He didn't have a choice now. Kill or be killed.

Eric whipped around before the wolf had a chance to attack. He dove for the wolf's right foreleg, hoping to bring him down before he had to deal with the other wolf. The wolf wasn't prepared for Eric's quick assault, and with two hard chomps in quick succession, Eric brought the wolf down. The wolf yipped and growled, backing away from Eric on three legs, favoring his injured one.

Eric swung around to face the new threat. The wolf he'd been following had tried to sneak up on him silently, like a wolf on a hunt. Eric feinted, then swung around and bit into the wolf's other leg. With a snap, he broke the wolf's leg.

Neither wolf was totally disabled. That was the

ALPHA WOLF NEED NOT APPLY   311

problem with just breaking their legs. He knew of a
wolf—a real wolf—that had lost a leg in a trap. She
continued to have pups, and when she lost her mate,
she began attacking sheep as a way to provide for her
young. Luckily, the sheep owner humanely caught her
and took her to a wolf sanctuary where she and her pups
were cared for. But it proved a wolf could still manage
to survive on three legs. Which meant these wolves were
still dangerous to him.

Neither attacked, but both eyed him, growling, which
made him suspect they were both beta wolves. When
one lifted his chin to howl, Eric knew he was calling
his pack for help. And then Eric would really be a dead
wolf. He leapt in a single bound and tore into the wolf.
He bit him in the throat just as he felt the other wolf
tackle his back.

Once Eric took out the first wolf, he twisted around,
but fell on his side. The wolf took advantage, but not for
long. The injured wolf couldn't manage well on three
legs. He was in pain, trying to kill Eric with all his might,
but it wasn't good enough. Still, the wolf managed to bite
Eric's flank, and then he lifted his snout to howl.

Hell. His heart racing, furious with the damn wolves
for doing something illegal and putting all their kind
at risk, Eric tore into the wolf. He only wanted to take
him in. He didn't want to have to kill him. But when
he heard another wolf coming, Eric finished the injured
wolf off, and raced back down the mountain. The other
wolf would have to deal with his dead pack members.
Eric could fight another, but not a whole pack if there
were even more of them in the vicinity.

His flank was burning, but he tried to ignore it as he

ran full-out as if a whole pack of wolves were on his tail.
With the enhanced healing abilities of the *lupus garou*, it
would heal up sooner than if he were just human, but it
could still take some time, depending on how bad it was.

Eric reached his truck and shifted, the shift warming his muscles and bones, though his wound burned
even more. The shift was instantaneous and he quickly
unlocked his door using the code, grabbing his medical
bag and fumbling around inside it for the disinfectant.
Then he bandaged the injury. It wasn't too deep, thankfully. He hurried to pull on his clothes when he heard a
wolf yip about a half a mile away, in a different direction than where he'd just been.

His need to protect a wolf kicked in, yet the wolf
could very well be from the same wolf pack that was
growing pot. What would the odds be that members
from two *lupus garou* packs besides his were here in
the park?

He grabbed his medical pack and headed out at a
run, calling CJ, his deputy sheriff brother, at the same
time. "Killed two of the wolves involved in the drug
operation. Left when a third was on its way. Now I'm
investigating a wolf injury." He gave coordinates for the
drug site.

"Wait for me to get there. I'm calling it in to Darien
and the sheriff, but I'm on my way."

"Can't wait, little brother. I'll be cautious."

"All right. I'll let everyone know what's going on."

Eric approached the area, careful to stay downwind.
When he was close enough to see what the problem was
without the wolf seeing him, he witnessed five wolves
around an injured she-wolf. She was lying on her side

near the base of a cliff where evidence of a recent rock slide littered the area. By the way the other wolves were reassuring the injured wolf, Eric assumed they were *lupus garous*, which surprised the hell out of him. He hadn't seen any in the park before his run-in with the other wolves earlier today. But owing to the size of the national park, it was understandable. Unless they were just visitors and not from the area.

He smelled their scents and was assured none of these had been near the cannabis plants he'd already located. Although they could still be members of the same pack and involved with the operation in other ways.

He slowly walked out of the cover of the trees toward the rocky cliff, wanting them to know he wished to help the injured wolf. He quickly told them who he was, since he was off duty and no longer wearing his uniform. "I'm a park ranger. My name is Eric Silver. I can take her in my truck to the clinic in Silver Town, two hours south of here. It's wolf-run."

Two of the wolves snarled and growled at him, but they didn't draw closer. He assumed they were betas, trying to figure out what to do. They couldn't take care of the wolf themselves, not as wolves. And running around in the woods as naked humans carrying an injured wolf was going to take a lot of explaining if they ran into anyone else.

The injured wolf was still lying on her side. She tried to sit up and yipped, lying back down.

"Just lie still," Eric said, motioning for her to stay put, his voice gentle and reassuring.

He needed to get closer so he could examine her, but he was cautious about the wolves who were threatening him. Even beta wolves could tear a person apart, so he needed permission to draw closer. Though they probably wouldn't hurt him, he couldn't risk injury by ignoring the threat.

When they wouldn't back down, he tried again to convince them he only wanted to help. "I can carry her to my truck, only a mile from here. Some of you can come with me so you know I'm serious about getting help for her."

They continued to snarl at him, protecting her, but Eric wouldn't back off either. He wasn't leaving until someone took care of her.

Then one of the men shifted. He was maybe in his forties, with black hair and hard amber eyes. "We don't need your help." Even so, the man was obviously in a quandary.

Eric took the wolf's shifting as a good sign. Not of friendship, but the wolf would have remained a wolf if he had felt threatened, especially since he appeared to be in charge. He would have led the wolves into attacking Eric if he was going to do it.

At that point, Eric slowly drew closer to the injured wolf. Then he crouched down to examine her, hoping they would finally let him help.

When he touched her right hind leg, she yipped. "Okay, girl, I'll be gentle. I just need to check to see if it's broken or something else." He carefully ran his hand over her leg, and she pulled it away from his touch.

"Is it broken?" the man asked, sounding worried.

"I don't feel any break, but it's obviously tender. It could be a bruised tendon, torn ligament, or even a hairline fracture of the bone."

"She can't walk on it. We're parked about five miles out."

Eric said again, "I'm parked only a mile from here on one of the official-use-only trails. I can carry her to my—"

"No. We don't need your help. We'll take care of it."

"But—"

"I *said* we'd take care of her."

Eric raised his hands in a sign of truce, but he wasn't leaving until he saw that they could provide her with the care she needed. "How are you going to do it? I'm trained in first aid. I can call in some others from my pack to help get her out of here, or I'll carry her to your vehicle." As much as Eric hated offering, he'd carry her the five miles to their vehicle if that was the only way they'd go for it.

"All right. You can carry her to our campsite then."

Eric let out his breath in exasperation. Every mile he moved her would cause the poor wolf more pain.

The man in charge had already shifted back into his wolf form and was watching for signs of anyone else coming with the other males, while the female stood by the injured she-wolf, looking concerned. Eric made a makeshift splint, and as soon as he bound her leg, she whimpered. He hated that she was in pain and wished he could give her something for it. As gently as he could, he lifted her in his arms. This was going to be the longest hike he'd ever made. He wished the wolf in charge had listened to reason.

As a wolf, this would have been no problem, even though he was feeling some pain of his own. But as a human carrying an injured wolf, the trek was all the more difficult. He stumbled over too many exposed roots to count because he couldn't see the path, making the she-wolf whimper or yip in pain. He fought groaning himself a time or two.

When they grew closer to a creek, he heard feminine laughter and worried human women would see him carrying a wolf, surrounded by wolves. One of the wolves in the lead ran off. The darkening sky was sprinkled with twinkling heavenly lights, the round moon on full display. Eric loved the wide open spaces in the park, the seventy-degree temps during the day, and fifty-degree temps during the night—even though in the summer things became rather hectic with all the visitors.

He wanted to make a wide berth around the women in the creek to make sure he wasn't seen.

But the lead wolf made Eric stay to the path closer to the creek.

Despite how chilly it was, the women were splashing around in the creek, which intrigued him. They wouldn't see him—not when he blended in with the lodgepole pines, oaks, and the shadows—unless the wolf forced him to go to the rocky bank.

Which the wolf did.

When Eric grew near enough, he observed five women in goddess-like semi-sheer dresses. He knew he had to be dreaming. Their silky pastel creations, in blues and pinks and mint green, fluttered about them in the summer breeze. The women were standing in the water up to their calves, the pocket water temperatures higher. Above them, the creek water was mostly gentle with a few small rapids. Down here, the rapids were much more common and significant, which had created the pockets of water. The women were laughing and talking. A petite brunette, her hair short and curly, really caught his eye. She was wearing a robin's-egg-blue dress, the water plastering the bottom half of the gown to her calves and thighs in a sensual way.

Another woman with her back to him had long brown hair and a mint green dress. She moved in the water, which effectively blocked his view of the woman in the blue dress.

The area was great for fishing, and he was mesmerized by the woman in blue, thinking what a delicious catch *she'd* make.

"You know, Pepper," a blonde said to the woman in the blue dress, her voice darkening, "he wants you for his mate."

Eric straightened a bit. No one used the term mate but *lupus garous*. He couldn't smell their scents from where he was, nor could they smell his. He would have to cross the creek upwind of them to learn if they were really wolves. But he suspected the woman he was carrying must be a member of the same wolf pack these women belonged to. Why else would the wolf lead him in this direction?

The male wolf suddenly detoured and Eric was taken away from the creek and back into the woods, on a path that led straight to a small cabin. A few more people were there, warily watching him. So the pack was camping here, not just visiting for a few hours. As many of them as there were—he'd seen about fifteen—they must have rented a couple of cabins.

The door opened for him, and a man stepped aside so Eric could carry the wolf inside. To reach these more isolated cabins, the pack would have had to hike in on foot. There were no vehicles here and no parking next to the cabins. Another reason he would have preferred to take her to Dr. Weber in Silver Town.

The wolf in charge ran into a room, then came out wearing a pair of jeans. "I'll take it from here. Just lay her down on the bed."

"Is your pack from around here? Our town is only two hours south," Eric reminded the man, hoping he would listen to reason. If the pack didn't have its own doctor, Dr. Weber would welcome the chance to take care of her.

"We'll take it from here," a woman said, and Eric swung around to see the brunette with the short, curly hair from the creek—Pepper, the other woman had called her. The other women were with her and some of the wolves were at her side, as if guarding her. "Thank you for bringing Susan here."

She was even more enchanting up close, and his image of her as a goddess remained the same. She was beautiful. He wanted to make an impression on the she-wolf standing before him, who was obviously in charge, and not in the least bit hesitant. She was an alpha and he was in love. It was the first time since he'd lost his mate that he'd felt any interest in another she-wolf.

Eric bowed his head a little to her. "I'm Eric Silver, a park ranger, and I'm with the pack of Silver Town. I was telling this gentleman we have a wolf doctor in town if you don't have one of your own who can see to her. It helps to see one of our own kind."

"We're fine. Thank you. We'll take care of her."

Did that mean they had someone in the pack with

medical training? Most packs had some, but not many that he knew actually had trained doctors in the pack.

Eric turned and said to the injured wolf, "Take care, young lady. I hope you heal up soon." Then he took one long, last look at the she-wolf in charge and bowed his head again before taking his leave.

The whole way back to his truck, he couldn't stop thinking about Pepper. Was she running the pack? Or was she just a sub-leader when the pack leader wasn't around? Either might be the case, since she made the decisions once she arrived, and not the male who had lead Eric there. She didn't seem interested in mating the other male, who was clearly interested in her. Which was good, if Eric could meet up with her again. Then his law enforcement training kicked in. What if the reason the woman didn't want him to take care of her pack member was because they were involved in the illegal activities in the park? Perhaps she didn't want to have anything to do with anyone who was in the business of law enforcement, particularly when that someone was a wolf too and could smell things that humans couldn't?

Hell, he hated when his law enforcement training took control. He really wanted to listen to his wolfish side on this one. Damn it.

When he reached his truck, he tossed his medical pack inside, stripped off his clothes, and looked at the bloody bandage on his waist a second before yanking it off. Stinging and a roaring ache accompanied every movement, and he bit back the pain. Then he locked up his truck and shifted. If the wolves had been forag-ing for new places to take cannabis plants, he wouldn't smell anything in the camp. But he hadn't smelled all the wolves who were there, either. If he didn't check out the campsite, he couldn't clear them for certain, but the possibility of another pack's involvement in the illegal operations would seem more viable at that point.

He raced back along the path and when he finally reached the area near the cabin, he slipped around to where he could see it from a distance. They were packing up. *Good*. The campsite would be cleared out, so he could sniff around to his heart's content.

He remained silent. No one would be able to smell his scent unless they ventured in his direction. He watched the party as they all hoisted packs and began to move the injured lady. Their movements were quiet, but complementary, as if they'd been together as a pack forever.

A few of them took off down a trail leading away from him when Eric saw a flash of gray and beige fur in the woods off to his right. Before Eric could react, the large, male gray wolf lunged from the trees and attacked him. Why would they need to post a guard?

"Ohmigod," one of the women said as the attacking wolf growled and snarled.

Adrenaline pouring through his veins, Eric shot around to defend himself against the male wolf's vicious attack.

Eric didn't know if the pack continued to move away or if they were monitoring the situation, but he couldn't understand why the male wolf would attack him. Unless they were doing something illegal. Or maybe this wolf didn't know he was the same man who had carried the injured wolf to the cabin. Unless they'd seen him before as a wolf, or could smell he was the same man who had helped them, he could be anyone. Even a wild wolf.

Eric snarled and bit at the hostile wolf, telling him to back off. The wolf was aggressive, alpha, not like any of the beta wolves he'd met in the pack. Since Eric hadn't met this wolf, it made him wonder where the wolf had been all this time. He had to be the pack leader, and should have been helping the injured wolf long before this.

Eric intended to take off, his stance firm as he eyed the snarling wolf, who now stood still, half listening to the people clearing out of the cabin, half concentrating on Eric. Eric didn't dare turn his back on the wolf just yet.

He didn't take a step forward to dominate the space, instead waiting for the wolf to give up and take off with his pack mates. When the wolf didn't, which was real alpha posturing, Eric had a choice: run off and leave the wolf's territory, or wait him out until his pack was far enough away that he felt the need to keep up with them to protect them. Without proof the wolf was involved in anything illegal, Eric didn't want to take him down. Protecting his pack would be a natural instinct for the wolf, one Eric could understand.

The wolf took a few steps back and turned as if to go, and Eric assumed the wolf wanted to rejoin his pack. Eric turned slightly to race off toward his truck, with every intention of returning when all the wolves were gone so he could conduct his investigation. Then the wolf swung around and lunged at him, biting Eric in the shoulder.

Hell and damnation!

Sharp pain wracked his shoulder, he swore it went straight down to the nerves on fire in the wound to his flank. Eric pivoted and clashed with the wolf. Snarling and growling, he matched the alpha's anger, the pain of the wounds fading into the background as their teeth clashed.

Eric didn't want to kill the wolf and upset the pack, when Eric was damned interested in the she-wolf named Pepper. Even so, he wanted to prove he wasn't about to be bullied by another wolf. *Any* wolf. He'd had his fair share of wolf fights over the years, and he never backed down from a fight another wolf started.

Before he tore into the wolf and killed him for the unprovoked attack, Eric ran off, his tail straight out behind him, not tucked between his legs. It was his way of saying he wasn't afraid in the least, but he wasn't going to fight him.

Even so, the wolf doggedly tracked him, though Eric had a good lead on him by several hundred feet, until he heard another wolf growling and snarling at his attacker. Eric figured the other wolf was warning the alpha that the wolf he was chasing had just helped them out, and he didn't want him fighting Eric. Or maybe they were afraid Eric would get suspicious of their activities because one of them had attacked him.

Then the woods were quiet. Eric assumed the guard wolf and the other wolf had caught up to their people.

His shoulder and flank still burning where the wolves had bitten him, Eric finally stopped and listened to the sound of the breeze rustling the tree limbs and crickets chirping. He heard an owl hooting in a tree several hundred feet away.

Despite how much he hurt, the woman in the blue gown—Pepper—fascinated him. He was dying to know more about the mystery wolf pack and this woman who had pinned him with a look that said she was in charge and he'd better mind. She could challenge him any day. He couldn't help but love it. Then he wondered if the wolf who had attacked him was the one who wanted to mate her.

Ah, hell, that would be his luck. He wasn't into stealing another wolf's potential mate—at least not normally.

Still, he was dying to check out the wolf smells at the campsite. But he had to take care of his injuries first.

When he reached his truck, he shifted, got his clothes out, and quickly threw on his briefs, jeans, socks and boots.

Tomorrow early, he'd go back to the campsite.

Then he pulled out his medical pack, reapplied a bandage to his waist, and did the best he could to bandage the shoulder wound. He pulled on his shirt just to keep blood off his seat, climbed into the truck, and drove to Silver Town to see Dr. Weber.

Eric never would have thought he would be the one injured when he only meant to help a wolf in need. Now *he* would have to see Dr. Weber about his *own* injury instead. He was about to call CJ with an update when the truck's digital screen lit up with an incoming call. It was his brother Sarandon, and Eric knew he'd have to tell him what had happened, even though he'd rather not mention the second wolf fight to anyone. His own pack would be furious he was attacked when helping another wolf pack out.

Chapter 2

PEPPER GREYCOAT COULDN'T BELIEVE IT WHEN SHE heard two wolves fighting in the woods. She'd seen a glimpse of both male wolves, the snarling big tan and gray that bit at Waldron Mason, a beige wolf with a white front and a smattering of gray hairs. The mystery wolf had snapped at Waldron before he raced off. The way he didn't tuck tail meant he wasn't cowed by the aggressor. And that had intrigued her.

She was furious that Waldron was pulling her away from her own pack to deal with him when she wanted to ensure Susan was properly cared for. As quickly as she was able, she stripped off her clothes, shifted, and ran like the devil to chase Waldron down. Whoever the other wolf had been, he had posed no threat to them. When she ran after the two wolves, she smelled their scents. The mystery wolf was indeed Eric. No way had she wanted Waldron to hurt him after Eric had helped Susan.

She was so angry, she could have killed Waldron for his unwarranted actions.

When she spied Waldron still chasing after Eric, she tore into Waldron, growling and snapping to let him know just how angry he'd made her. He whipped around as if to attack, then recognized her, and realized he'd lose any chance he had with courting and mating her—not that he had any—so he backed off. From his narrow-eyed, harsh gaze, she could tell he was irritated to the max with her. If he could have, he would have continued to hunt the other wolf down and finished him off. She worried about Eric—she smelled his blood on Waldron. How badly had Waldron hurt Eric?

But she knew Eric had been injured even before this because she'd smelled both an antiseptic and blood on him when she first met him.

She listened, but didn't hear any sign of Eric. Growling at Waldron again, she turned and ran off. She continued to pay attention to the sounds around her, making sure he wasn't following her back to their camp-site. She didn't want to have to say a word to him about any of this when she reached camp. Her only intent at that point was seeing that Susan was taken care of.

She wondered if he'd gone after Eric again when she didn't hear him follow her.

As for Eric, she already had trouble with one alpha male wanting to court her. She sure didn't need a second one bugging her, if Eric had any such notion. Still, she felt badly Waldron had attacked him, and she really hoped he wasn't hurt too seriously.

Later that night, after a doctor had x-rayed Susan's leg and found her cousin had suffered a hairline fracture, Susan and Pepper settled on the couches for a late night glass of wine and chips at Pepper's home in the woods. Susan had her wrapped leg propped up on Pepper's coffee table to help reduce the swelling.

"You should have played in the creek with us instead running off and starting a rock slide," Pepper said, unable to let go of the annoyance over Waldron. "It would have been safer that way." Had Waldron been watching the women playing in the creek before he attacked Eric? Most likely. She was certain Waldron wouldn't have been spying on the rest of the pack.

She still couldn't believe that Eric Silver had stood up to her about taking Susan to see his own pack's doctor. The challenge in his whole expression had said he didn't agree with her and that he wanted to do things his way. She didn't know anything about his pack, and she had no intention of relying on a doctor she didn't know. She and her pack might not have a wolf doctor, but they trusted the human ones they saw. Not that their doctors knew anything about the *lupus garous*.

She still could envision Eric finally bowing his head in concession, giving in to her ruling.

"Yeah, but then the most handsome of wolves wouldn't have carried me back to the cabin," Susan replied. "I couldn't believe it when Richard told Eric he couldn't take me to see their doctor. Their pack actually has a doctor! Now how cool is that?"

"Cool." Pepper thought it was great, but she didn't want to get involved with another pack. She was surprised there was another pack living only four hours south of where she and her people lived. Still, since each pack tended to run in their own territory, Pepper could see how they wouldn't have encountered each other before.

Susan snorted. "You wouldn't know a hot wolf if he knocked you down and licked you all over." Susan smiled. "Now that gives me some interesting ideas. Let's see." She lifted her phone off the table.

Pepper wondered what she was up to.

"He said his name was Eric Silver, and he's a park ranger." Susan pulled up an Internet browser. "Yep, here he is. Giving a lecture to a group of senior citizens. With his dark hair and eyes, his height, and that gorgeous smile, he looks like every woman's fantasy." She sighed dreamily. "And," she said in a pointed way, "he's all smiles with the gray-haired women and men, so he wasn't putting on a show just for you."

"He *wasn't* putting on a show for me. He wanted me to do what he said. If he'd wanted to put a show on for me, he wouldn't have suggested taking you to Silver Town."

"He's clearly an alpha wolf, not a beta. And he's a park ranger, so he knows something about taking care of people in the park who are injured." Then Susan frowned. "Ohmigod, you don't think he's the wolf Waldron attacked, do you?"

"Yeah, he was. Though I'm surprised Eric returned to our campsite as a wolf."

"See? He's interested in you. Or, well, maybe he ditched his clothes somewhere nearby and was watching us as a wolf. *Although*"—Susan elongated the word, putting her phone over her heart and looking up at the ceiling—"in *my* fantasy of him, he would be thinking only of me and not you."

Pepper laughed.

"Did you bite Waldron?" Susan asked. "Richard said you took off after him and you smelled of blood when you returned. Not your blood. I was in the car by then and missed out on all the action."

"Waldron was chasing him, though I didn't see any sign of the wolf. Waldron had bitten him, and I had to do something to get Waldron's attention. He was definitely in hunting mode and determined to catch hold of his prey."

"And kill him?" Susan sounded horrified.

"If he could have gotten hold of him, I'd say that was a good bet." That brought back memories of the alpha who had killed her mate—though her mate had been a beta—and Pepper shuddered.

Susan closed her gaping mouth. Then she set her empty glass on the table. "So, where did you bite Waldron?"

"His tail, the first part of him I reached. I didn't bite too hard, but I still drew some blood."

"Was he pissed off at you?"

"We had a wolf-to-wolf confrontation. Yeah, he was pissed, but I wasn't backing down either, and if he wanted me to look at his courting favorably, he had to mind me."

"Oh, wow, I bet that nearly killed him." Susan shook her head, taking another chip from the bowl and biting into it.

"Yeah, he didn't like it. If we'd been mated wolves, I'm certain he would have growled and snapped at me to back off."

"You're not going to, are you? Consider courting him?"

"No way. Look how aggressive as he is toward another male wolf who hadn't provoked him in any way. We aren't even courting."

"Agreed. But now, Eric? He's my kind of guy."

Pepper waved a potato chip at her. "You should have given him your number."

"I would have, but I was a wolf. I wish he'd given me his business card."

"He might have. But you were a wolf."

"I should have shifted and given him a big smile and a big thank-you for his help."

Pepper laughed. "You would have been way too shy to do that."

"Yeah. I keep telling myself I need to overcome that. I couldn't believe Waldron was watching our pack tonight. Well, and that he tore into the other wolf. He's becoming a real stalker."

Pepper refilled their wineglasses. "He thinks he's protecting his 'property.' But I won't be his mate no matter what."

"Richard said Eric growled and snapped back at Waldron. I've never seen anyone stand up to him. *Besides you*. I wish I'd been there." Susan sighed.

"Eric is a real alpha wolf. I was surprised he didn't stay and fight Waldron to the end." But Pepper was glad for it. She wouldn't have wanted to see Eric hurt further since he'd already been wounded. Even now, she wondered if he was okay.

She didn't want to call and check on him though.

She let out her breath on a frustrated sigh.

She hadn't expected to have any trouble on their camping trip into the national forest. She was a forester and used to working with groups on forest management. Many of her pack members worked in some forestry job or another. Susan supervised their own forest nursery and Christmas tree farm. Some of the pack members worked there or on other tree farms and some worked on other forestry projects, such as tree removal. But they hadn't been to this forest together as a pack in the last five years or so. It had been a vacation, and before Susan injured herself, they'd been having a blast.

Pepper had a lovely log home for pack meetings, with 250 acres of woods and a covered stone patio for outdoor gatherings. Most of her pack members had log homes of their own situated all over the territory to afford them privacy, but close enough that they could gather as a pack whenever they needed to.

"What if Eric could chase away Waldron permanently?" Susan asked.

"Then what? What if he expected something in return for his help? Our pack? Our land?"

"You? If I were the pack leader, I'd seriously be considering it."

"Yeah, well, I'm not interested. We'll continue to deal with Waldron like we have since he moved into the area with his pack two weeks ago."

"I don't think Waldron will get the message without someone taking him to task, physically. As alpha as you are, you couldn't beat him as a wolf. Not one on one. Not like you took that other wolf down." Susan moved her leg off the table and winced. "I'm going to call it a night. When do you see the Boy Scout troop tomorrow to talk about being a forester?"

"First thing in the morning, and another after that. And I have two sessions after lunch, so I'll be hanging around the area. I'll have someone stop in to feed you while I'm gone." Because Susan was using crutches, she was staying with Pepper for a couple of days. Longer, if she needed to. But Pepper didn't want her to have to try and do for herself right now.

"Thanks for putting me up for a couple of nights."

"No problem, Susan. You know I always enjoy your company. If you think of it tomorrow, you could give Eric Silver a call and tell him that you're all right. I'm certain he'd like to know that. While you're at it, you can thank him for the rescue, and if it comes up in the conversation, ask him if he's okay."

Susan smiled broadly at her. "You *are* interested in him! But I doubt he'd want you to know if he was injured. Macho wolf syndrome, you know."

"Possibly. Unless he wanted to get our sympathy. The doctor said it should take about four weeks for your leg to mend, which means half or less time for us. Just don't put any stress on the leg for now. You don't want to increase the fracture."

"No, that's for sure. It already hurts enough. I hope Pauline can run things until I return to work."

"Pauline will be fine, but I'll run over there to check things out. You don't have to worry about anything. Just rest." Then Pepper raised her brows. "You didn't do this on purpose did you, to get some time off? You know I'd spell you for a while if you needed vacation days."

Susan laughed and hobbled off to bed, saying good night.

Pepper retired to her bedroom, hoping she could figure out a means to keep Waldron away from her pack and her lands without having to take more drastic measures. He'd been scent-marking all over her territory, and so had some of the males of his pack. She'd taken him to task for it, but what else could she do? They outnumbered her more than two to one, from what he'd said. She couldn't complain to human law enforcement that Waldron and his men were peeing all over her property. She still wouldn't give in to him no matter what. But it could be a real problem for a wolf pack if they ignored it.

She tucked herself into bed, thinking about Waldron attacking Eric and drawing blood. She should have told Susan to call her when she learned how he was, *if* he was willing to tell her the truth.

—◦◦◦—

His injuries throbbing, Eric answered Sarandon's call while he got on the road to return to Silver Town. "Hey, what's up?" Like Eric, his brother loved the outdoors. He was a guide for anyone who needed one—photographers, nature lovers, hikers, and rock climbers. He loved doing it all.

"Just a heads-up; I might be a little late to the forestry careers talk tomorrow," Sarandon said. "I've got a Lepidopterist Society meeting first thing in the morning so the members can count butterflies and identify different varieties. If we have a big showing, we'll be there a while. So I might have to talk after you do."

"I'll let the Scout leaders know," Eric replied. "I've got other business to attend to after I speak, so if I'm not there, just give your lecture and I'll meet up with you after lunch at the next Boy Scout campground. They'll love hearing what you do. I have something I have to do afterward, and I'll take care of it during lunchtime."

"I thought you said you had the whole day scheduled to talk to troops."

"I do. We have two other Scout troops camping in

other areas to meet, but when everyone's busy with lunch, I have other business to take care of."

"I thought we could get lunch together. We don't often see each other during the duty day."

Eric suspected his brother sensed something was up. He couldn't get anything past Sarandon. His younger brothers, sometimes, yes, but not Sarandon. Even though the quadruplet brothers were only minutes apart, he and Sarandon were the closet to each other, just like Brett and CJ were close.

"Okay, so what are you going to do that's so important?" Sarandon asked.

"Nothing. Just checking out an area on the nearby creek." He wanted to learn more about the pack that had rented the cabin, like where they lived. Which meant checking their reservations. Since he worked for the park, it would be easy for him to do. He had to know if they were involved in the illegal cultivation of cannabis.

"For...what?"

Eric couldn't lie to his brother. After their father had lied to Eric and his brothers, Eric wouldn't do that to them. But he wasn't about to tell him he had seen a fantasy in the forest he wanted to know more about, and wanted to prove to himself in the worst way that Pepper was innocent of any wrongdoing. Pepper was the only name he had to go by. And she was just as hot and spicy as her name. "Just checking it out."

"Okay, well, let me know if you discover anything interesting."

"Will do."

"I bet," Sarandon said, sounding skeptical.

Eric knew he had to get his injuries looked at, and

better Sarandon hear about the fight from him rather than pack gossip. "A couple of wolves bit me."

"Is it bad? It has to be or you wouldn't have told me. Do you need me to come get you?"

Sarandon knew not to make a big deal of it.

"Not a problem. And I wouldn't have mentioned it if I hadn't wanted Doc to look at it."

"Hell. It is bad or you wouldn't be seeing Doc."

"Just to be on the safe side."

"How bad—"

"Minor." Though both wounds were still bleeding and hurting like crazy.

"This has to do with the drug wolves?"

"One of them, yeah. CJ and the rest of the sheriff's department are checking into it."

"One? What about the other?"

"He was a…guard wolf for another pack, just visiting the park."

"You're going after the wolf tomorrow then?"

"No." Not *that* wolf. The she-wolf.

"Then—"

"I think he was protecting his pack. Anyway, I was just curious where their pack is from." Eric pulled onto the main road going to Silver Town.

"Related to the drug business?"

"I don't believe so." He sure as hell hoped not.

"Any woman you're interested in seeing more of in particular?" Sarandon asked, his tone bordering on amused, but he was also curious. "You wouldn't be interested if there wasn't more to it than that."

"As if it's any of your business, but yeah. There were women in the pack."

"Hell, Eric." Now Sarandon sounded surprised. Which, given Eric's disinterest in women for the past two years, was understandable.

"They might be mated." Eric knew Sarandon would assume he was interested in one of the women in particular. He didn't want to tell him about the possibility that her pack, or some of her pack, could be involved in illegally raising cannabis. Not without proof.

Then again, Pepper had been the leader of the group of women at the creek, not necessarily a pack leader. The other women had fluttered around her like she was a goddess, everyone attentive to her, and when she entered the cabin, she'd definitely been the one in charge.

"Do you want me to go with you when you check the area out?" Sarandon sounded worried.

"No."

"The wolf who attacked you could be her mate."

"She didn't have one. Apparently some wolf has been wanting to court her though."

"Do you have a name for her?"

"Pepper is all I got."

"All right. Let me know what Doc says about your injuries."

"Sarandon…"

"All right, all right. See you tomorrow if we can get together. Otherwise, I'll talk to you later."

"Sounds good." They ended the call. Despite the fact that Eric's shoulder was hurting like crazy, he was trying to see the point of view of the wolf who had bitten him, but he was having a difficult time of it. He called Doc, hating to make this a late night call, but Dr. Weber always took calls anytime of the day or night.

Not that he would be happy about it. Doc wasn't a late-night person.

Still, Eric was damn glad they had a wolf doctor in their pack. Reporting that a wolf had bitten him to a human doctor would be bad news all the way around for wolves, his kind and otherwise. And lying and blaming a dog could cause problems too. Of course, Eric could have called their pack vet, because he didn't mind taking care of anyone any time of day or night, but Eric really didn't want to see the vet.

"Hate to be calling you like this," Eric began.

"Another snakebite?" Dr. Weber asked, sounding grouchy.

Eric was still irritated with himself for not spotting a coiled-up rattler only a week ago while he had been out searching for a missing hiker. He'd been wearing heavy-duty, snake-proof boots, but the rattler had struck out at him from a stack of rocks, and had dug his fangs into his thigh.

"A couple of wolf bites this time. I probably shouldn't even be bothering you with it."

"Wolf bites? While you were in the national park? A regular wolf? Couldn't have been one of our pack. If you're calling me at this hour, it needs to be seen. How long before you get here?"

"Half hour. Yes, I was at the park. No, it wasn't one of our people, and before you ask, it was a *lupus garou*."

"I'll be ready."

"You don't need to tell Darien." Eric knew he would anyway.

"When a wolf bites one of our people, Darien needs to know about it. I take it you didn't provoke the wolf."

"One of them is involved in the drug business. The other bite happened in a different location, and the wolf was just being protective of his pack." Eric didn't want Darien sending out a hunting party to take down the "dangerous" wolf.

"All right. I'll let Darien know."

Fifteen minutes into the drive, Eric got a call. *Darien*. Eric let out his breath and explained about the woman's injury and the subsequent events.

"It's a national park, not a place a *lupus garou* pack can claim for their own," Darien said angrily after Eric had finished. "And you didn't act aggressively to the wolf or threaten their pack in any way."

"I know, but it's okay."

"I know you, Eric. It's not okay. You're going to try and locate the pack."

"Yes, as a human and in my capacity as park ranger, I am checking on the status of the woman's injury. I won't be running as a wolf. They have to respect the uniform."

Darien didn't say anything. Eric knew Darien didn't want him going alone, not after what had already happened between him and the wolf. He *was* concerned about the woman's injury, but he was also bothered by the notion that some wolf was hassling Pepper. Not that she'd appreciate Eric stepping in and chasing off the other wolf if she thought she could handle it herself, but if it worked out well for her, he was certainly willing to help her out.

"I haven't had a chance to check in with CJ. What happened when he and the others investigated the trouble I had up on the cliffs?"

"No bodies. No marijuana plants. But all the wolf prints and trace evidence of blood, including your own, were there. The wolf pack had to be close by to clean it up as fast as they did and move out. Eric, you're not to investigate these people on your own any further. You're not immortal."

"I had to take a chance. This is the first time any of us have actually encountered the wolves responsible." Not that it did a whole lot of good, since the wolves were now dead. What if he learned Pepper and her pack were involved up to their wolf ears in this shady business?

"Take Sarandon with you," Darien said, breaking into Eric's thoughts. "You said you both were giving talks to Boy Scout troops in the area. Take him with you when you investigate this visiting wolf pack."

Darien was giving a pack leader order, and Eric didn't like it. He knew Darien was concerned for him, but that's what irked Eric the most. "Eric? I know you're perfectly capable of handling this on your own, but for my peace of mind, will you take him along?"

Eric was surprised Darien would change his tune. He normally wouldn't have altered his command to a request with any other pack member—except when it came to his pack leader mate, Lelandi, and no way did he order her about.

"They packed up and left already."

"Okay, but I still want you to take Sarandon."

"Yeah, all right." What else could Eric do? He had gone against Darien's rule on occasion, but not when it might involve another wolf pack and get his own into trouble.

"Let me know what you learn."

"Will do." Eric hadn't wanted the whole pack in on this. Sarandon would keep Eric's injury secret from their younger brothers, Brett and CJ. But Eric was afraid news would somehow get out that he was bitten by a wolf from a neighboring wolf pack and was trying to track down the pack.

Others in the Silver pack would want to help him. Including his brothers. He really didn't want anyone's help in this. The more who got involved, the more the she-wolf would feel he was being too pushy. He'd been accused of it before; well, of being too bossy when he wanted to help the three new she-wolves in the pack to renovate the Silver Town Hotel. He wasn't one to stand by and not offer advice when he came up with some brilliant ideas of his own.

Eric was also worried that if the wolves *were* involved in the drug business, they could get spooked and run off to another park that he didn't have jurisdiction over.

When Eric arrived at the clinic, Doc Weber let him in, glanced at the blood soaking his shirt, and shook his head.

"Did you call Darien about this?" Doc asked as Eric stripped off his shirt in the exam room. He then removed the bandages Eric had applied.

"I did."

"So how did it happen?"

Eric had to explain all over again.

Doc stopped stitching him up for a moment to consider him, his white brows deeply furrowed. "I'll have to give Darien a medical report."

"Over a couple of lousy stitches?" Eric snorted, wishing he could have pretended nothing was wrong, but because of the location of the second bite, he couldn't have stitched the wound closed himself. Plus the antibiotics could help keep the bite from becoming infected. Suturing it would help it heal faster than if he'd just let his enhanced wolf healing abilities take care of it.

"Twelve on one shoulder, ten on the other. And they're fine stitches, if I do say so myself. I'd tell you to take it easy for a couple of days, no running as a wolf, and by the end of the week you should be mostly healed. But I know you won't listen to me."

Eric grabbed up his shirt, but didn't put it on. With the suturing and the new bandages, he wouldn't bleed on the driver's seat and he didn't want to put on the bloody shirt.

"Take it easy, and if you need anything for pain…"

"Nothing. Thanks." Eric left the clinic and when he arrived home, he called Sarandon one last time for the night. He really didn't want to take Sarandon with him tomorrow, but pack leader orders. He began washing the blood out of his shirt when Sarandon answered.

"Hey, what did Doc say? You must have already seen him by now."

"Couple of stitches. Why don't you come with me to try and locate the pack tomorrow? I want to check on the woman and see how she's faring."

Sarandon was so quiet, Eric thought he'd lost the connection. "Okay?"

"I know you didn't threaten the women or this wolf, or you would have taken a chunk out of him. You didn't, did you?"

"No. I just left the area."

"If he's a *lupus garou*, it seems he wouldn't react so aggressively unless he were provoked."

"I *didn't* provoke him."

"I know. I'm just saying, it seems odd. It seems he has more at stake here."

"Alpha male pack leader, I suspect. Anyway, no big deal."

"And the woman you're interested in?"

"Yes, she's alpha. At least around the women she was with at the creek, and then later when she met up with me at the cabin."

"You were alone, together?"

"No. Give me a break."

"Then the guy was most likely her mate."

"One of the women said a guy wanted to court her but she wasn't interested."

"How many are following *that* wolf then?"

"The one who attacked me was probably with her pack. She might be a sub-leader or just another alpha in the pack. He might be the pack leader, or a sub-leader or just another alpha in their pack. We have several alphas in ours. She might have several in hers. And if he's not with her pack, he could be a lone wolf."

"All right. I'm just saying don't get your hopes up. Wait, you've been trying to catch up to the wolves growing pot in the remoter areas of the park. Don't tell me you think this pack has anything to do with it."

"Do you want to come with me or not?" Eric couldn't help being annoyed. He wasn't declaring his interest in courting the she-wolf. Yeah, he found her attractive, and just the fact she was an alpha intrigued him. But she hadn't trusted him enough to help take her pack member to Dr. Weber. Then again, maybe that was some of his problem. The need to prove he was trustworthy and not in the least bit bossy. As to the other matter, he wasn't going to say they might be the wolves who planted the weed if they were innocent.

"Did Doc say you should rest up a bit?" Sarandon asked, abruptly changing the subject, as if he knew Eric was about to leave him out of this.

"Yeah, he did. But you know him. He always thinks anyone who has been injured should be abed for days afterward."

"Of course he does, because he doesn't want to have to redo his work if the wolf doesn't mind him and pulls out the stitches. And, hell yeah, I want to go with you. Did you want to ask CJ to come with us? As a deputy sheriff, he would lend a little extra weight."

"No. I don't want to escalate this into something more than a case of reaching out to show friendship."

"All right. I'll make sure the group I'm working with gets an early start counting butterflies so I can make it in time to give my lecture, and then we can see to this other matter at lunchtime."

Acknowledgments

Thanks to my beta readers, Donna Fournier and Loretta Melvin, who were the only two I had time to send the manuscript to this go-around! Thanks to Deb Werksman, my editor, and to the whole production staff. The covers are phenomenal!

About the Author

Bestselling and award-winning author Terry Spear has written over fifty paranormal romance novels and several medieval Highland historical romances. Her first werewolf romance, *Heart of the Wolf*, was named a 2008 *Publishers Weekly* Best Book of the Year, and her subsequent titles have garnered high praise and hit the *USA Today* bestseller list. A retired officer of the U.S. Army Reserves, Terry lives in Crawford, Texas, where she is working on her next werewolf romance, continuing her new series about shape-shifting jaguars and cougar shifters, and having fun with her young adult novels, when she's not playing with her two Havanese puppies, Max and Tanner. For more information, please visit www.terryspear.com, or follow her on Twitter, @TerrySpear. She is also on Facebook at www.facebook.com/terry.spear. And on her blog, *Terry Spear's Shifters*: www.terryspear.wordpress.com.